HELL HATH NO FURY . . .

"You gonna cry, pretty girl? Gonna do that female boo-hoo thang right here in front of all us big bad men?"

Don't guess she was as bad off as he thought. Her eyes narrowed up on him like the sights on one of those old rolling-block rifles. Her lips curled back like a mother wolf protecting newborn cubs when she said, "Damn you to an eternal burning hell, you sorry piece of human trash. You murdered my entire family."

Her eyes blinked real fast a couple times, and tears coursed down her cheeks right before she screamed, "You even killed my mother, you low-life scum-sucking dog!"

Then, as God is my witness, a short-barreled Remington .44 appeared in that angry gal's hand like a sideshow magician's rabbit. . . .

Berkley titles by J. Lee Butts

HELL IN THE NATIONS
LAWDOG

HELL IN THE NATIONS

J. LEE BUTTS

BERKLEY BOOKS, NEW YORK

HELL IN THE NATIONS

A Berkley Book / published by arrangement with the author

PRINTING HISTORY
Berkley edition / November 2002

Copyright © 2002 by J. Lee Butts.
Cover design by Jill Boltin.
Cover art by Franco Accornero.

Visit our website at
www.penguinputnam.com

ISBN: 0-425-18732-2

BERKLEY®
Berkley Books are published by The Berkley Publishing Group,
a division of Penguin Putnam Inc.,
375 Hudson Street, New York, New York 10014.
BERKLEY and the "B" design
are trademarks belonging to Penguin Putnam Inc.

PRINTED IN THE UNITED STATES OF AMERICA

10 9 8 7 6 5 4 3 2 1

For Carol,
whose patience and support are boundless,

and

Linda McKinley,
whose talent and skill make me a better writer

ACKNOWLEDGMENTS

Once again, special thanks to Michael and Barbara Rosenberg for their invaluable efforts on my behalf. To Kimberly Waltemyer for turning me into a published author. And finally, all those buckaroos and buckarettes at the DFW Writer's Workshop whose invaluable knowledge, experience, and weekly contributions are apparent in every word of my work.

Why . . . consign these men to death and exterminate them from the earth? Because they are preying wolves . . . unfit to live and unfit to remain at large.

—*Western Independent*, 1871

Hell. That's what it were like. Hell in the Nations.

—Carlton J. Cecil, 1948

Near as I can figure, living has always caused dying. . . .

—Hayden Tilden, 1884

PROLOGUE

ON AN ICY morning, when frozen tree limbs clicked against the windowpanes of my sun porch kingdom here at the Rolling Hills Home for the Aged, Franklin J. Lightfoot, Jr., slid silently into the chair beside me and flipped his notepad open again. The boy looked to have just shaved, his face glowed, and instead of witch hazel, he'd switched to something new, Old Spice, I think, or maybe Bay Rum. My nose might be big as a South American parrot's bill, but it doesn't work as well as it used to.

"Well, I'll just be damned. Been wondering when you were gonna get around to coming back by, Junior. Looka here, Carlton, the prodigal pencil-pusher hath returned."

Cecil's heavy-lidded eyes opened slowly, and then sparkled when he recognized our young friend. "Junior, my God, son, it's good to see you again. Actually, it's good to see anybody when you get our age. Want a lemon drop?" He fumbled around in his blanket and came up with a fuzz-covered ball of stickiness.

Franklin J. examined the candy like it was a bug on a pin, scrunched up his nose, and said, "No, thanks, Carlton. I'm just here to talk with Mr. Tilden a bit." He smiled and winked as Cecil popped the sugar-covered fur ball into his mouth, then went into a spitting fit trying to get rid of all the blanket lint.

"Well, Junior, what's on your mind?" I took General Black Jack Pershing, leaned over, and dropped him into the reporter's lap.

"You read the *Lawdog* series?" Franklin J. scratched the old cat behind the ears with his left hand and held a pencil at the ready with his right.

"Couldn't hardly avoid it, since you made a point of seeing everyone here at Rolling Hills got a free copy of the paper. Some of these old farts that hadn't read much of anything in ten years got hooked on the stuff you wrote. I've got women so ancient they can barely push their walkers up and down the hall chasing me around my bedroom at night. 'Bout to wear me down to a nub."

He smiled so large, every tooth in his mouth got some sunshine. "Glad to hear that, Hayden. *Lawdog* has generated more interest than any article of its type I've ever written. We've had inquiries from publishers all over the country who want to serialize a version of your life story, and most importantly, they want more."

"More?" Tried to sound innocent and uninformed at the same time. Wanted to give him the impression the possibility of such a prospect had taken me completely by surprise. "You're just pulling an old man's arthritic leg, aren't you, Junior?"

"Hayden, right now the level of interest from our readers is such that I think we could go on for about as long as you can stand it."

Carlton almost ruined my trick, though, when he kicked in with: "We knew you'd be back, boy. Didn't we, Hayden? Hell, they's just too much more to pass on. You'd barely scratched the surface with Magruder and that bunch in your first installment. We've got a lot yet to tell you, don't we, my friend?"

Junior looked pleased. "A lot more? How much more?"

Before I could stop him, Carlton blurted out, "Oh, you've got your Charlie Two Knives and your Albino Bob Thornton, Lonesome Edgar Steele, L. B. Ledoux, Chief Buffalo Head Long Feather, Three-Toed Willie McCord, and uh-uh-uh . . ."

Either his memory completely failed, or he couldn't get his mouth to work around one of those lumps of candy at that exact moment. No idea what caused his rambling old mind to burp, but he just kind of mumbled off into nowhere—thank goodness. I didn't want to let everything out at one time anyway. Figured we had our red-faced reporter hooked, and wanted to string him along for all he was worth. Whatever that turned out to be.

"Well, if it's agreeable with the two of you fellows, why don't we start this session sometime around the point where you'd just put Magruder in the ground and go from there."

Thought it nice of young Franklin J. to include Carlton in the mix, even if the crazy old coot couldn't keep his mind on much of any one thing for more than a few minutes. But of course, that was only if you didn't include candy or pretty young nurses and whatever else his fractured mind might want to latch onto as important. Right kind of bribe and his prehistoric thinker mechanism worked just fine, thank you very much.

"Why don't we pick it up around 1880–81, or something in the neighborhood. Just tell me anything. You know—like who the worst criminal you encountered about then might have been. I don't see how you could have happened on too many as bad as Magruder, but just try to think of one." He glanced up from his pad and threw me a mischievous grin. "You can remember 1881, can't you, Hayden?"

Scratched my head, then my chin, squirmed around in the chair, picked at my fingernails, and stared up at our dormant ceiling fan for about ten seconds before I kinda mumbled, "Well . . . let me see here. Do I remember 1881?" Then I perked up and snapped, "Hell, yes, I can remember '81, Junior. The *Fort Smith Elevator* used up a lot of good ink on a bunch of famous dead people that year. We're not talking run-of-the-mill bandits, thieves, and killers. We're talking folks everyone still remembers. Pat Garrett shot the hell out of Billy Bonney over in New Mexico Territory. Newspapers said The Kid was slain by Sheriff Garrett. Never have believed you could slay murdering weasels like him. Seems like The Kid checked out kind of early in the year, if I remember correctly. Anyhow, my friend Wyatt Earp, his brothers, and Doc Holliday rubbed out two of the Clantons and a couple of their cronies over in Tombstone. And '81 was the year President Garfield got blasted by some disappointed churnhead that didn't get the job he wanted. So, yes, by God, I do recall most of 1881 for those and some particularly tough-to-take personal reasons."

A roguish Carlton J. Cecil squirmed in his chair and grinned. He had the look of a kid behind an outhouse who'd just seen his sister's best girlfriend in the altogether.

"Smilin' Jack Paine," he wheezed, "he 'uz a bad 'un."

The fact my own private loony bird remembered the name astonished me. Of the hundreds of people he could've brought up, it was easy to figure out why he'd picked that one, but it still irritated the hell out of me.

"God Almighty, Carlton. You could've talked till dark and not mentioned that low-life son of a bitch."

Of course our exchange just lit a fire under Franklin J. Junior. "Who was he, Hayden? Come on, tell me about him."

"Don't care to talk about Smilin' Jack, if it's all the same to you, Junior."

"Why on earth not?"

"Smilin' Jack Paine did, and personally caused, some things so awful I've never forgot 'em. Having Carlton bring him and his nefarious deeds back to mind again is really irritating. Besides, while Jack was a bad one, there were others just as bad and some even worse."

Jerked around on the comforter over my legs for emphasis. Tried to put just the right amount of righ-

teous in-dig-nation into my voice. Wanted to make
sure he jumped on board the Hayden Tilden Special as
it ripped off into the wilds of Judge Parker's Indian
Nations full tilt, belching steam, its whistle screaming
for notice from everyone.

"Come on now, Hayden. Gimme the whole animal—
fur and all. Tell me everything you can remember
about Smilin' Jack Paine. You know I can go to the
Fort Smith Elevator's archives and find out everything
I need to know about him anyway—now that you've
dropped the name."

"I didn't drop Smilin' Jack's name. That bonbon-
sucking piece of ancient wheeze over there beside you
is the one who remembered Jack and his bunch."

Carlton grinned, his head snapped back, and he
twirled the lemon drop around in his almost toothless
mouth with a tongue the size of a Pony Express rider's
saddlebag.

Junior's eyes lit up. "Bunch? This just keeps getting
better. Did he lead a gang like Magruder's?"

The cat jumped out of the boy's lap when the scribbling got more furious than he wanted to deal with.
Having someone scratch his ears pleased Black Jack
more than just about anything, but he tended to be a
somewhat persnickety two-hand feline, and if one of
yours wasn't busy with him, he would just abandon
you altogether for someone who'd shower him with
their total attention. As a consequence, Carlton accused
the big tomcat of being somewhat "female" in his at-
titudes, and often blamed Chief Nurse Leona Wildbank
with having had Black Jack fixed. A fate worse than
death as far as Carlton was concerned.

Knew we had Franklin J. on the line again, and kept jiggling the hook just to make sure. "Well, Junior, sometimes Smilin' Jack ran with others, sometimes he ran alone. But he spent most of his life running one way or another. That is—till Hayden Tilden caught up with him."

"Just how much do you remember?"

"How often have I told you before, Junior? I've been cursed with a memory longer than an Arkansas well rope and clear as that water those folks from Hot Springs sell for five dollars a bottle to Yankee tourists who aren't paying attention. Some old people can't remember how to tie their shoes; others can't forget the slightest details of their lives from sixty years past. At times its does seem a curse, because I fall into that second bunch."

"Are you going somewhere with this, or was Smilin' Jack Paine hiding in that gob of bull feathers and I just didn't hear about him?"

"Smilin' Jack's sorry assault on the world is an open book just waiting for me to read it out for you. As had been the case with others, Judge Parker's private bailiff, Mr. Wilton, presented me with the package that contained everything anyone could ever have wanted to know about the worthless piece of vermin."

"Well, let's get on with it."

"Where do you want to start?"

"How far back can you go?"

"I can go all the way to Mount Joy, Ohio, where Jack taught school in a one-room shack just a few miles from the river. Guess he'd been there for several years when a new family moved into the tiny community and placed their sixteen-year-old daughter in his classes. Her conduct with local boys—and men from all over south Ohio—drove her into the open arms of her trusted *instructor*. Before Mr. Paine knew what hit him, he was running down the Ohio headed for the Mississippi and all the freedoms available in that world-class capital of sin, New Orleans."

Junior glanced up from his notepad. "Let's back up for a minute. Go to the very beginning. Tell me how you and Mr. Wilton met, and give me all the particulars in as much detail as you can recall. Want to get everything down just right for all your new fans out there in Tildenland, now don't we?"

"You're right, Junior. Be especially hard on the inmates here at Rolling Hills. So, I'll give you the whole bird. Feathers, beak, feet, and all."

1

"HAYDEN TILDEN, AT YOUR SERVICE"

I MOTIONED JUDGE Parker's personal bailiff toward a brocaded armchair in Elizabeth's spanking-new month-old parlor. She'd purchased the house just before Easter of '81. I'd been out in the briars and thickets at the time, chasing a two-tailed skunk named F. Evan Polk. Polk killed Buckskin Elroy Tatum near White Bead Hill in the Chickasaw Nation. Story I heard had it that the men fought over the results of a horse race. According to witnesses, Polk lost the fistfight, but caught Tatum on the trail home and emptied both barrels of a twelve-gauge into the back of the surprised winner, who was then robbed of approximately a thousand dollars. Most of the money was still drenched in the dead man's blood when I took it off Polk. Spent almost two months of living on the ground before I caught that murdering scoundrel. Man was slicker than a hand full of watermelon seeds.

My approval of Elizabeth's purchase had its basis in the quiet we'd achieved by moving away from the hustle and bustle of downtown Fort Smith. Never minded living in the apartment over the store we'd inherited from her father, but noise from the street tended to go on late into the night. After being so close to nature while in the wilds for weeks on end, sleep often came hard for me during my visits to civilization.

Our new home, north of town, sat on a hill overlooking a bend in the Arkansas. From the veranda that encircled the entire house, I could see Van Buren to the north and all of Fort Smith to the south. A good road led back to the Marshal's office and Judge Parker's chambers. In emergency situations, I found it easy to make myself available for duty in less than thirty minutes.

Loud ticking from the grandfather clock just inside the foyer rippled through the silence as Wilton made his way across Elizabeth's highly polished hardwood floors to the chair I'd offered. She was in town at the store, and we had the house to ourselves. He seated himself like an overdressed fussy old woman and kept picking at his clothing.

"Judge Parker has another special assignment for you, Marshal Tilden." The carefully barbered and immaculately dressed black gentleman leaned forward in his seat and gently placed a thick envelope on the table between us.

Since the day of my secret agreement with the Judge to take on the mission of being his personal bounty hunter, Mr. Wilton always performed the task of acting as our go-between. His responsibilities included the provision of all necessary information available and instructions about disposition of those scalawags so beyond the pale of justice they required the Judge's own private lawdog to dole out a "special brand" of handling.

"Rather than read all of that pile of paper, Mr. Wilton, I'm certain you can tell me exactly what I need to know about the man portrayed in your carefully prepared file." ·

"Of course, I can acquaint you with most of the facts. The biography contained in those pages is of one Alonzo Jackson Paine, known as Smilin' Jack to those bold enough to count him among their circle of friends. He is an evil one, Mr. Tilden, and needs immediate attention."

"Smilin' Jack Paine. I've heard the name, but can't say I have any substantial knowledge of his criminal activities."

Wilton crossed his legs, ran a manicured thumb and finger along the crease of his trousers, and flicked at little bits of dust as he drew the hand back. "His descent into murder and depravity began when as a teacher he vacated the tiny hamlet of Mount Joy, Ohio, in the company of one of his female students. A girl named Veronica Boatman, if memory serves." Wilton's deep Southern voice had the seeming power to both soothe and invigorate the listener at the same time.

"Unfortunate, but not all that unusual, Mr. Wilton. I've heard several such stories about teachers and students right here in Fort Smith."

"You are quite right, Marshal. But Miss Boatman possessed an astonishing beauty, and Paine soon forced the girl into selling her flesh to keep them in funds as they made their way along the Ohio to the Mississippi and thence to New Orleans. Upon arrival in that den of iniquity, Mr. Paine discovered a hidden talent for poker and other games of chance. The young lady worked the bars and saloons along the waterfront whilst he gambled and drank."

"Well, I haven't heard anything yet that would inspire Judge Parker to set me on the man's trail."

Wilton twisted in his chair. "Do you mind if I smoke, Mr. Tilden?"

"Not at all. You'll find an ashtray on the table to your left."

With a stag-handled pocketknife, he clipped the end from and lit a maduro panatela. The dense smoke had a hint of rum, and quickly filled the room with its heavy aroma.

"About two years ago, Paine's reputation as a gambler and gunman started to spread from New Orleans to the outer reaches of civilization. He claimed responsibility for at least five killings as the result of disagreements over his card-shuffling ability, and two more that involved men who made the mistake of falling in love with the beautiful Miss Boatman. Then—for reasons as yet unexplained—he added Veronica Boatman to his list of murders."

"He killed the girl?"

"So far as we can determine. At any rate, he fled New Orleans shortly before authorities there discovered her brutalized body in their living quarters. Her throat had been slit and the corpse exhibited numerous stab wounds. His trail led directly to the Nations. He has been operating there and on the fringes of Texas, Kansas, and Arkansas for some time now."

"But why do we want him? The only crimes you've told me about should involve Louisiana lawmen."

"Two weeks ago he and another bad one named Orvis Blocker stopped at the home of a Mr. Titus Burton on the line between the Choctaw and Creek Nations. They asked to come inside and warm themselves by the fire—a common request out in the wild places. Mr. Burton, a trusting soul and friend to everyone, admitted them. Once they gained entrance, Paine further requested that they be allowed to sleep on the floor. Burton agreed, had his wife make a pallet near the fire, and left them in the room with his hired man, Able Stoddard, who slept on a cot that occupied one corner of the main room." Wilton stopped for a moment, picked a piece of tobacco from his teeth, and dropped it in the ashtray.

"I have the feeling we're about to get to the crux of this matter, Mr. Wilton."

"You are correct, Marshal. At about two A.M., Paine and Blocker arose, skulked into Burton's bedroom, and shot the man dead while he slept next to his wife and children. Stoddard, awakened by the shooting, leaped from his cot. The killers fired on him, but—as he went down—he grappled with Blocker and wrestled him to the floor. Paine seized an ax from beside the fireplace and struck the unarmed man a blow in the neck that left a terrible wound. Stoddard fought them bravely, only to have his right hand chopped off in the fray. As he lay on the floor bleeding profusely from horrendous wounds, Paine struck the fallen man several more times in the back and legs, then left him swimming in a pool of his own blood. Next, they turned their attention to Mrs. Burton and assaulted her in the most brutal fashion before the very eyes of her four children."

"God Almighty—what finally brought the insanity to an end?"

Wilton tapped his cigar on the lip of the glass bowl, drew more of the thick smoke into his lungs, and sighed. "The family dog set up a racket outside and the killers rushed into the night. They obviously feared someone was approaching the house. Mrs. Burton drew the children about her, slipped out a back door, and walked barefoot for almost a mile to a neighbor's home. Miraculously, the much-abused Mr. Stoddard survived."

I couldn't believe my ears. "The man managed to live through being chopped up with a double-bit ax?"

Wilton pointed with his cigar toward the package of documents on the table. "Yes—and you'll find his statement, along with that of Mrs. Burton, on the bottom of that sizable stack of paper. We had a stenographer take the poor man's deposition as quickly as possible for fear he still might die from the dreadful wounds inflicted by Smilin' Jack Paine and his friend."

It might have seemed a trivial matter, but the image of a grinning fiend hacking away at the wounded Mr. Stoddard flashed across my mind and wouldn't go away. "Is there any indication in your record of how he got the moniker Smilin' Jack?"

"According to those who know him, he smiles almost all the time—no matter the situation. Such a countenance tends to fool most people into misinterpreting his grinning expression as being one of friendliness. At least that's what I'm told. Others maintain that he tends toward the slack-jawed idiot in appearance."

"Has he been seen since Burton's murder?"

"We have some sketchy reports from near McAlester's Store that he and his accomplice robbed several people along the M.K.&T. line near Atoka. They've shot at least two other men and had their way with another woman caught alone and too far from protection. Some believe he headquarters in an area between Tishomingo on the west, Durant on the south, and Atoka on the north. However credible, these reports might well be little more than conjecture."

I thought the meeting had drawn to an end, and stood to bid Mr. Wilton farewell. "I'll get on this as soon as possible. Please inform Judge Parker of my hope to put these men before him for judgment or before God for punishment. One way or the other, their outlaw days are about to come to an end."

Wilton rose, but made no move to leave. "There is one other thing, Marshal Tilden."

"Yes."

"Judge Parker asked me to request that you go about this particular hunt in a somewhat different manner."

"How so?"

"He would like you to accompany another marshal as one of his posse."

"Who did he have in mind?"

"Barnes Reed." He allowed the name to hang in the

air like a heavy cloud between us before continuing. "Would you have a problem with that, sir?"

Barnes Reed enjoyed a hard-earned reputation as one of the bravest and best of my fellow marshals. He'd been with Judge Parker from the earliest days of the law's arrival in Fort Smith. Hadn't had the chance to work with him in the past, and only knew the man by sight.

"What would be the point of me accompanying Marshal Reed on this hunt?"

Wilton leaned over and crushed his burning cigar in Elizabeth's crystal ashtray. "Marshal Reed has arrested Jack Paine before and knows him. Paine was a prisoner in our jail for almost a year before being bonded out by friends. Reed was already in possession of a fugitive warrant on Paine for failure to appear in court. Now these additional charges make his arrest or death more urgent. We felt a joint effort might expedite the matter of his capture or disposal. Judge Parker wants Paine and any accomplices, including Orvis Blocker, out of circulation as quickly as possible. Murderous rapists running amok tend to make the entire population of the Nations and northern Arkansas uneasy, Marshal Tilden."

"Is Reed aware of my understanding with Judge Parker?"

"No, he is not. As promised, the Judge, you, and I are the only three people living privy to the secret nature of your unique efforts on his behalf. I can assure you no one will ever learn the facts of the arrangement from us."

"Does the Judge wish me to make certain these men do not return for trial?"

Wilton studied on that one for a moment before answering. "Given the nature and history of Paine and his friends, we doubt you'll have much choice in this matter. Murder is one thing, but they've also raped at least two women. Be assured, resistance to arrest and return to Fort Smith is a virtual certainty."

"Barnes Reed has a well-known reputation for bringing his men back, Mr. Wilton. Doesn't care to kill them unless absolutely necessary, or so I'm told."

"In this particular set of circumstances, Mr. Tilden, we feel certain they will resist." He smiled again, bowed slightly, and left without saying another word. I knew beyond any doubt I'd just been given license to rid the countryside of Smilin' Jack Paine and anyone in his company by whatever means necessary. He and his friends' days among the living could be counted like grains of disappearing sand in the top half of an hourglass.

Junior tapped the eraser of his pencil on the notepad and waved at me like a man trying to bring a footrace to a halt. "Hold it just a minute."

"Look at this, Carl. We haven't seen the boy in over four months, I've been talking less than ten minutes, and he's already stopped me."

Cecil rolled a lemon drop around in his mouth and sputtered, "What didn't you understand, Junior?"

"Well, who was Barnes Reed? You've never mentioned him before. Could you tell me about him?"

"Sweet Jehoshaphat riding a buffalo! He don't know about Barnes Reed, Hayden. Can you believe that?"

"Yeah, actually it's easy to believe. In spite of the fact that Barnes was probably a better man than all the rest of us combined."

By now Lightfoot had pretty much figured our little act out, and instead of getting red in the face like he had during the first series of interviews, he just smiled, wrote a few more words on the page of his notepad, and asked the same question again.

"Can either of you tell me about Barnes Reed?" He sounded like a father talking to a couple of his sons who'd been caught stealing fresh-baked pies off the neighbor's windowsill.

Carlton perked up and sounded almost intelligent for a change. "Hayden's right. No one commanded the kind of respect Barnes got from friends and enemies alike. Even the worst of 'em knew if he hit the trail carrying a warrant what bore their names, the wild times of bein' out on the scout were pretty well over."

"Cannot recall seeing his name in any of my initial research materials, and you didn't mention anything about him in your last group of recollections, Mr. Tilden."

"Well, Junior, doubt you'll find much on Barnes in any of the handful of books written about our exploits in the Nations. Have to go a little deeper. Check out some of the Indian newspapers published in the territories during the '80s, or perhaps one of the weeklies put out around Paris, Texas, in the 1890s."

"Why do you suppose that is, Mr. Tilden?" He

scratched at his ear with his pencil and shifted further
back into his chair. Few more inches and he'd have
been lying down. Mr. Franklin J. Lightfoot, Jr., had
become considerably more relaxed around the two of
us old killers. Thought at the time I liked him more
that way. The tension between us while he wrote *Lawdog* had been a novelty at first, but tended to tire me
out just watching it.

"Barnes Reed was a black fellow, Junior."

The only outward sign of my revelation's impact on
the *Arkansas Gazette*'s star features writer was a brief
fluttering of the eyelids, kind of like a window shade
that slips from your grip and bangs around on its roller
for a few seconds.

"I am aware some black deputy marshals did work
out of the Parker court, but must admit nothing in my
research netted the name Barnes Reed. At least, I don't
remember having run across such a person."

"Need to check again, Junior. Bet you'll find him
mentioned prominently among those feared by bad
men all over the Nations, Arkansas, Texas, and Kansas.
Barnes Reed was a hell of a man."

"Hell of a man," Carlton chimed. "If'n I had to go
back into the wilds today and could pick between Hayden Tilden and Barnes Reed—it'd be a damned tough
choice. Of course, since Hayden's still alive and sittin'
right here with us, you can tell everyone that I'd pick
him." His mouth fell open in another gap-toothed grin.
The lemon drop rested on top of his tongue and swam
in a tiny pool of saliva like a little yellow boat.

"Suppose you met this fabulous manhunter in the
U.S. Marshal's office or Judge Parker's chambers."

"Wrong again there, Junior. Met him in the Napoli Café and Pie Shop on Rogers Avenue in Fort Smith. Barnes had an astonishing sweet tooth. He could put away an entire custard pie faster'n any man I ever knew."

Carlton sat up and mined for more candy in his covers. "Personally always liked that Italian feller's chocolate pies best. Me'n Barnes used to race to see who could polish his off the fastest."

Junior looked considerably surprised. "You knew this man that well, Mr. Cecil?"

"Sure. I was the other posse man who went out after Smilin' Jack. That's how me and Hayden met."

Day after I talked with Mr. Wilton, I stepped into the Napoli Café just in time to witness a pie-gobbling contest between Barnes Reed and a little red-haired feller who looked like it would be a pretty good trick if he could even hold that much at one sitting. They managed to finish off at almost exactly the same instant. Whole competition appeared too close to call, as near as I could tell. Barnes probably could have won the race, but spent most of the time laughing at his opponent, who'd managed to smear toasted meringue all the way up into his eyebrows. The black marshal, wide as a doubled-up barn door and thick with ropy muscles, beat on the tabletop with his right hand and laughed so loud the windows rattled. His shirt, large enough to make a sideshow tent, strained at every seam, and sleeves too short for arms the size of tree trunks stopped about two inches above his wrists.

When I walked up, he spotted my badge, glanced at

the Winchester, and immediately invited me to take a seat. "Mr. Tilden, I believe. Heard plenty about you and your big rifle." A voice so deep it seemed to come from somewhere outside the man rumbled across the table. His enormous right hand found mine and shook it vigorously. I'd never felt such strength from another human being. He motioned toward his laughing friend and said, "Meet the other member of our posse, Mr. Tilden. This here's my good friend Deputy Marshal Carlton J. Cecil."

Cecil wiped creamy bits of filling and crust from his fingers and greeted me in much the same way as his cohort. "My pleasure, sir." He smiled, and immediately went back to sopping the remnants of his feast with sticky, crumb-covered fingers.

"You appear ready and primed for the chase, Marshal Tilden," Barnes commented as he wiped his hands with a spotless napkin.

"Always prepared for the worst when more than a few steps away from the front door of my home, sir. I'm told you prefer to wait until tomorrow morning for our departure."

"Yes. Carlton and I must give testimony in Judge Parker's court later this afternoon. We brought a scoundrel named Grantland Dillworthy to heel 'bout a month ago. He couldn't make bond and only just now got a trial date. So, if it won't be too much of a problem, we'll meet you out by the ferry slips tomorrow morning at your convenience, and get after Smilin' Jack and his friend Orvis Blocker."

"I'm told you know Paine by sight."

"And Blocker as well. Smilin' Jack's a medium-built stack of cow dung, with long stringy hair he lets hang out on his shoulders. Has a scar across his left cheek where a member of the Union cavalry slashed him during the Battle of Pea Ridge. Usually sports a heavy mustache and chin whiskers. When we find Jack, Blocker will most surely be nearby. The men are rarely out of one another's sight."

Cecil nudged me with his elbow. "Cain't miss that peacock Blocker. He tends to dress hisself in leftover military duds. Don't know where he finds the stuff, but every time I've seen him he's managed to dandy up in another cavalry officer's long dress coat and hat. Carries a pair of old Colt Navy conversion pistols in military-style holsters, and has been known to hide a sawed-off shotgun from a sling he loops over his right shoulder." He held his right arm in the air and made a circular motion with his left hand to illustrate what he'd just said. "These men are a pair of real bad 'uns, and they probably won't be all that willing to come back considering the charges again 'em. Look for 'em to fight this time no matter how we approach 'em, and hell, I think we should give 'em whatever they want."

"I have no objection to that, Mr. Cecil, or an early morning exit, Marshal Reed. In fact, rather prefer it that way. Like to spend the eve of all my raids on the Nations in the company of my wife. So if you gentlemen would excuse me for now, I will see you in the morning."

Tipped my hat and started my exit. Before I could make the boardwalk, heard Barnes say something about having to nickname Carlton Ole Pie Face. They broke into table-banging laughter again, and were still in full hoot when I pulled the door closed.

Climbed aboard Thunder and headed north on Rogers. Hit Towson just a few blocks south of Reed's Mercantile. Elizabeth's father taught her well, and when he died—after Tollman Pike and Crouch Albrect stormed the store and shot him in the eye—she took over the business and turned it into a fabulously successful moneymaker by catering to Fort Smith's more affluent female shoppers. She visited New York twice a year on buying trips, and always amazed me with her ability to bring back the most desirable fashions of the day.

The front of the store had been rebuilt according to her specifications. Large false pillars in the Greek style now decorated our façade, and the entire thing had been sloshed with a new coat of white paint. Gave the appearance of substance, like the front was made of marble. The second floor, site of our old apartment, now bustled with women and girls from Fort Smith and Van Buren who had money enough to clothe themselves in much the same manner as their more affluent sisters back East.

Tied Thunder to the hitch rail I'd used my first day in town. She must have spotted me as soon as I stepped through the door. A flurry of blond-haired motion and sound flew into my arms.

"Hayden, dear man, how wonderful of you to stop in," she whispered as her lips brushed my ear. "Could you find nothing to do at home? No postholes to dig, animals to feed, or barns to clean out?" A playful grin danced across her lips and she dug at my ribs with her thumb.

"No, darlin'. I spent my morning visiting with Mr. Wilton."

Her eyebrows knotted up and deep creases slashed across her forehead. "Ah. He brought another assignment, no doubt."

"Yes. Unfortunately, I must leave early tomorrow."

"I see. So I'll have the privilege of dinner at Julia's and a quiet evening at home with my husband?" She flashed a wicked grin and pulled my hand to her waist.

"I can't think of a better way to spend my time than having a meal with the most beautiful woman west of the Mississippi." Kissed her hand, then her forehead, and whispered, "This bud of love, by summer's ripening breath, May prove a beauteous flower when next we meet."

She leaned heavily against me—her head buried in the folds of my coat—and said, "How can any woman resist a man who quotes Shakespeare, especially *Romeo and Juliet*."

I felt sure my arrival at the ferry across the Arkansas would be well ahead of my new associates. Couldn't have fired that shot any farther from the mark. They had been on the scene long enough to cook coffee and smoke half a cigar each by the time I made my appearance.

Barnes stood and offered me a cup of remarkably good up-and-at-'em juice that he called Reed's Special Early Morning Belly Wash. Other marshals, jailers, and posse men turned out the kind of wake-me-up drink that could float a windmill wrench. Never could ferret out Barnes's special recipe, but it sure was tasty stuff.

Carlton got a puzzled look on his face as he blew over the surface of the dark liquid in his cup. "What the hell is that?" He pointed to a spot behind me.

"That's Caesar. He'll tag along, if you don't mind."

Barnes rested his chin in his hand and studied the dog like he'd just discovered a whole new species of animal. "You sure that's a dog, Tilden? Looks most like a little fuzzy bear to me. Ain't never seen a dog that big before in my entire life."

"Well, I think he's a dog. Acts like one, most of the time."

Carlton pulled his hat off and scratched his head. "What the hell does he act like the rest of the time?"

"My guardian angel. Don't make any kind of move like you are about to do me harm. Several years ago— out in the wilds just this side of the Arkansas before you cross over into Dodge—he bit a Texan's entire ass off."

"Aw, go on with you. The whole thing?" Carlton turned away from the dog and held his hat over his own backside.

"Yep, took off the whole thing. Poor old boy never sat another saddle or drove another steer. Heard tell he shriveled up and died a few days later. You know, when you take off the most important part of a Texican, they don't usually live very long."

Barnes burst our laughing. People on the other side of the Arkansas must have heard him. Carlton got all red in the face, slapped his hat against his leg, and said, "Well, let's get this traveling doo-dah parade and animal show on the road, boys. We're losing time and money standing around here listening to lies about how dangerous your goddamned dog is. You don't have any more surprises for us, do you, Mr. Tilden?"

"Haven't seen him yet, but I'm fairly certain a friend of mine might be tagging along at a distance. He'll probably come into camp later this evening, or maybe just be there when we wake up in the morning. Then again, he might not show up at all. I just never know for sure."

Barnes kicked at the coals of their fire, then pushed the soot-covered coffeepot into his saddlebag. "Done heard 'bout your Indian shadow, Mr. Tilden. Old Bear you call him, I think. Goodly number of bad men from the territories sure do hate to hear it when you and that red gentleman set out on their trail."

"Well, he isn't really an Indian. Captured by them early in his life, lived with various tribes in the Nations off and on for almost fifty years, but he's still white underneath all that time and previous education."

Didn't take us but a few minutes to get everything together, load onto the ferry, and hit the far bank of the Arkansas, where the only law in evidence was pinned to our chests. Barnes set a steady and easy-to-maintain pace. Thought he'd be in a bigger hurry, but we started south and west like we had plenty of time. Most of the morning no one spoke, but after we stopped for a bite to eat—and then struck out again—Marshal Reed seemed ready to talk.

He pulled up beside me on his monster of a sorrel once we got under way again, and I couldn't resist the opportunity to get the conversation going with a little dig of my own. "You know, Marshal Reed, you can make fun of my dog if you like, but that's the tallest horse I've seen in years. Most men could get a nose-bleed from way up there where you are. Gotta be all of sixteen hands."

"Almost seventeen, Marshal Tilden. Man my size needs an animal with some mass and muscle to him like this here big ole sorrel gelding. He's powerful beyond describing and can run with the best of 'em."

From behind us Carlton called out, "Don't race with him, Hayden, unless you're just determined to lose your money. Seen him take the poke of many a man seated on some little sprinter that was supposed to be a real dirt-burner. Ole Big Red there took them all down."

"Well, pretty sure my horse Thunder here could give Big Red a run for your money, but we'll wait and do it another time when we don't have quite as much action in our futures." I said it with a smile and tipped my hat in Barnes's direction.

Reed chuckled and patted the sorrel's neck. "Can save you the money and Thunder's pride, Hayden. This red hoss would shuck the two of you right down to the cob in a full-bore two-mile race. And when it comes to stamina—I've not seen the animal yet that could hold up the way he can."

Carlton pulled alongside on the black marshal's right and said, "Well, when you two get finished bragging about these oat-burnin' rubber necks, it'd be nice if we could talk for a bit about where we're going. I know you've already got your mind made up, Barnes. Sure would like to be in on our destination."

Barnes swung his head back and forth as he tried to keep us both included in his assessment of our situation. "Couple of days ago I talked with some gentlemen who'd been out in the Nations doing maintenance work for the M.K.&.T., Flat Thumb Chester Waits and Beadle Davis. They both be a-knowin' Smilin' Jack and Blocker. Said they seen them fugitives at Drinkwater's Store 'bout ten days past. Them bad boys were traveling in the company of at least two other men— Lawerence Westbrook and One-Eyed Bucky Stillwell. Paine and Blocker would be a double handful all by theirselves. With Westbrook and Stillwell added to the mix, it's probably gonna be a real hair ball if we don't handle it right. Ole Smilin' Jack would take great pleasure in killing any or all of us, but that damned crazy Bucky Stillwell would laugh the whole time he was a-cutting our heads off afterwards."

"Isn't Drinkwater's that place out near the foot of the Arbuckle Mountains about forty miles west of Tishomingo?" I threw the question up in the air. Either one of them could have answered, but Carlton jumped right in.

"That's the one. But do you think they'll still be there by now, Barnes?"

"Maybe not, but they'll be back. Smilin' Jack tends to set up shop in an area and stick close to whatever hideout he's done wallowed himself down into till things get less hot. Be willing to bet they're camped somewhere 'tween the Santa Fe Railroad tracks and Tishomingo, and are coming in to Drinkwater's every so often for supplies and the like. Lot safer than visitin' the Chickasaw Nation's capital."

• • •

Three days later, we'd camped a bit west of the Muddy Boggy when a scab-covered fellow who looked like a farmer rode up on a scrawny mule. Old Bear still hadn't made an appearance yet, and I wasn't sure if he was nearby. I'd got to the point where I thought I could feel his presence, but never knew for sure till he turned up. The raggedy farmer slid painfully off the back of his bony animal and addressed us as a group.

"Ye'ns be them lawdogs from Fort Smith?" He had trouble getting anything much through split lips and a mouth crusted with dried blood.

"That's right, but how did you know who we were?" I asked. We had avoided all the ranches, country stores, well-known watering holes, and railroad stops. So it came to me as something of a surprise that he'd found us so easily.

"Hell's fire, they's folks been a-watchin' you boys ever since you crossed the Arkansas. Ain't one of you lawmen leaves Fort Smith but the whole countryside don't know of it. News travels ahead of you faster'n a Kansas cyclone. Bet they ain't been ten minutes of the past two days that I couldn't of found ye if'n I'd been in any shape to travel. Had to wait fer ye to come to me. The wife and me live 'bout two mile yonder ways."

He pointed to the southeast, but did so with what appeared to be some pain. "Five day ago Smilin' Jack Paine and three other'ns come to my place askin' fer water and sech. Couldn't very well refuse 'em. Knowed 'em fer bad boys. So I tried bein' neighborly. Thought they's gonna leave when they got what they asked fer. But then the wife came out'n the house.

She's a Chickasaw gal. Fine-lookin' woman. I suppose that's what they actually wanted 'stead of the water and sech. Anyway, they beat the red-eyed hell out of me and had their way with her. Thought we'uz dead 'uns sure as hell's hot, but fer some reason only God can explain, we still be with the livin'.''

Carlton shook his head. "They've done this before, friend. Tonight, when you hit your knees, best heap a pile of thanks on that God of yours for watching over you and your wife."

The battered plow-pusher nodded, mounted the skeletal mule, and led us to his home. Compared to what most people now call a house, it wasn't much. Raw, rough-cut boards for walls and split shingles for a roof over a single room housed the entire family. Chickens, guinea fowl, cats, dogs, and several children occupied the same dusty, manure-splattered spots in his meager yard. Cows and a few horses grazed in fields that surrounded the sad place. Only thing I noticed that might have indicated a woman's presence other than the kids was a patch of flowers at one end of the house under the only window.

Marshal Reed questioned the man closely along the way, and determined Matthew Conrad had legally lived in the Chickasaw Nation with his wife Sarah Little Crow for at least five years. But Barnes surprised me when he asked that I speak with the man's wife. It turned out to be one of the most difficult question-and-answer sessions I ever conducted.

She was already seated behind a curtain of rough cloth hanging from the ceiling in one corner of the room. Her English was remarkably good. Guessed later that such knowledge had to have originated at local Indian schools before she met her husband.

We lawmen all filed in together. Barnes and Carlton waited by the door. Took my seat on a crude chair that creaked and complained under my weight. I addressed my questions to the coarse drapery.

"Mrs. Conrad, my name is Hayden Tilden. I am a deputy U.S. marshal and part of a posse from Fort Smith. Your husband informed us you have been brutally assaulted by men who stopped here about a week ago. Please tell me as much as you remember so I can write it down as your legal statement to me and the other two marshals present here."

For what seemed a long time, no sound or movement emanated from behind the cloth wall between us. Then the most musical of voices, tinged with sorrow and humiliation, came to me through that piece of pitiful rag.

"I heard Matthew talking with someone and went outside. Four white men, bristling with pistols and knives, stood a few feet from the front door drinking from our water dipper and laughing. They all stopped when they saw me. I knew immediately what they intended." She paused and, for at least a minute, the silence allowed the clucking and other barnyard noises from outside to creep back in on her confession. Thought I heard a sniffle and a soft, stifled cough.

"The one Matthew called Smilin' Jack chased me back to this corner. He was on top of me so fast the possibility of resistance vanished with my dress and underthings. I could hear a commotion at the door. The others took turns beating Matthew. Thank God my children are too young to understand what happened. My husband fought them till I heard one of them say, 'I think ye've killed him, Bucky.' When Paine finished with me, the others filed in one at a time and took their turn. That one-eyed man was the worst. He smelled of stale whiskey, an absence of soap, and in the end— me." She never spoke another word while we were all present.

Not a dry eye remained when I handed Matthew Conrad the sheet of paper and pencil. "Both of you must sign this. It is of the greatest importance that Mrs. Conrad put her mark at the bottom of the page. We will need it as evidence—if there is a trial."

Didn't amount to anything more'n a mouthful of wasted words. I'd already made up my mind. No matter how Barnes or Carlton felt about it, none of Smilin' Jack's bunch would live more than a few minutes once I found them.

The sad farmer disappeared behind her flimsy wall. We waited outside the shack for almost five minutes before he returned with the paper. She had signed her name in a beautiful and much-practiced script.

"Marshal, my wife would like to take a final word with you, jus' you," he said as he handed me the deposition.

Stepped back inside the cabin and waited a few seconds for my eyes to adjust to the darkness. She had moved to the table in the middle of the room. Long black hair pulled over her right shoulder flowed down her chest to a tiny waist. A small, pure white flower behind her left ear cut through the darkness. Likely she'd picked it from the patch below her window. But for a bluish-purple bruise on her right cheek, her ordeal was physically undetectable.

Dark brown eyes searched my face. She sounded puzzled when she asked, "Are you the man who just spoke with me?"

I removed my hat, bowed slightly, and said, "Yes, Mrs. Conrad. Hayden Tilden, at your service."

"Marshal Tilden, my husband says you will try to arrest the men who attacked me." A single tear slid down her left cheek.

"You can be assured of it."

"Thank you, sir, for your efforts on my behalf. But if it would be the same to you, I'd prefer you killed them. Until they are all dead . . . my heart will never know any peace."

There was an awkward silence between us. I couldn't think of anything to say. When I finally found my voice again, whispered across the room to her, "Don't trouble yourself any longer, Mrs. Conrad. If there is any way under God's blue heaven to accomplish the end of their sorry existence, you can sleep well tonight knowing I'll do exactly as you wish. From this moment you may think of them as dead, until I have the opportunity to put them in the ground where they justly belong."

She blessed me with a halfhearted smile, mouthed the words "Thank you," and burst into heartrending sobs that racked her body and shook the table she leaned on. Her husband pushed past me as I stumbled through the door and to the company of my waiting friends. We ran from that place as fast as strong horses could take us.

I pushed Thunder harder than any time since we'd chased Saginaw Bob from the Wild Horse River country to Dallas. She seemed to get better the longer we went. In spite of the boasting about their animals' prowess, Barnes and Carlton had to work to keep up.

The vision of Sarah Little Crow Conrad's face floated before me—between that of my mother and sister—every step of the way to a spot about five miles south and east of Drinkwater's Store. Men who could, and would, do such things to a woman now swarmed across the Nations like a carpet of ravenous locusts. The thought of it damn near made me sick.

Barnes brought us to a halt. "We'll stop here." He scratched Big Red's ears, then patted the sweaty animal's neck.

"Why quit now?" The fire of revenge for Sarah Little Crow's depredation raged in me like a dead cedar tree put to torch, and the anger came though in my voice. "We can be there in thirty minutes and get this over."

The huge black marshal and Carlton, who at the time could stand under a clothesline in a thunderstorm and not get wet, stepped from their animals, removed their saddles, and hobbled the horses to graze.

Barnes spread his blanket, reclined with his head against his saddle, then pulled his hat down over his eyes. "There be plenty of time, Hayden," he said. "Bet them ole boys be around tomorrow or the next day or whenever we gets there."

"What makes you think that, Barnes?" The question had a somewhat bitter edge on it that I regretted as soon as it came out of my mouth.

He lifted his hat from his face and said, "Because, Marshal Tilden, they be a-thinkin' they's safe."

We'd barely had time to make camp when Carlton threw his saddle roll on the ground, pulled out a set of the most ragged, nasty clothing I'd ever seen, and began shucking what he had on.

They both smiled and winked as I shook my head in disbelief. "What the hell are you doing?" I asked.

"Little disguise, Hayden. Them boys know Barnes by sight, and I'd be willing to bet a year's pay that if you strolled up to Drinkwater's carrying your Winchester, they'd figure out who you are pretty quick too. Fortunately, Carlton J. Cecil ain't nearly as famous or as good-looking as either one of you fellers, yet. These duds here and my ugly face should fool 'em if they're still around. Once we know whether they're about or not, plans for taking them should be easier and it'll make the whole thing safer for all of us."

I still couldn't believe what he was about to do. "So you're gonna dress yourself up like a broken-down drunk and just stroll up to Drinkwater's like you belong there."

"Thash it, Tildrink, my man." His slurred speech was punctuated by a splash of homemade whiskey from a bottle he sloshed into the air and walked into as the drops headed for the ground. Before my disbelieving eyes, Barnes's laughing companion transformed himself into the most pitiful-looking inebriate in the Indian Nations—and it took less than five minutes.

"Shee you boysh sometime tomorrow or the nesh day." He took a snort from the bottle and strolled off in the direction of the frontier mercantile, notions center, and watering hole where Smilin' Jack and his bunch waited, if our luck held.

I turned to Barnes and said, "He'll be all right out there by himself, won't he? It is at least five miles, you know."

"Needn't be a-worryin' yourself about Carlton. Better to harbor considerable concern 'bout any thang or anybody what he comes up against. He knows the way. Been there at least a dozen times. And don't be fooled by his rough ways and sorry grammar. Out here in the wild places, the man's smarter than a greased copperhead and meaner than an outhouse rat."

Well, all that could have turned out to be true, and then again maybe not. At the time, I remember thinking we'd probably never see Carlton J. Cecil again. If we did, he'd most likely be dead. And if One-Eyed Bucky Stillwell had anything to say about it, we'd find the head and the body in two different places.

2

"MAN NEEDS KILLING AND DAMNED QUICK"

LIGHTFOOT FLIPPED THE cover closed on his pad and shoved it into his jacket pocket. "Sorry I have to leave in the middle of a semi-cliffhanger, boys, but another appointment down at the State House requires my presence for about two hours this afternoon. Be all right if I come in tomorrow morning around nine-thirty or maybe ten, Hayden?"

"Hey, you know it's all okay with me, son. Show up whenever you want. Keeps us from having to spend much time talking to each other, faking a checkers game, or trying to make peace with Leona Wildbank every time we turn around."

Carlton woke up when our friend stood. He cupped his palsied right hand over his ear and did his I'm-so-deaf-the-Second-Coming-probably-won't-wake-me act. "What'd you say, Hayden?" His scraggly head bobbed around like an apple in a tub of water.

Raised my voice just enough to make him happy. "Said we're always here, aren't we?"

"Oh, hell, yes." Then he mumbled off to himself for a second or two. "Cain't go nowheres. Closed all the saloons and beer joints years ago. Ain't seen a lewd woman in so long, done forgot what one looks like. By God, soiled doves, now there's a phrase none of these young'ns get to use much, I'll bet. My all-time favorite handle for a bawdy woman, though, was alley bat. That's a good 'un."

That night, after the staff got all us inmates in our respective cells, I slipped back out onto the porch. Figured if Ole bony-fingered death had plans to come for me unexpected, I would rather be in a place I actually liked more than my room. Being able to look at the night sky reminded me of sleeping on the ground in the Nations. Missed that part of my past life. No doubt about it, though, our veranda got cold after dark came in the winter, but the blanket off my bed could keep a hibernating grizzly bear warm.

Pulled a chair over to a corner where the nurses couldn't see me, and lit one of the cigars I kept hidden in a stash above the ceiling panel over my bed. Night nurse Heddy McDonald caught me standing in the middle of my stony hospital cot one night as I fished out my loot. She promised not to tell on me. Liked her more than some of the others because of her thoughtful gesture that let me retain some of my independence, however tiny the amount.

Anyway, I sat in the dark, enjoying a rum-soaked

Italian stogie called a Barotti Twist, which closely resembled a rotten tree root, and I saw them sneak Essie
Bryant out. Leona did stuff like that, you know. Bet
Essie had been dead all afternoon. Maybe even passed
the night before. Couldn't remember seeing her in at
least a week. Guess it was altogether possible she had
laid up in there for so long the smell got to somebody.

We had a terrible incident one weekend in August
a couple of years ago when they forgot to check on
lonesome Edgar Eastlake. Hell, he was younger than
Cecil or me, but death came and got him and no one
even noticed. Man had a case of the halitosis that could
take paint off a Kansas barn door, and not many friends
because of it. Carlton claimed a skunk got between
Edgar's teeth and died. More than once Carl yelled at
Edgar and told him he should have his skunk surgically
removed. He even left bottles of Listerine sitting
around in Edgar's room a time or two. Poor stinky-
mouthed wretch's mind worked kind of like a broken
pocket watch, and he never could understand what Carl
was ranting about or why big jugs of antiseptic mouth-
wash kept appearing on his dresser. Shameful thing for
a poor old man like him to go out alone the way he
did, though. He seemed like a nice enough sort—just
cursed with a case of the feeble mind and a mouth that
smelled like the bottom of a recently emptied chamber
pot.

Anyway, Leona didn't want us to see the dearly departed lugged out. So she would make the staff wait
till about one or two in the morning and try to slip
them past us. Said she didn't want her little family—
that's what she called us—to get upset. Never could

imagine what the woman thought we would be distressed about.

Most of us antique discards had seen more dead folks than Leona would in two lifetimes of working around one of these depots for used-up people. Some of those, feeble in mind, body, or both, even wanted the end to come. Life had worn them down to the nub, and the only thing left was the answer to the greatest of all questions. Every once in a great while, I got to feeling the same way myself. But not since the day Franklin J. Lightfoot Junior showed up. Cherry-cheeked boy made me feel like I could make it to a hundred. God almighty! 1960. Would that be a hoot or what?

Seriously doubt if it would be worth the trip, though. Between Carlton and me, we've seen about everything a person could imagine. The world can't change enough between now and the sixth decade of this century to make it worth sticking around for another twelve years. Even if the answers to all our questions got revealed, how many ancient, decrepit, hundred-year-old people would give a big rat's ass.

Back in my youth, death chased me all over Parker's Indian Nations head down, horns out, kicking dirt in every direction trying to get in my face. Now, he creeps around behind potted plants, hides in old ladies' comforters, and often stands by my bed when I sleep. I've awakened in the night and peeked at him through slitted eyes as he tried to dart behind my curtains. Saw the tricky bastard when he followed Essie out. He turned, smiled, and shook a skeletal finger at me. I was surprised by how old he'd become. For some reason I remembered him as being much younger.

"Carlton's not coming out this morning?" Lightfoot asked, pulling out his pen.

"Afraid not, Junior. He had another one of those trying-to-die nights. Don't expect to see him up and around for another week or so."

"He'll be okay, won't he?"

"Oh, sure. He has one of these things he likes to call spells about once every two weeks or so. His diabetes puts him in bed pretty regular now. Course he don't do a lot to help stop it. Man has all the table manners and eating habits of a rabid weasel."

"Well, let's get back to it. We were camped outside a place called Drinkwater's Store, if I remember correctly."

"You got it, Junior."

"Oh, by the way, where was Old Bear?"

"Don't know. Hadn't shown up. He always came and went any time he wanted. Grew not to expect him till he put in an appearance, and most of the time he'd just materialize like a ghost. Usually when I needed him most."

Barnes and I fished a shallow creek near our camp and just generally led the lives of layabouts for the next few days. Once farming made its brutal exit from my life for good, I readily assumed the mantle of one who had decided he would never drown himself in his own sweat—unless absolutely necessary. So, I took the lull in stride and used it to learn as much as possible about my new associate. We'd not had much chance to talk until then, and I learned pretty fast that, unless you asked him directly, Barnes Reed didn't give out much information about his life and times.

"How long have you worked for Judge Parker, Barnes? Heard you signed up right after he got to Fort Smith."

We were stretched out by our fire the first night after Carlton left. I'd noticed that although the Negro marshal liked to talk, it usually didn't involve anything of any substance. Once he started on this horse thief, or a favorite gun, or land he secretly coveted, he hardly slowed enough to let me get a word in crooked. But even then, he revealed so little of himself I had to keep boring in on him to get what I wanted.

"Took a job with the Judge in '75—July or August, as I remember it. He'd been in Fort Smith for near 'bouts three months." His voice had the hypnotic power and depth to put a man to sleep. Knew I'd have to fight off the heavy eye to stay with him.

"What about your life before you took on a deputy marshal's commission?"

He peered through the flames, studied my face intently. It felt as though he searched for some assurance that the things he revealed would be to a friendly listener.

"Started off like most black folk in the South. Be born in Arkansas, I think."

"You think? You don't know for sure?"

"Not for absolute certain. Not important anyway. Ended up living on a farm in north Texas near 'bouts the community of Gainsville." He poked at the coals with a stick and threw me relaxed, friendly glances.

Stared across the crackling flames at his smiling, open face and remembered that my father never owned slaves. He felt it a practice beyond contempt. I always agreed with him wholeheartedly, but had to admit to my secret self I found the darker aspects of our national shame interesting because of my lack of knowledge on the subject. I suppose an inquisitive attitude about such things had its root in romanticized feelings toward warfare, chiefly the war of my childhood's fancies.

Born in 1860, I had no memory of the death and destruction brought on by what my mother referred to as the Unpleasantness. So I made up my mind to simply plunge ahead and blurted out, "Did you have a difficult life as a slave, Barnes?"

Not sure anyone had ever asked him the question so directly. He thought it over for some time before he answered. "Not *so* difficult, I suppose. Not as thorny as some others when I spend a spell thinking on it. Bad times and mistreatment ain't the point anyhow, Hayden. Was the being of the thing, don't you see?"

Thought I knew what he meant, but wanted him to continue. "Sorry, but I don't understand, Barnes."

"Well, what I meant was, just being a slave was bad enough. The thing didn't require beatings, poor food, or bad clothing. It was the being of the thing made me hate it—and Master Chauncey Ledbetter." He quickly lapsed off into silence again and made me retrieve the thread.

"Ledbetter. I've heard of a family from Texas named Ledbetter. Well-known politicians and such, I think."

"Yes. I became body servant to the family's eldest

son, Chauncey. We grew up together as children. For all the years of our early lives, I never knew a waking moment not linked to his. Owe a classic education money couldn't buy to our shared experience. Sat next to him during instruction, listened, and kept my mouth shut about what I learned. Had it not been for my position in the Ledbetter house, I'd most likely still be illiterate and scratching out a meager living on a piece of hardscrabble, barren land somewhere in Arkansas. As you might have now noticed, I can lapse in and out of a cotton-patch version of grammar with the greatest of ease."

"But you came to hate Chauncey Ledbetter?"

"Children grow up, Hayden. Most become their parents in spite of everything life presents them. They can't help themselves. Chauncey turned into a young man given to the worst aspects of his brutal father's personality. Year by year our relationship soured, and by the time the Civil War arrived, his conduct bordered on the unbearable."

Rolled onto my back and stared into the inky darkness. Always felt closer to God sleeping on the ground. The great separation of earth and sky vanished when the blackness came. The whole of heaven seemed to press down on me like the love I'd left behind in Fort Smith. I've always believed that any night on the ground looking at a sky decorated with millions of flashing dots applied to the great void as though by God's silver-tipped brush beat sleeping in bed by a mile.

"He fought for the South, didn't he, Barnes?"

"Yes, and for a time, I fought with him at Chicka-

mauga, Missionary Ridge, and Pea Ridge. Hellish
places no one should have to have seen. But we made
it out alive. All that counts in war—just getting home
alive. Managed to stick with the man for another five
years. But he finally stepped over the line one time too
many. Guess you could say we had a difference of
opinion and went our separate ways."

"You ran away?"

"Well, in a fashion. Was a free man by then, you
know. I decided to leave, and he decided to let me.
Course all them knots I put on his head might have
had something to do with his decision. First, he threat-
ened to call out the night riders on me. So I hid out.
Then when things got quiet, headed for Van Buren and
laid low for a couple of years."

"How'd you get into the criminal-chasing business?"

He relaxed into his bedding and, for a second or so,
we stared at the night sky together. "Started out doin'
deputy marshal work in Van Buren back in '72. Sorry
job that one. Mostly, we picked up drunks and tried to
keep trash off the streets. You know, things like dead
pigs and horse manure. In '74 took a job as deputy
sheriff for the county. Got to travel in the Nations some
with the sheriff. Found out I had a talent for Indian
languages. Speak enough to get by with several of
them now. About a year later, worked myself into an
assistant jailer's job. Never really cared for the work
much, but it beat dragging drunks in and picking up
garbage.

"Then, in '75, Judge Parker came to Fort Smith. His
bunch of lawdogs was a whole new deal. Been working
for him ever since, and can't say I've regretted a min-

ute of it. Enjoy the work. Like catching bad people and dragging their sorry hides to Judge Parker's court for their just deserts. Jesus ain't the only one what knows we've got some bad ones out here."

Wanted to get a definite idea of how he felt about Smilin' Jack and whether he had intentions of bringing the outlaw back alive, so I said, "You think Paine and his bunch will be as much trouble as Carlton claims?"

"Oh, yeah. They'll fight. You can bet your grandpa's Kentucky farm on it. Best get some sleep, Hayden. When Carlton gets back, things will start happening pretty fast and you want to be sharp. Smilin' Jack's kin to a rattler on his father's side and a black widow on his mother's. God reserved the man his very own rocking chair in Satan's front parlor the day he got born. Lord willing, we'll be the ones what send him to a much-deserved eternal rest." He yawned, stretched, and rolled onto his left side.

For a long time the fire snapped, popped, and threw flashing sparks toward heaven. The horses stamped and snorted. Night birds called to one another like lost souls searching for safety, and every once in a while, a breeze brought me the smell of some kind of blooming flower. Then I heard Barnes mumble as though in his sleep, "Aim to see he gets where he belongs, Hayden. The man needs killing—and damned quick."

Next day, after the noon sun passed over, Carlton strolled back into camp, danced a jig around our fire, and grinned like he'd just come in from an all-night social where the liquor was free and the women were easy. "You boys been fishing, I see," he said, and grinned.

He picked through some of our leftover bream, poured himself a cup of Barnes's coffee, pulled up a piece of broken timber for a chair, and went right into his report.

"Didn't take much to fool them ole boys. Hell, I waltzed in there just like I owned the place and they didn't even notice me. They're all suckin' on individual jugs of Who-Hit-John so hard, they barely had time to take a breath between swallers. There's five of 'em now. Paine, Blocker, Westbrook, Stillwell, and"—he hesitated and stared at Barnes as though to give the last name emphasis—"Billy Standing Bull."

Barnes groaned like a man in the throes of grief, pitched his coffee onto the fire, and rubbed his forehead with the back of his left hand. "Well, the only way it could be any worse is if God sent Jesse James and Cole Younger over to Drinkwater's before we get there."

Carlton blew on the liquid in his cup, then said, "Oh, hell, Barnes it ain't that bad. They don't know me. They don't know Tilden here, and if we play our cards right, we just might be able to catch 'em all without firing a shot."

Sounded pretty good to me. "You really think we can take them so easy, Marshal Cecil?"

He threw his head back and laughed. "Oh, hell, no. I just said it to make you and Barnes feel better. Sure as we ride up to Drinkwater's, they're probably gonna blast the bejabbers out of us. Billy Standing Bull would most likely open fire just for the fun of hearing his guns go off."

Well, after his comical but hard-nosed assessment,

none of it sounded too good. We sat around and jawed it over till almost dark, and finally decided we'd move in on the place from three different directions and hope we caught them off guard. Barnes said the chances of such luck were damn slim and none, but it was the best we could do under the circumstances. I suggested we wait till the killers left Drinkwater's and catch them out on the trail somewhere. Carlton didn't like my idea. Said it'd be too easy for them to get away, what with five of them and only three of us. Having them all holed up in the store seemed like the best way to take the whole bunch at one time. Barnes agreed, but made the point that we needed to go in ready to burn up a lot of powder. Taken altogether, I didn't like the sound of the plan a bit, and remembered feeling considerable better the time Billy Bird, Handsome Harry, and I walked in on those Texas boys down in Black Oak.

When I take the time to look back on the thing and give it any serious thought at all, guess I'd have to admit to myself we couldn't have planned it any worse.

Next morning, shortly after the sun came up, we got ourselves spread out around Drinkwater's. The one-story rectangular building ran east and west with the front facing south. The backside butted up against a pile of rocks about sixty feet high that dribbled down from the foothills. Carlton took the east side, Barnes moved in from the west. I reluctantly agreed to meet the evil scoundrels head-on by coming up from the south.

Sycamore trees hovered over each end of the rough store like big umbrellas. The west end of the buck and battened structure supported a lean-to shed used as a makeshift barn for horses kept in the corral stretched around it. The lumber for the whole thing appeared to have been nailed up and ripped down several times in other constructions, and had the washed-out color of greasy gray mud. Out in Carlton's direction, the sickly sweet odors from an outhouse wafted around on a swirling dust devil that kicked up at the exact same time we started moving in on the place from about two hundred yards out.

Guess Thunder couldn't have taken more than twenty or thirty steps when the shooting started. At least three men busted through the door, and windows on either side of it, guns blazing. I recognized the sorry bastard described to me as Smilin' Jack. He was the first one out, and levered shells into a Henry rifle as fast as he could pump it. First one burned a hole in the air so close to my ear I could feel the heat and smell the powder.

Thought the man on Paine's right was One-Eyed Bucky Stillwell. Didn't recognize the other fellow. Had my Winchester up at the ready, but didn't react fast enough for their first volley. Then things got scary as hell when it seemed like all those sons of bitches lined up together and fired directly at me at the same time.

A single tongue of flame melded from the three barrels of their weapons and spat death my direction. There was this odd *thump, thump, thump* beneath me. Went to put the spur to Thunder, but she twisted awkwardly, stumbled, and dropped like a felled tree. Landed on her left side and flung gouts of black blood back and forth as her head swung from side to side. Poor beast tried to run lying there on the ground. She shook for a few seconds like she was cold, her legs stopped moving, and she sighed so loud I could hear it over all the gunfire aimed my direction. Then, she stiffened up like she was frozen for a bit, and almost all the air rushed out of her at the same time.

I had tried to pull out of the stirrup on the way down, but my left leg got wedged under her anyway. Knew it was gonna take everything I could do to kick myself free and drag away. Wasn't making much headway with the thing when she kinda flopped like a fish out of water—just enough to break me loose. Then, she let go of one last, long, blood-saturated breath.

Only God knows for certain, but I'd swear to this day she knew I couldn't get loose and used up everything she had left to get off me. All the while, bullets kicked up dust around us and punched more holes in her. Kept thinking Thunder had saved me by the way she died. Other than all the air kind of whooshing out of her at one time, she never made another sound.

By the time I got completely loose, turned around, and could defend myself, the gunfire was pretty general, and hard for me to tell where it all came from. At least three men made for the horse pen, but Barnes was moving in on them as fast as Big Red could carry him. He stood in his stirrups, had the reins in his teeth, and pumped bullets through a pistol in each hand as fast as he could thumb the hammers.

Turned back the other way and saw Carlton jump from his horse. He carried a cut-down shotgun and hid himself behind the outhouse. Both barrels from his big boomer opened up just about a second after he hit the ground running. Buckshot peppered the entire front of

the store, and someone on the porch screamed. Big
fellow I took to be Billy Standing Bull went to yelling
and whooping. He hopped up from behind the water
trough over on the end of the building closest to Carlton and started running toward the outhouse. He
poured a steady wall of lead in and around the rugged
outdoor reading room. Guess he used up all the powder
available about a second before Carlton stepped from
behind a boulder a bit right of his original hiding place.

Heard him yell something like, "Hi there, you worthless pile of weasel shit." Then he blasted Billy Standing Bull completely out of his moccasins.

Well, I kept steady spraying lead at anybody running
toward the horses or shooting in my direction. Barnes
and Smilin' Jack appeared to be in a two-man gunfight.
Paine put one through Barnes's hat brim, cut his reins
with another—that one set the big marshal afoot. The
murdering bandit kept up such a volley of fire from his
iron-framed Henry, I feared he just might kill my
newly made friend.

Swung my rifle around on Paine, but every time I
squeezed one off, the man managed to move just
enough to keep my shots from finding him. Barnes
dropped to one knee to reload. Put himself in a hell of
a bad spot. I got up on both my knees and really showered Smilin' Jack with everything I had. Thought I hit
him at least twice, but was so far away I couldn't be
sure, and it didn't slow him down any. He made it to
the corral, jumped into the saddle on a dun horse, and
was gone faster than a Baptist deacon taking up a col-
lection. He passed to within fifty feet of Barnes on his
way out, and let off another round of fire. One slug

sliced across Barnes's back and burned a streak in his jacket from one shoulder to the other. My friend did manage to get the last shot off, and even though it seemed to hit home, Paine stayed upright in the saddle and made good his escape.

After he disposed of Standing Bull, Carlton waded into those ole boys who'd vacated the corral and bunched up on the porch. The man could shoot and reload a shotgun faster than anyone I'd seen, except Billy Bird. Inside of thirty seconds, he'd managed to rip off about ten shots and put so many holes in two of Paine's three remaining gang members, you could of held them up and read the *Fort Smith Elevator* through their perforated hides.

The whole dance couldn't have lasted more than a minute or so. Standing Bull kept twitching for quite a while after the smoke started to clear. Carlton hopped up on the porch and kicked the other wounded men.

"That 'un there's Orvis Blocker." He talked so fast his words came out like one long word as he pointed to a scrawny pile of dirt seated upright in Drinkwater's doorway. The front of the wounded man's shirt had at least twenty holes from the buckshot, and a Smith and Wesson pistol lay in his lap. Wispy smoke curled from the barrel and cylinder.

"Is he dead?" I asked.

"I damn sure hope so. I shot the hell out of him. If he gets up and tries to walk away, I'll knock him back down, stand on his chest, and you can shoot him a time or three." He grinned and kicked Blocker onto his back. The blood-covered outlaw man moaned. "Just be damned, guess he's still with us. Worthless bastard's tougher'n I thought."

A stocky man with gray hair had fallen off the porch and rolled up against one of the posts of the hitch rack. "Is this the one called Lawrence Westbrook?" I pulled his head back so Carlton could see the face just as Barnes walked up.

"That's him, and the one over here"—he pointed to the end of the plank porch nearest the corral—"is none other than the infamous One-Eyed Bucky Stillwell. And slap me nekkid, but the son of a bitch is still alive."

While Carlton and Barnes grabbed Stillwell by the feet and dragged him up on the porch, I stumbled back over to Thunder. Sometimes terrible things have a way of not really making any impact at the moment they first happen. When you're real busy trying to stay alive, death has a way of sneaking up beside you and taking someone or something else so fast your mind just can't get itself around the thing. Thunder had been a fine companion at times when I was out on the scout alone. More than once she'd saved my hide when things got a lot hotter than I cared for. Hadn't been for that horse, I never would have caught Saginaw Bob and his bunch. Thunder was special, and Smilin' Jack Paine killed her with no more feeling than if he'd squeezed the head off a tick.

Barnes eased up behind me while I stood looking down at her. "Sorry about all this, Hayden. We probably should have tried it all a little different. Maybe we could have come up with a plan that would have kept something like this from happening."

Took my hat off and wiped my forehead on the sleeve of my shirt. "Barnes, as God is my witness, if it takes me the rest of my time as a deputy marshal, I'm going to find that horse-killing son of a bitch and erase him from the world like yesterday's lesson on a schoolmarm's blackboard. He did this on purpose. His first shot went right by my ear. When he realized he'd missed, he plugged her dead center. She was gone when she hit the ground. If Thunder hadn't dropped the way she did, Smilin' Jack would've put so many holes in my hide, Old Man Drinkwater could've sold me for a flour sifter."

Barnes patted me on the back.

Well, somehow Orvis Blocker had managed to live through the curtain of lead we'd dropped on that bunch. Carlton propped him up next to One-Eyed Bucky, and was standing on the wounded man's leg when we walked up.

"Where'd he go, Orvis?" Carlton punctuated his question with more pressure from the heel of his boot.

Blocker squealed like a stuck pig. "Sweet Jesus, Marshal! Christ Almighty, that hurts! Please stop."

"I'll stop when you tell me where Smilin' Jack was headed. Figure you boys must have had some idea of a place to run and hide before we showed up. So where'd he go?" Carlton backed off about half a step and kicked the wounded outlaw in the side where a purple stain slopped from his shirt and spilled into the waist of his pants. I swear, the sound that came out of Orvis Blocker was enough to jerk tears out of a glass eye.

"Oh-h-h, God Almighty! He went to Martin Luther

Big Eagle's place! I swear it. That's all I know, Marshal. Goddammit, please don't kick me again!" He hunkered over to protect the wound and wept like a baby.

Carlton bent down into the brigand's face and sneered, "You'd better be damned sure of that, Orvis, or so help me God, you'll wish you'd never seen my face. How'd you boys spot us?"

One-Eyed Bucky picked at the bloody left sleeve of his shirt and mumbled, "Hell, you lawdogs ain't so damned smart. Larry Westbrook seen you in Fort Smith more than a time or two, Marshal Cecil. He remembered who you was after you left here t'other day. Been looking for you boys to show up ever since. Billy Standing Bull was on watch and seen you coming this morning. Recognized that feller with the big Winchester too. Said he seen him a-standin' on the gallows the day Parker hung Bob Magruder. Billy and Magruder wuz old drinking compadres."

Barnes and I loitered by the hitch rail and listened to it all. I'd never heard of the newest killer who'd just got dropped into the mix, and felt foolish when I asked, "Who's Big Eagle and where can we find him, Barnes?"

He shoved shells in the last of three pistols he carried and said, "It don't matter. We can just forget about catching' Smilin' Jack for the time being. Might have to get him on the ricochet."

Well, that really walled my eyes and bowed my neck. "What the hell do you mean? I promised Sara Little Crow Conrad I'd try my best to kill the son of a bitch, and I aim to do exactly that. He doesn't have so much of a head start on us we can't catch up with him."

"That's true enough, Hayden. But he'll make it to Martin Luther's place long before we could nab him, and once he does, the man might as well be on the backside of the moon as far as we're concerned. Besides, you kept your promise. You did about as much as any man could to kill ole Jack. Just not in today's cards."

"Would you mind explaining some of that to me? I'm totally lost here." By that point I was madder than a bullfrog in a tack factory. "If you know where Smilin' Jack's going, we can ride him down and kill him, or bring him back. That is, if he's of a mind to come back. As you well know, I'm all for doing for him the same as we just got through doing for some of these ole boys." Waved in the general direction of the two men we were about to have to put to bed with a pick and shovel.

Barnes looked at me like a man who understood, but knew the dice hadn't rolled our way. "He's headed for Red Rock Canyon up on the Canadian. Big Eagle has a place there that's about as close to a fortress as any in the Nations. Calls it Robber's Roost. It's supposed to be dug into the face of a bluff. I've heard claims that from his perch, he can see everything for miles in three directions. Least that's one story. Another tale we keep hearing declares the thing is down inside the canyon and controls the entire canyon floor. Either way, it'd take a company of cavalry to get at 'em, and even then, we'd probably lose half our men or maybe more. None of our fellow deputies has ever managed to get in there—and several have tried—so you might as well just give it a rest till we can run across Smilin' Jack Paine at some more opportune time in the future."

Carlton snapped a thumb toward Thunder. "Till we get you another horse, Marshal Tilden, you ain't gonna be riding much of anybody down."

Well, didn't like admitting it, but they were right, and after we buried Lawerence Westbrook and Billy Little Bull, it took a day and a half of riding double and dragging Orvis and Bucky on litters before we found a horse ranch north of Atoka where I bought a sorrel gelding that was almost a dead ringer for Big Red. Named him Gunpowder. When he got to picking his feet up and laying them down pretty good, the sound boiled up around you like you were in a tunnel and drowning in a wave of explosive noise.

We cleaned those sorry outlaws' wounds with carbolic and made a suitable poultice for all the holes we could find. Some of the shot had barely punched through the piles of filth-encrusted, ragged clothing they wore, and easily popped out of the newly made dents in their worthless hides. Most of the holes in both of them came from Carlton's shotgun pellets and didn't appear life-threatening.

Our trailside doctoring kept those boys alive till we made it to McAlester's Store. Finally found a real people doctor there who just barely managed to save One-Eyed Bucky. He almost bled to death from the rifle bullet in his arm in spite of everything we had already done for him.

He whined and cried to the point that I'd had all I

could take from him when I bent over next to his ear and said, "I swore to Sarah Little Crow I'd kill you, Bucky. And if Barnes Reed had managed to turn his back on me for about one second at Drinkwater's, you'd be deader than Judas and roasting in hell right now. But while I listened to you brag about Smilin' Jack's escape and reloaded my rifle, I got to figurin' it'd be a lot more fun to see you mess your britches when you swing from the cross-beam of the Gates of Hell. So shut your blubbering mouth or I'll put one in your skull and save Judge Parker the expense of having Maledon string your sorry ass up." Don't think he made a sound after that.

Blocker turned out to be one tough ole bird. He had a cupful of shot still in him and at least two rifle bullets, but none of it seemed to bring him down all that much. Man was so pleased to be walking and talking, his spirits just naturally kept him among the living and laughing in spite of the fact that we were taking him to Judge Parker for a certain hanging.

By the time we reached Fort Smith, I'd come up with a sketchy plan for Big Eagle's outlaw roost. Barnes didn't think much of it, but Carlton laughed for almost half an hour after I told him about it, and said he'd be glad to help me see it happened just the way I'd described it.

Funny thing happened on the ferry back to Arkansas. One-Eyed Bucky Stillwell all of a sudden up and died. I went out and watched them dig his grave a few days later. Smiled the whole time they shoveled dirt on him because in spite of poor aim, questionable decisions on my part, and just general bad luck, I'd managed to keep most of my promise to Sarah Little Crow. Smilin' Jack was the only loose end left. Way I had it figured, he was already dead and just didn't know it.

Lightfoot sat up in his chair and reached for the coffee Nurse Heddy McDonald had brought out for us. He held the cup and saucer up to his lips and blew across the steaming liquid before he took a careful sip.

After several nibbling runs at the lip of his cup, he said, "You want me to believe the gumdrop-crazed old coot you play checkers with was the man you just described to me? The Carlton J. Cecil who sat in the chair across this table from me the whole time we worked on *Lawdog,* and yesterday spent most of the afternoon with candy juice dribbling on his chest, shotgunned wanted fugitives like cotton-patch rabbits?"

"One and the same, Junior. Carlton is an object lesson in the old saw that you should never judge a ninety-two-year-old Cecil by the scratches on his wheelchair. For about fifty years, that dried-up little prune was about as dangerous a man as you'd ever want to run up against, and the kind of gunhand anyone would want on their side if things got too hairy. Man was tougher than the calluses on a barfly's elbows; snake blood flowed in his veins; and when lead flew, he was as cool as a skunk in the moonlight. His life is a whole book all by itself. Maybe when you finish up with me, you can go to work on him. If he lives that long."

The cup rattled back down onto the table and Lightfoot scrunched up his eyebrows. "I hope he'll be well soon and can verify some of this stuff. We'll worry about his life story later. You said you'd formulated a plan for the Big Eagle hideout. You gonna tell me what it was, or do I have to come over there and read the bumps on your head to see if I can figure it out?"

"Now, now, Junior. You're getting all pissy again. No need for that. You know full well I'm gonna tell you all about it."

"Guess you were just gonna round up all your friends—Billy Bird, Handsome Harry, Bix Conner, Old Bear, and the rest—and storm the place like Custer did at the Little Big Horn."

"Damn, Junior. That's really perceptive of you. There's only one thing wrong with your prediction, though. Everyone knows Custer got snuffed because he wouldn't wait for his Gatling guns to come up to the front. I just happened to have the acquaintance of a man in Mulberry, Arkansas, who owned a cannon. Nice Napoleon six-pounder. Great for wall-busting."

"A cannon? You planned to use a cannon on them?"

"Absolute truth of the thing was that I had less than fond memories of the night I dynamited Morgan Bryce's cabin down in the Choctaw Nation. Shower of debris when that one stick blew his table through the roof put several bumps on my head, and if any of the heavier stuff had managed to find me, I'd probably be buried in his front yard today. Folks like Bryce and Big Eagle had a habit of digging in like badgers, and about as hard to root out. Figured if I went after Smilin' Jack and had to blast him loose, Cletis Broadbent was the man I needed to see. On top of my Smilin'

Jack problem, I'd just managed to sink into my favorite chair and pull my boots off when Elizabeth presented me with even more reasons not to spend much time soaking my feet."

3

"The Worst Kind of Men"

"HAYDEN, I HAVE something important I must discuss with you." Her eyebrows pinched together and caused deep furrows across her forehead. Last time she sounded that serious was when she told me about her father's death. She'd pulled a footstool up next to my chair. A folded piece of the roughest kind of paper rested on her lap, partially concealed in her favorite lace handkerchief.

Reached out for her, placed my hand on her shoulder, and said, "What's the problem, Elizabeth?"

She covered my hand with hers and gave me that painful, more-serious-than-yellow-fever look again. "Several years before you arrived in Fort Smith I had a friend named Birdie Mae Blackwell."

"I've never so much as heard you mention anyone by that name." Like most men, I flattered the bejabbers

out of myself and harbored the rather elevated belief
that my wife told me absolutely everything. The abrupt
revelation about Birdie Mae was the first time I realized Elizabeth had deep, perhaps dark secrets, and an
astonishing skill for keeping me from finding out
things she didn't want known.

"Birdie Mae arrived in town in the back of a spring
wagon very close to being dead. She'd delivered a
baby on the side of the road just outside Fort Smith.
The loss of blood and lack of treatment almost killed
her. A family on their monthly trip in from Dyer found
the poor girl and brought her here. The first place they
stopped was our store. I nursed her back to health."

"Sweet Merciful God, Elizabeth. Did you know her
prior to any of that?"

"No. I'd never seen her before the day Lester Mc-
Intyre and his wife appeared out front with the girl in
her wagon."

"What about the child?"

"She had already passed." Pained sorrow filled her
voice. "We buried her out in the Little Angels section
of the town cemetery under a stone with the name Ramona chiseled into it. Birdie Mae stayed on with Papa
and me for over a year. We became close friends in
spite of the fact that she had one serious and evidently
insurmountable character flaw."

"And what was that?" Couldn't have imagined the
answer I got back then. But now, today, it would be
real easy.

"She had an almost lethal fascination for the worst
kind of men. Birdie's beauty captivated everyone she
met—men and women. Auburn hair cut like a boy's,

beautiful brown eyes, a willowy figure, and all the attributes to accentuate it served to gain the attention of men for miles around Fort Smith. And, of course, it didn't hurt that she had a face like one of those angels used to illustrate passages in our family Bible. On top of everything else, she never met a stranger and, all too often, that overly friendly attitude was misinterpreted. We had a constant parade of randy males milling around the store the entire time she stayed with us."

"Did you ever learn where she came from and how she managed to get here?" I asked.

"She did finally tell me most of her story, but only after extracting an ironclad promise not to act on anything she revealed."

Secrets were like puzzles to me, and I couldn't resist asking, "And what did she reveal, Elizabeth?"

"She came to us from Memphis where her father was a well-known and highly respected lawyer, judge, and local politician. They had been very close because of her mother's untimely death from consumption when Birdie was but a child." Elizabeth picked nervously at the lace handkerchief twisted around her left hand, then caressed the letter in her lap as though to gain enough strength to keep going. "Once she reached her early teens, the tender connection to her father vanished in the cloud of her promiscuous behavior. Judge Blackwell caught her more than once unclothed and in the arms of a man he'd never seen before. On more than one occasion he grew so violently incensed with her wanton actions that he beat her senseless with a buggy whip. As long as she could, Birdie harbored the secret of a child that resulted from one of her unfortunate liaisons. Then, in the seventh month of a pregnancy she could no longer hide, she took one of her father's wagons, fled Memphis, and simply headed west. I suppose the harshness of a month on Arkansas back roads in a wagon hastened the miscarriage of poor little Ramona."

"Where is all this leading, Elizabeth?"

"As I said, she stayed with us for about a year, then left in the company of one of the most awful men you can imagine."

Well, having just heard Birdie Mae Blackwell's history, it didn't come as too great a shock. The story seemed all too common and one oft repeated about women and girls who managed to make their way to wild places like Fort Smith and the Nations. "Who?"

"His name was Martin Luther Big Eagle and he leads a band of brigands who live in an infamous criminal refuge out on the Canadian called Robber's Roost."

You could have knocked me over with a feather from a baby duck's behind. There he was again, Martin Luther Big Eagle himself. A man whose name I'd never heard spoken as little as a week before.

"This note came while you were out in the Nations with Barnes Reed. I was helping a customer in the store one day last week when a short, filthy man dressed in the most raggedy clothing you can imagine just appeared behind me. He handed me this note and said, 'Tole her I'd brang it to yuh,' then disappeared like a puff of smoke." She handed me the ragged piece of paper. "Read it."

It appeared to have been written on the rendered portion of a heavy page ripped from the back of a family Bible. Don't remember the exact words in the beginning, but she said something to the effect that her life had turned into a living hell since leaving Fort Smith. Big Eagle had become brutally abusive, and she'd sought refuge in the Good Book in an effort to find some comfort from her persecutions. She admitted the error of her ways, and begged Elizabeth to do anything she could to help rescue her from a life she felt would soon drive her to self-destruction. The final few words are still etched in my brain as if by acid. "I have secured a small pistol and, if my situation does not see some alteration soon, I will be forced to bring an end to my own life." Her cry for help was a piteous thing and brought tears to my wife's eyes again as I read it aloud.

Guess I could have told Elizabeth I already had plans for Big Eagle, and the rescue of Birdie Mae Blackwell would just be icing on a great big cake, but didn't.

"Can you help her, Hayden?"

Suppose it was one of the few times a husband has a chance to look heroic to his wife without really having to put out much effort, so I took it.

I kissed her on the forehead and whispered, "I'll do what I can."

Next morning, Carlton and I started our search for Cletis Broadbent's place. After a day or so of ambling all over the rolling hills surrounding the Mulberry Community First Baptist Church, we finally came upon a crude farmhouse so far back out in the sticks the chickens carried big clubs to fight off the wildcats. Pretty sure Cletis worked body and soul at the contraband whiskey business in an effort to make enough money to stay alive. Most likely, he did his share of introducing over in the Nations, but he was smart enough to cook the stuff away from the house. Besides, I hadn't come there to arrest him for bootlegging.

When we presented him with my proposal of a fifty-cent-a-day fee for the use of his military fieldpiece, the man almost broke down and cried. I figured we'd need the thing for at least a month, and fifteen dollars was probably more money than ole Cletis had seen at one time in most of his adult life. Less than five minutes after our arrival, we stood around a heap of canvas in a rickety, crumbling barn and listened as he described his favorite toy.

"Yessiree bob, sir. She's a beaut. Know yew boys've seen me set her off at the Fourth of July celebration in Fort Smith. That old cannon out front of the courthouse is plugged, yew know. Cain't be fired. So every year since that spell of well-known Yankee-inspired unpleasantness back in the sixties, I drags Miss Beulah here over and shakes the ground a little. Usually shoot her off five or six times."

He pulled the heavy tarp away from the gun, stood back, and admired it. A tobacco-stained smile sliced across his round, hairless face. Dark brown juice from a piece of homegrown Arkansas twist dribbled off his chin and decorated the front of his faded, heavily patched overalls.

"Yew boys want to take her out back and shoot her off a time or two so's yew get the hang of it?" He grinned like a kid asking if a friend wanted to take a turn rolling his hoop down the street.

"Think that's an absolutely capital idea there, Cletis. Carlton and I don't have any experience in the use of artillery this size." My partner punctuated that assessment by placing his hands behind the grips of bone-handled Colts and pushing them forward. The happy farmer hooked a team of mules up to the caisson and pulled the whole contraption out into a field behind his house. The short, stout man talked the whole time.

"Just a few days after that bloody skirmish at Pea Ridge, I slipped back up there scoutin' around for anythin' that might be valuable. Them ole boys left an awful lot of stuff scattered around. Hell, they was bodies everywhere, and some of them poor Yankee boys rotted right there on the ground. Lord God, I found 'em under bushes, behind rocks, all over. Most of them poor kids had mighty nice boots, though. Still have eight or ten pair of 'em. Praise God, it was the only fight I saw during the war, and I'm damned glad Gettysburg and places like that were so far away I couldn't make 'em. The Ridge was my first and last battle. Had all I wanted with that 'un. Packed my kit and came the hell back home.

"After the Ridge, President Davis started conscripting every man 'tween the ages of eighteen and thirty-five. Guess them officers would of arrested me for a deserter if'n the war had gone the other way and we'd of won. All that killin' lasted three more years, and they'd probably have shot me without so much as a trial, but they couldn't ketch me."

He pulled everything up to a spot on the edge of a

plowed field behind his cabin that appeared to have been used for practice before. Wheel ruts caused the carriage to drop about six inches into the ground.

"Them grooves help cut down on the recoil," he said as he detached the gun from the caisson.

Tobacco juice flew in every direction as he flipped the lid back on the ammunition box and pulled out an oblong paper cartridge filled with powder that appeared to be just slightly larger than the six-pound balls the thing fired.

"Found four of these munitions chests full of kat-tridges same day I come across Miss Beulah. She got dumped in a ra-vine, but I ain't sure by which side. Think it was them Union fellers. Hard to tell, though, 'cause both parties in the disagreement used some of the same kinda stuff." He shrugged his shoulders and threw us an impish smile. "Had to steal the carriage off another'n what had a cracked barrel. The beautiful Beulah had a busted axle. Hell, it took me more than a week, but I finally got her all home."

Carlton's enthusiasm for the weapon bordered on the way you'd expect a five-year-old kid to act at Christmas. "Well, now, Cletis. Were you an artilleryman?" he asked.

"No, Marshal Cecil, I were not. When it comes to knocking thangs down and blowing thangs up, I'm completely self-taught."

He pushed a long pole with a brush he called a "screw" into the muzzle of the little howitzer, swabbed it out with a wet sponge, then shoved the cartridge home with a ramrod almost six feet long.

"Yew'll need to do everything I just did each and

every time yew reload. Clear it with the screw, swab it out, push the kat-tridge down gingerly. Don't pound on it with the ramrod. Then yew roll a ball in, tamp her down, and take this piece of wire—yew call this a pick—clean out the touchhole here on top, and punch on through to the paper kat-tridge. Pour a little more powder in the cleared-out touchhole like this, and she's ready to shoot."

"Any special instructions on how to sight the beautiful Miss Beulah?" a grinning Carlton asked.

Our bootlegging cannoneer dipped into a leather pouch and pulled out a pair of fairly simple-looking brass instruments. "Friend of mine over in Mountainburg served in the field artillery fer a while in the fighting back East. He give me these thangs. This here one is the level. Think he called it a hausse. Yew set it on the base of the gun to help get it level. This 'un here is the sight. Yew set 'er up on the gun like this and line 'er up with that 'un on the end of the barrel." He grinned, and continued to decorate a spot at his feet with more tobacco juice. "Yew can do all that if'n yew've half a mind to. But hell, boys, if'n I wuz yew I'd use the Cletis Broadment method. Just have to eyeball it, Marshal Cecil. Always worked better fer me anyways. After yew fire her the first two or three times, yew'll have the range and elevation down pretty well." He struck a lucifer and put it to a piece of wick about a foot long.

"Yew want to light her up, Marshal Cecil?" His gap-toothed grin displayed a mouth full of rotted teeth covered with a thick brown layer of tobacco stains. He held the glowing match out for Carlton and used his tongue to roll the wad around in his mouth.

"Yew betcha," Carlton said as he took the smoking cord and stepped to a spot Cletis pointed out.

"Put this here cotton in your ears too." My happy friend quickly plugged his ears and stretched his arm out to put fire to powder.

"Mr. Tilden, yew'd best stand over here next to me, and if'n yew want to continue hearing for the rest of the day, yew might want to cover up too. She's sighted in for that big elm tree across the field yonder, Marshal. Stepped that off at least ten times. Almost exactly two hundred yards."

Carlton threw us a wicked grin, turned, and pushed the burning lighter onto the howitzer's touchhole. After a quick flash on top of the barrel, a thunderous explosion engulfed the whole area around us. Billowing gray-black smoke filled the air, and the acrid, sulfurous smell of burnt powder singed our nostrils as Cletis quickly pointed out the iron ball rocketing toward the target. A resounding crack shot back across the field when it hit about five feet above the ground almost dead center of the already damaged tree. Bark and wood splinters flew in all directions and showered an area for ten feet around all the gnarled roots that stuck out of the ground like an old man's bony knees. Carlton hopped around the cannon, giggled, and danced. Man seemed demented in the childlike joy brought on by all the noise and smoke.

Before Cletis could think to react, the newly enthused, freshly trained, novice artilleryman ran over to the caisson, grabbed another cartridge, and started to stuff it in. Broadbent almost had a stroke. He screamed, darted toward Carlton, and knocked him to the ground a split second before the hot debris left in the tube ignited the second load and detonated in a cloud of deafening, but harmless smoke.

Our farmer, bootlegger, and amateur cannoneer jumped up and started beating on Carlton with his chewed-up piece of a hat. My astonished friend rolled around on the ground for a second or so before he managed to get to his feet and use his own hat in self-defense.

I couldn't believe what had just happened. Two grown men were now slapping on each other like kids in a schoolyard fight. Epithets like "stupid damned ya-hoo" and "crazy goddamned farmer" got pitched around for about a minute before I stepped between them and stopped the physical part of the dispute.

Cletis's head looked like it just might go off like the cannon. "Done tole yew to do exactly like what I done. Have to clean it with the screw, use a wet sponge to put out any chunks of paper or sech that might be burning, and then—and only then, dumb-ass—yew load the kat-ridge. Good thing yew hadn't got to the point of using the ramrod on that load. Beulah coulda shot that thing through yew like a giant Comanche arrow."

Carlton got real quiet. He turned, stared at Beulah's still-smoking barrel, and scratched his head. "Well, you know, I wondered why you had to do all that silly-assed stuff. Hell, you don't have to go to all that trouble loading a Navy Colt, but I suppose a pistol wouldn't have the kind of residue left you'd find in this gun."

I pulled on his sleeve, turned him around, and said, "Apologize to Cletis, Carlton. He might well have saved your silly hide."

Cecil was a big enough man to say his sorrys without so much as a twinge of phoniness. That seemed to satisfy Cletis and calmed him down. We got the red-faced clod-kicker to go through his whole song and dance one more time to make sure we both understood every step of the loading process.

By late that afternoon, Cecil had fired the gun at least five more times. His studied performance convinced our sodbusting bootlegger we would take care of his plaything like it belonged to us.

Loaded up our ammunition box with fifty of his paper cartridges, the same number of six-pound balls, the additional necessary equipment, and agreed to pay another ten cents for every shot fired once we found Big Eagle's nest. I figured the extra charges were well worth it and if we couldn't bring any wall in the Nations down with fifty blasts from Miss Beulah, we might just as well give up and drag back home with our tails between our legs.

Paid Broadbent ten dollars in advance out of my own pocket. Swear the man got a look on his face like he'd just inherited enough money to make him the financial equal of any Texas cattle baron or the richest Eastern railroad magnate.

"Marshal Tilden, yew've been mighty righteous 'bout this from the beginning. I mean, yew 'splained everthang and paid like yew said yew would." Then, he got real quiet and all conspiratorial. "So, I've got one more thang might help yew out when you get out into the wild places."

Couldn't imagine what he was talking about. "What might that be, Cletis?"

He got up close and talked low like he feared someone might hear him. "Well, sir, if'n yew'd like 'em, I've got several boxes of Ketchums in the barn too."

That one left me completely in a fog. Couldn't figure out what he meant. Thank goodness Carlton saved me the trouble of embarrassing the hell out of myself, though. He blurted out, "What the hell's Ketchums?"

"Wait right here. I'll get some of 'em fer yew." He sprinted back to the barn, and we could hear him dragging a lot of heavy stuff around inside for a good bit. After a couple of minutes more, he reappeared with a small wooden crate across his arms and sat it on top of the cannon's ammo box.

"They's eight of 'em in here. You can have 'em. Cain't imagine I'll ever have any use fer 'em."

Carlton pulled the lid back and lifted out what looked like a silver rocket with red paper fins. Broadbent was so proud of himself he almost glowed. "They's called Ketchum grenades. Yew throw 'em like a big dart. They's nose-heavy as hell, and when they hits on that flat plate there on the end, yew get a hell of an explosion. Only good fer close-up work, though. If'n I wuz yew boys, I'd only use'm if'n nothing else worked. Oh, keep 'em in this here box. Wouldn't want to bump 'em around overmuch neither."

Carlton gazed into the crate and said, "Hell, man, these things are fifteen years old. How do we know they'll actually work?"

"I keep 'em up high and dry. Trust me, they's still good. But if'n yew want, we'll try one out."

Devilment jumped around in Carlton's eyes again as he said, "Now that sounds like a damned good idea, don't it, Hayden?"

Couldn't do anything but nod while Cletis raced back into the barn and came out about a minute later gingerly carrying one of the grenades in front of him like an offering to some hidden god of thunder who was about to make a surprise appearance.

We strolled back out to his cannon range, and stood behind a busted-up piece of wagon that looked like he'd put it there just for the trick he was about to perform. "The kids like these 'uns. I throws one fer 'em 'bout once a year. Ain't got but fifteen or twenty lef' now. I'll count to three and pitch her out. We gonna have to duck down behind this here wagon on three."

We stood behind him while he counted. When he got to three, we all ducked. Guess ole Cletis managed to pitch that thing about sixty or seventy feet. Then there was a hell of an explosion. Little pieces of hot metal flew in every direction and rattled our wagon-bed screen like someone hit it with a sledgehammer. Damned thing blew a hole in the ground about two feet deep and ten feet across.

Carlton gandered at the damage like a man amazed and muttered, "Goddamn, Hayden. If I get a chance, I'm gonna throw one these things right into Big Eagle's drawers."

Cletis made a heavy-duty point of warning Carlton to be careful with the grenades again before we pulled out. We carefully strapped their crate to the top of the ammo box after Carlton padded the inside with some extra straw—and that just about did it. Hitched our horses up to the rig, waved good-bye to ole Cletis as he stood in his scruffy yard counting his money, and dragged the whole shebang back to Fort Smith. Gunpowder didn't seem to mind the pull much, but that meaner'n-hell dapple-gray mare Carlton called The Beast snorted, honked, flounced in the traces, and tried to bite everything in site for miles before she calmed down.

Started hunting for a posse soon as I got back in town. Even though it was beginning to get dark, didn't take but about ten minutes of Beulah sitting outside the courthouse door to draw every marshal in from the Nations for a gander at Carlton's new toy. Just about had my pick of anybody I wanted. Course it shouldn't take a genius to guess who I asked to go with me.

Handsome Harry Tate ambled up, caressed the cannon's barrel, and smiled. He'd traded his monstrous beaver hat for a brand-new felt Plainsman with the brim pushed back out of his heavily mustachioed face. His pearl-handled pistols glistened in the dying sunlight, and I noticed he'd added a matching third gun and holster across his lower back.

He strolled around Cletis's cannon, chuckled, scratched his chin, then stopped and shook my hand. "Don't know why someone hadn't thought of this before, Hayden. Might well be the only for damned sure way to get at Big Eagle. You need some company?"

"Love to have you, Harry. You seen Bixley Conner lately?"

"Think the Marshal sent Bix to Mobile, Alabama, to

serve an extradition warrant on Elton Bob White, that
Choctaw gentleman who cut his wife into four or five
fairly equal pieces several months ago. Probably won't
be back for two or three weeks. You gonna take Old
Bear with you?"

"As you well know, that hairy sometime-Indian
tends to come and go as he pleases. To tell the absolute
truth, I haven't seen him in more'n a month. Thought
he might show up when I went out with Barnes Reed,
but didn't spot hide nor hair of him. When Thunder
fell and Smilin' Jack was dusting me with rifle fire that
sounded like a Gatling gun, hoped he'd pop up and
save me."

Harry smacked the leg of his shotgun chaps with a
leather quirt and laughed. "Billy Bird's upstairs in the
Marshal's office. He's spent the past few days trying
to whittle a six-pound chunk of stove wood down to
something like a toothpick. Man's so bored, someone
claimed they heard him say he was going to carve himself a sailboat. Bet he'd jump at a chance like this."

"Well, why don't you go tell him we'll be leaving
in the morning? Love to have him along for the hunt.
Figure four of us should be plenty. Carlton Cecil
agreed to go. Hell, he's so worked up about firing this
thing, he can hardly sit still. He and Billy can pilot the
tumbleweed. We'll hitch the ammo box and cannon to
it. We can tie the extra horses and a couple of mules
to the tail end of this rig. Sound good to you?"

"Judge Parker couldn't have planned it any better
himself." He smiled and started for the courthouse
door, then stopped with his hand on the knob and
called to me, "Hayden, I'll throw a few sticks of dy-

namite in with our supplies just in case things don't work out the way we want them to. You just never know."

"Good idea, Harry. See you in the morning." Cannon, Ketchum's, and dynamite. If there was any other kind of weapon we needed and didn't have, I couldn't bring it to mind.

Thought we had everything pretty well set when I started for home that evening. Rode up to the house and spotted a horse I didn't recognize out front. Knew it couldn't be Elizabeth, she never got in from a long day at the store before dark. Real rough looking feller had a comfortable seat in my favorite chair there on the veranda. He stood and ambled up to the porch rail as I tied Gunpowder off at the hitch rack.

"You Tilden?" Silver spurs of the Mexican type attached to high-heeled boots jingled and sang as he came to a stop and looked down at me from his perch on my porch. Heavy canvas riding pants were stuffed in the tops of the leather stovepipes that came up almost to his knees. White Texas stars and fancy colored stitching you couldn't miss seeing, decorated the front, sides and backs of them.

"You are correct, sir. And who might you be?"

He flashed a toothy grin at the world in general and said, "Might be Andy By God Jackson or Abraham By God Lincoln, or even Sam Houston, but they're all dead—so I must be Lucius A. By God Dodge, Texas Ranger extraordinaire, and I know you're gonna be glad to meet me." Another five-pointed star inside a circle of silver twinkled and glittered on the left pocket of his rough vest.

Made my way up the steps as he sheathed a foot-long bowie knife he'd been using to carve up a piece of wood about the size of an eight-foot-long two-by-four. Man had so many pistols and knives hanging on him, it became something of a puzzlement for me to figure out how he managed to stand and walk.

"Pleasure to meet you, Ranger Dodge," I said as we shook hands. Pointed to his gunbelt. "You figure on running into some serious trouble from all appearances."

He glanced down at the twin Smith and Wesson .45's hanging on his hips. With an itchy left forefinger, he tapped the grip of the hideout gun in a shoulder rig under his right arm that was made almost invisible behind a cowboy bandanna. He pushed his bear-killer of a knife forward and checked the Colt snugged against his back before he grinned, made a clicking sound at me, and said, "Well, a man in our business just can't be too careful these days, now can he, Mr. Tilden?"

Found it hard to argue with reasoning as sound as that. "Guess not, Mr. Dodge."

Motioned for him to resume his seat, and took the chair next to the table. He seemed perfectly at home, like he'd been sitting in my chair on my porch all his life. He crossed his right leg onto the left and dropped his palm-leaf sombrero—crimped and formed in a stylishly Western manner—onto the toe of his boot. A leather case from his inside vest pocket produced long, thin, black cigars. He offered me one and took another for himself.

"Think we . . . can be of . . . some help . . . to one another, Mr. Tilden," he said while at the same time lighting the panatela and puffing it into action.

"How's that, Mr. Dodge?"

"Well, there's a rumor going around you might be about to take a party up the Canadian to Martin Luther Big Eagle's nest." He pulled a lung of the heavy smoke down and blew it into the air. "Heard you're looking to catch a no-account named Smilin' Jack Paine. Way I've got it figured, anytime you come across Smilin' Jack, you'll probably also run into a slithering bag of pus named W. J. McCabe."

"Never heard of the man."

He pulled an official-looking pile of paper from his belt and dropped it on the table. The top sheet was a wanted poster for W. J. McCabe. My new Texas Ranger friend went on talking like I wanted to know everything he could tell me about a subject he clearly enjoyed discussing.

"Ah, W. J. McCabe. Been after the man going on a year now. All started when he celebrated his departure from the clutches of education in the town of Posey, Texas, by beating hell out of the schoolmaster and burning the community's one-room center of learning to the ground. He scampered away before Mr. Harvey Monday—the aforementioned much-abused school-master—could bring charges. W. J. took umbrage at the audacity necessary to put the law on his back, and promptly returned and shot Harvey Monday deader'n last week's beefsteak. Killed him on the steps of his classroom while he was ringing the morning bell. About twenty terrified kids witnessed the bilious shooting of a man most of them liked and respected."

"And I take it that was just the beginning?"

"Absolutely. Witnesses have identified him as having taken part in at least three robberies, another killing, and there exists some evidence he's done his share of horse theft, stage holdups, and cattle rustling. Think he probably robbed the Jacksboro stage at least three times. He evidently stole so many cows from the Bow and Arrow Ranch down in south Texas, the owner put up a five-hundred-dollar re-ward for his capture."

"You figuring on taking the ever-lovely W. J. back to Texas for the money, Mr. Dodge?"

"Couldn't care less about the re-ward, Mr. Tilden. Harvey Monday was my mother's brother. I intend to watch W. J. swing for that killing—or put so many holes in his sorry hide that the state of Texas won't have to waste the money, time, and effort to hire a good hangman."

"And you want to ride along with my posse in the hope McCabe is nesting with Big Eagle and Smilin' Jack up at Robber's Roost in Red Rock Canyon."

His face lit up and he smiled like a man who'd just been told about the birth of his first son. "That I would, Mr. Tilden. Yes, sir, I would indeed."

"Why don't you call me Hayden, Lucius? If we're going to be on the trail together for a spell, I'd get real tired of being called Mr. Tilden."

"My pleasure, Hayden. You reckon I could camp out here on your place till we start for the Nations?"

"Throw your stuff in the barn. There's a cot in the tack room. Elizabeth, my wife, should be home soon. I usually start supper a-cooking and she finishes up. Call you when it's ready." I figured we'd have to forgo our usual pre-departure dinner at Julia's. Knew Elizabeth wouldn't stand for us leaving a guest in the barn with nothing to eat.

He stood, picked up the warrants and other paper on W. J. McCabe, and stuffed it all back into his belt. "An actual home-cooked meal would be much appreciated, friend Tilden," he said as he tipped his hat. He jingled down the steps to his gray mare and pulled the reins loose.

Couldn't help but notice the arsenal that decorated his tough-looking mustang. "How many guns you got hanging on that poor animal, Lucius?"

"Oh, just the usual. Four Colt's Dragoons and a '73 Winchester. Don't really need the rifle, though. These Dragoons are still the most powerful pistols known to man. When me and Hateful here get to running and shooting, we can pump out almost sixty shots without stopping to reload." He smiled, patted the animal on the neck, and pulled at her mane. "Makes it real hard for men like W. J. McCabe to put us down, and even the wildest of Injuns just naturally give us a real wide berth. There's men of every race all over Texas what ball up in knots of fear when they see Hateful coming."

He'd already started for the barn when I called out, "You named your horse Hateful?"

Over his shoulder he threw back, "Once you get to know and love her the way I do, you'll understand." The animal must have sensed he was talking about her. She snapped at his hand, then tried to push him aside with her nose.

"You see?" he said as they disappeared into the barn.

Dodge turned out to be something of a lady-charmer.

He came to the table freshly shaved, dressed in a clean shirt—minus all the weapons I'd seen earlier that afternoon—but still wearing those Mexican spurs. His deep-fried accent and courtly Southern manners had Elizabeth dithering around the table like a girl half her age. When our evening came to a close, and I told him we'd be leaving first thing in the morning, he seemed genuinely disappointed his stay had ended before it got started. He kissed Elizabeth's hand as he took his leave. Thought the woman would pass out. She flushed up and got to batting her eyelashes so fast, I thought she would lift off the floor and fly around the room.

Stood on the porch, had a whiskey, and smoked another cigar with him after dinner. He took his liquor mixed in a cup of coffee and said, "I do like a dab of stump juice with my sour mash."

"Pretty sure you'll find all your traps in order when you get back out to the barn, Lucius. Not many around here would have nerve enough to come on my property and take anything."

He started out grinning, then laughed so hard he had a coughing fit that caused him to have to sit down for a moment on the porch rail. "Hell, Hayden, left all my stuff in the stall with Hateful. Any of these bold sons of bitches here in Arkansas, or the Territories for that matter, with brass enough to get within ten feet of that animal can have every damned thing they're man enough to carry off." Then he started laughing again, winked, and ambled off toward the barn. Those big Mexican spurs sang jingling songs to a moon that floated silently overhead in an inky black sky. Just before he disappeared inside, he held the cup up above his head in salute.

When first light came, Lucius A. Dodge, Texas Ranger extraordinaire, got to witness something not even Billy Bird or Handsome Harry had ever seen.

Every time I had to take my leave of Elizabeth—it got more difficult. We'd worked my actual departures down to a little ritual. She always fixed a good breakfast on the morning I left, and sat at the table while I ate. Walked me out and watched until I got to our gate at the bottom of the hill. When I turned and placed my hat over my heart for her, she waved good-bye. Just nothing like my memory of that glorious woman standing on our veranda with the sun coming up behind her. Even now, sixty years later, when I close my eyes at night, I can still picture her waving farewell like we might never see each other again.

As Lucius and I turned toward Fort Smith, he said, "You are one truly lucky son of a bitch to have a woman like that, Marshal Tilden."

I remember blinking back a tear when I told him, "No one knows it better than I do, Lucius."

4

"Done Fount Me a Body."

"HAYDEN, IT'S GETTING a bit late in the day. Much as I'd like to hear the rest of this business about Smilin' Jack, think we might better take it up again sometime tomorrow. Maybe around one in the afternoon." Lightfoot leaned forward in his chair and brought shaking hands up to his tired hollow-eyed face.

"You sure you're going to make it back tomorrow, Junior? Hell, you sure you're going to make back it to your car?"

Poor drag-assed boy waved absently over his shoulder and mumbled, "Hey, the only thing that could keep me from an appointment with you would be an unexpected late-night visit from Veronica Lake."

"Who?"

"Never mind. See you tomorrow afternoon."

Watched him all the way to the front door before I

called Jerimiah Obidiah Samuel Henry Jones over and got him to help me get myself out of the wicker torture instrument that seemed to have caved in a bit since I first sat down in it. Hell, the minefields just seemed to pop up all over the place when you get as old as Carlton and me. Something as simple as sitting in the wrong chair had the possibility of turning into an ordeal, if you didn't keep a sharp eye on where you were and what you were doing.

Hobbled down to Carlton's room. Stood in the hall and peeked in through the crack between the hinged side of the door and the frame. Nurse Heddy McDonald fussed around his bed. Kept talking to him as she fluffed his pillow and straightened his sheets. She checked all the tubes and rubber hoses flowing into his worn-out old carcass, and then bent over and whispered something in his ear. Swear she looked almost like someone in love. Managed to sneak into the room before she spotted me.

"You shouldn't be here, Mr. Tilden." She shook a scolding finger in my direction.

"Think he'll die this time, Heddy?"

She came over, linked her arm in mine, and winked. "Oh, he'll be all right. Dr. Matthews just left. He said this was just a small one. According to him, Carlton should be up and around in a few days."

Thing I liked most about the beautiful Heddy was her seeming lack of fear of old people. You'd be amazed how many young folks these days seem to think old age is something you can get on you like a glob of horse manure stuck to your boot. They act as if accidentally touching someone past a certain age will cause an instant condition of no hair, wrinkled skin, and paunchy bellies—and that it will just get all over them faster'n ugly on a loggerhead turtle. It's distressing as all kinds of hell. Sometimes think the thing I miss most about my youth is the fact that no one seems to want to touch me anymore unless it can't be avoided. Course I don't include Heddy in that bunch of idiots.

"What did you say to him when you whispered in his ear, my black-haired beauty?"

She blushed, batted long lashes at me, and rested her head against my shoulder. "You weren't supposed to see that, Hayden."

Liked it when she called me Hayden, and she knew it. "Well, I just don't want ole Carlton beatin' my time with the best-looking woman at Rolling Hills."

Her fingers tightened around my arm. "I told him he had to get better so he can take me to our Thanksgiving dinner in three weeks." When she looked back up at me, tears had formed in the corners of her eyes. "Thought maybe if he could hear me, it would give him something to look forward to."

"Well, I have a message for him too. Think it'd be okay if I sneak over there and whisper a little something in his ear myself?"

"You go ahead, Hayden. I'll stand in the hall and keep watch. Wouldn't want Leona to catch us, would we?"

Shuffled over to my friend's bed and just stood there and looked at him for a bit. Time had worn Carlton down the same way waves beat rocky beaches into sand. Then, all at once, it hit me like a Hereford cow dropped from the threshold of St. Peter's gate. We'd come a long way together and—if he died—I couldn't imagine the impact it'd have on me.

Placed my hand on his withered old arm and said, "Listen to me, you old coot. Those folks who make oatmeal and prune juice sent me in here to tell you they won't stand for you going out on the scout right now. Hell, way I've got it figured, you're single-handedly keeping Quaker Oats in business. Weren't for that shriveled-up chunk of gut you call a colon, those folks would have to close up shop tomorrow. Not going to be any dying done around these parts just yet— you hear me? We've got too many things to do. Too many stories to tell. Franklin J. Lightfoot's hooked big-time, and I don't know for sure if I can keep him interested forever by myself. Need your ugly carcass around to spice things up a bit. You go and croak out on me and I'll come back down here and beat hell out of you with this hand-carved cane your daughter gave me last Christmas. You get all of that, you stringy old bastard? One more jig, old man. You've got one more dance to do."

I'm not sure he heard a word of it, but he moved his head and his eyes opened up for a second. I've seen dead folks do as much. Thought I even spotted a faint smile play across his purple parched lips. Course I could have been mistaken. Maybe it was just gas.

Around three in the morning, I sat in a chair in my room and stared out the window. The old fart had me worried and I couldn't sleep. My door creaked open and the beautiful Miss McDonald stuck her head in.

"I knew you wouldn't be asleep, Hayden. Wanted

you to know he's turned the corner again. By tomorrow morning he'll probably be chasing the nurses up and down the halls like nothing ever happened."

Didn't want her to see the tears on my cheeks and tried not to let her hear the relief in my voice. "Awfully nice of you to think of me, Heddy, awfully nice of you."

Then she tiptoed across my room, bent over, and kissed me on the cheek. "You have my word on it. He's much better, and you can talk to him in the morning."

Sure enough, right before breakfast I went down and peeked in on him. He spotted me at the door and motioned me in.

His voice cracked, but got stronger as he talked. "You know," Carlton said, "had a dream about your wrinkled-up ugly ole ass last night. We were out in the Nations riding around looking for L. B. Ledoux. Remember that sorry son of a bitch? He's the one what met some Texas feller out on the trail outside Pawhuska, shot him in the head six or eight times, stole his fancy handmade boots and horse. Threw the body in a creek. Wasn't that just the way of it? All them stupid jugheads thought throwing the body in a creek or river covered up what they'd done. Anyway, you got mad at me about something, can't remember what, and started ranting about how you wuz gonna kick my sorry behind if I died out there on the trail and you had to break up all that frozen ground to bury a stinking old fart like me. Made me madder'n hell." When I grinned at him, he snapped, "Yes, it did, by God. Chased you all the way to Okmulgee and promised every step of the way to kick your skinny behind when you stopped running."

Well, the fight was on and I snapped back, "Tell you what, old man. You get your bony, rusted-up, cadaverous self out of that bed and I'll let you kick my behind right in front of Leona Wildbank's office door and give you a week to draw a crowd. Hell, I'll even buy ice cream for all the toothless drooling codgers you can keep awake long enough to witness such a debacle. Course I've never seen anybody kick anything while seated in a wheelchair. Should be a real enlightening experience."

"Well, by God, they's a first time for everythang. Just so's I do plenty of damage when that golden moment arrives, gonna have Heddy fish out my best pair of boots. You know, them with the pointy toes capped in silver and the big star on front. Tattoo your antique backside real good with them clod-kickers."

About then, Nurse Willett fluttered in and hustled me out. "You fellows get way too excited. Seems like I spend most of my waking efforts every other day trying to keep the two of you out of a fistfight."

Carlton grinned, tried to slap his own leg first with one hand, then the other, finally gave up, and called behind us, "That's right, Nurse Willett. Drag that troublemaking old fart outta here. Awful hard on a man in my kind of delicate condition to have to get off this here deathbed and beat hell out of a loud-mouthed old fool like Hayden Tilden."

Convinced me. Couple more days and the nursing staff would have to hike their knickers up pretty tight again, because Carlton J. Cecil—the Terror of Rollings

Hills Home for the Aged—had fought off the devil again and God help any part of a woman within arm's reach of his wheelchair.

Next morning, Junior came back all fresh-faced, rested up, and ready to go. He'd bought himself a brand-new pad of yellow paper and had a fistful of freshly sharpened pencils. Hell, the boy reminded me of a kid who was loaded for bear on his first day at school. Figured I'd give him one to remember.

Things went pretty slow what with our wagon, dragging the cannon, and extra animals to take care of. Since every outlaw in the Nations probably already knew when and why we'd left Fort Smith, I figured a stop at McAlester's Store couldn't do any harm. Course you never knew back then what might pop up out in the wild places—and sure enough something did.

Handsome Harry, Lucius, and I leaned against the side of the tumbleweed wagon while Billy and Carlton rummaged around in the mercantile looking for anything they thought we might need on the trail.

Just as we lit us one of Harry's panatelas, this reed-thin farmer whose rough pant legs came almost to his knees walked up with his hat in his hand and said, "Er, yew fellers lawmen from Fort Smith?" He shook so much, it got to be something of a question mark as to whether he might be able to keep from falling down.

Harry knocked the ash from his cigar against the front wheel of the tumbleweed and gazed at the glowing tip like a man interrupted while conducting the most important business of his day. But he smiled when he looked up at the quaking plow-chaser and said, "That's right, sir. Can we be of some service?"

"Well, done fount me a body in the creek not fer from my house, and was on my way to fetch any kind of law I could lay a hand to when Mr. McAlester tole me yew fellers was in town."

"We don't have time for this, Hayden," Harry said.

Carlton threw a burlap bag of commodities into the space under the jockey box and yelped, "He's right. Don't need to get distracted now. Seems like every time we come out here, one of these sad cases shows up and gets us going in a different direction. Let the Choctaw lighthorse police take care of it."

I moved away from the wagon and closer to the shaking dirt-kicker. "What's your name, mister?"

"Be Willard Rump, formerly of Sequatchie County, Tennessee, Marshal. Come out here during the last few months of the war. Married me a Choctaw woman so's I could farm and raise kids in peace. Done been a-thinkin' to get myself away from all the shootin' and killin'. Guess I needs be doin' some more thinkin'. Never expected to be a-findin' murdered-up bodies in my creek."

"How far away do you live from here, Mr. Rump?" Harry asked. He'd perked up and gotten a lot more interested with the mention of murder.

"Jest a few miles west of Atoka. Got a place not fer from the Choctaw-Chickasaw line 'bout a hoot and a holler off the Clear Boggy. Mill Creek runs from north to south behind my house fer about a mile. Went out day afore yestiddy to check on a five-acre patch of mine north of the house. Heard shootin' whilst the boy

and me was restin' a bit. Sent him home double quick.
Skulked my way up the creek fer a piece 'fore I fount
this here feller looked to be a cowboy a-layin' in the
water facedown. First off, I was so scared didn't know
exactly what to do. Watched him fer 'bout an hour to
make sure no one wuz around, then pulled him up on
the bank. That's where I lef' him 'fore I struck out
huntin' you lawdogs."

"How could you tell he was cowboy?" Lucius asked
the question like a man who needed convincing.

Rump didn't back off any, though. "Only thangs left
on him was his boots and hat. Ain't seen no farmers
round these parts wearin' hand-tooled, high-heeled
boots or Boss of the Plains sombreros. Looked to me
like he had a fallin'-out with some of his compadres,
and they done kilt him and went on their way a-takin'
most of his kit, clothes, and sech-like with 'em."

Harry blew smoke over his shoulder and said,
"Guess maybe we should take a look at this one, Hayden. If the dead man was Indian, I'd say pass on by
and let the lighthorse take care of it. But this one is
obviously ours. Carlton and Billy can strike out for the
Canadian, and we can catch up at Big Cougar Bluff as
soon as this all shakes out. Billy knows his way around
about as well, or better than any of us, and he'll know
when to stop even if we haven't shown up when expected."

I didn't care for the idea at all, but what could I do?
Man standing right in front of me had just told what
had to be a story of murder and robbery and was asking
for our help. Way I had it figured, we had to go.

"Mind if I tag along on this one too?" Lucius had

his right foot stepped up into the wagon's back wheel and was spinning the fancy rowel on his Mexican spur.

"What do you think, Harry? Reckon we'll be safe out here in the Nations in the company of a Texas Ranger?" Stretched the words Texas Ranger out so they sounded a bit like they might be something you wouldn't want to find on the bottom of your boot.

Harry pulled his hat down tighter on his head and laughed. "Hell, if we're not safe in the company of a man carrying as many pistols, rifles, and knives as Lucius By God Dodge, we wouldn't be safe anywhere in the civilized world. Personally, I kinda like the idea of traveling with a real live one-man army." Dodge grinned at the gibe, but Harry hadn't finished. "Now, if he could only play the fiddle and sing us to sleep every night out here in the big cold and lonely, things would be just about Georgia-peachy-perfect."

Well, that's the way it all shook out. Carlton and Billy took the tumbleweed, cannon, their horses, and the mules and headed straight west. The rest of us followed Willard Rump to his farm out on Mill Creek. Seems to me like these days there's a one-dog town named Clarita not far from the site where Rump spent a good part of his life raising kids and turnips.

Anyway, we pulled up there in the middle of the afternoon, but didn't stop at his good-sized log house to socialize. Willard wasted no time, and led us to the body in pretty short order. He'd covered the dead man with some heavy stones to try and keep the animals away. By the time we finally got to the poor departed gentleman, his four-day-old corpse had turned pretty ripe.

Near as any of us could tell, the dead fellow looked to be about twenty years old and had at least four bullet holes in him. One hit under his heart; one punched a hole about a finger's width above his left eye and was as big around as the end of my thumb; a third one fractured his right collarbone; and he sported a smaller, almost undetectable, wound in the lower right abdomen. None of 'em were as deep as the Palo Duro Canyon or as wide as the Red River, but taken altogether, they killed him deader'n Judas just the same.

Rump grunted, pointed back upstream, and said, "The blastin' me and the boy heard come from back yonder. Maybe a mile or so up and, 'less'n my ears done fooled me, the killin' got done on t'other side of the crick."

Before we scratched a hole in the ground, buried the corpse, and covered it back up with Willard's river rocks, Harry and I removed both the cowboy's boots. Some of the foot, and a toe or two, came off with the right one—nasty business for Harry. Found the name Jeff Diggs stitched in bright red on the inside of the left one. We were all somewhat puzzled at why the boots hadn't gone with the rest of his clothing and belongings. Lucius pointed out the obvious.

"Too conspicuous. Man spent a small fortune havin' them things made. Most likely, everyone who knew him would recognize snake-stompers that cost as much as these. Give 'em another look. Should be something on one of 'em somewhere that identifies the boot maker. Be willing to bet whoever took this man's life and other belongings knew him. He just might have even called them friends."

Harry pulled his bowie, ripped each boot down the back, and spread them out like filleted fish. Embossed around the top of the right one, but barely visible because of the water damage, were the words *Staples-Denton.*

"Ever heard of a leather worker by that name, Lucius?" Harry handed the boot to the Ranger.

"Yep. That's the mark of Bradford 'Big Foot' Staples from Denton, Texas. Made the pair I'm wearin'." He pushed the top of his right boot down, and there it was plain as day, a perfect match for the stamp in the one we'd pulled off the foot of the very dead Mr. Diggs.

Didn't take long after that for Harry to find where the killin' took place. Bloodstains, scattered clothing, and a pile of personal belongings like tintypes and letters made it pretty easy. We collected everything we could lay a hand on and wrapped it all in the fallen man's undamaged shirt. None of us could come up with a good reason to explain why he'd been stripped before getting shot. Even Lucius couldn't do anything but shake his head on that one. By then the sun had begun to fade, so we made our way back to Rump's house and set ourselves up to spend the night in his barn. Got us a fire going and cooked coffee. Laying in the hay and sipping on a hot cup of stump juice that could float a Colt's pistol almost made a man feel cozy.

About an hour after we arrived, Rump's wife and a daughter, who appeared about half-grown, brought out plates loaded with beans, corn, smoked meat, and hot bread. Those Choctaw ladies wore dresses decorated up with lots of brightly colored needlework. Vividly rendered belts and necklaces of detailed beadwork emphasized narrow waists and dark-eyed beauty. Harry and Lucius both got all fumble-fingered and stuttery in the presence of the stunning Eleanor Little Spot, eldest daughter of Willard Rump and Mary Bold Woman. Her mother must have seen the sparks flying. She hustled the girl away as quickly as she could, but on the way out the door the dark-eyed beauty turned and flashed a brilliant smile at my two wifeless friends. Lucius Dodge looked like a man who'd been hit in the head with a galvanized water bucket.

I couldn't let the opportunity for a little fun at his expense slip by. "Well, Harry, appears our heavily armed Texican compadre has a soft spot for black-haired, fiery-eyed females."

"Don't be making too much fun of him, Hayden. She's a beauty. Even caught my eye."

"Aw come on, Harry," I shot back. "Eleanor Little Spot caught more than your eye. Thought for a minute you two fellers were gonna be over here in the horse stall gnawing on trace chains and snapping at each other."

They grinned like schoolboys, and tried to put an end to it by devoting all their attention to abundant helpings of fried chicken and yellow squash.

Next morning, Mary Bold Woman brought us breakfast, but the girl didn't put in an appearance. Both my friends were sorely disappointed.

Lucius sopped a biscuit around his plate and mumbled through grits, sorghum, and bacon. "Most likely got that steamy, dark-eyed gal chained to a wall. Don't blame her mother for wanting to keep her away from me, though. Women and girls around the world just naturally find a good-looking Texas man such as myself downright irresistible."

Harry got choked on his biscuit, and spat a laughing piece the size of a barn owl's egg onto the ground, where a flock of wild, scraggly chickens cackled, fought, and pecked at it before a black rooster muscled his way to the front of the crowd, seized the prize, and strutted away with it over the heated and noisy objections of his flock.

When his coughing fit finally resolved itself, Harry growled, "Only two things uglier than hammered manure are armadillos and Texas men. Kind of amazing, isn't it, Hayden, both of them come from the great Lone Star State."

Lucius decided to take the funnin' in stride. "Well, just where in the hell are you from, Mr. Handsome Harry Tate?"

Harry picked at a piece of errant bacon caught in his teeth and over his finger got out a muffled "Boston."

Lucius took that one and ran with it like a scalded cat. "Bah-ston? Bah-ston? Where the hell's Bah-ston?"

"City of culture and refinement back East in the great state of Massachusetts. Not surprised a Texican brush-popper like you wouldn't recognize the name." Harry winked at me and finished off his last bite of bacon and biscuit.

The lanky Texas Ranger threw the remnants from his plate to the scrappy chickens and began strapping on his arsenal. "Oh, I've heard of Boston. Known a whole slew of you beaners. Evidently, the state doesn't have much hold on its citizens, though. Seems to me like damn near half of them live in Texas—and they're all bootleggers, thieves, or murderers. You must have come from a more refined section of town than the folks I'm accustomed to dealing with, Mr. Tate."

He grinned, whacked at the holsters of his pistols to get them in just the right spot on his hips, slapped on his hat, and said, "Marshal Tilden, Marshal Boston Beans, let's throw the coffee on the fire and put that big yellow hound on the trail. They's murderers to be caught and they've got four days on us."

We thanked Willard Rump profusely for his hospitality and said our good-byes. As we thundered away, heard Harry ask Lucius if he'd made a map that could get him back to the farm and Eleanor Little Spot. Lucius confidently replied he could easily find that beautiful girl again, even if her father's house was on the bottom of the biggest lake in the Nations.

We headed for the spot where Jeff Diggs saw his last few seconds of life. Hadn't been there but about five minutes when Harry and Lucius found the trail. They made a good pair in the brush. Felt safe with those men on either side of me. Hell, I just knew when things started to get rougher'n a petrified corncob, I couldn't have been in the company of better men. Good thing those feelings gave some comfort, because the corncob—armed to the teeth and ready for a fight—waited for us a few days up the trail.

5

"LUCKY'S ALWAYS BETTER'N BEIN' GOOD."

CAESAR TOOK THE scent of those murderous bastards with his nose to the ground, his tail in the air, and running for all he was worth like he always did. We'd only been following the dog for a matter of hours when Lucius said, "No point pushing our animals so hard for this bunch. They're not in any hurry. Appear to be meandering along like nothing happened. Near as I can make out, there's four of 'em. That sound right to you, Harry?"

We'd stopped for a minute, and Harry scratched around in the dirt as he examined each print to make sure he'd recognize all of them, even if crossed by someone else's tracks further along.

"Best I can tell, you hit the nail right on the head, Lucius. But I'd be willing to bet my next month's wages they aren't in any hurry 'cause someone's awaiting their arrival a bit further up. That's the only reason I can think of would keep them from scorching everything within shouting distance to get away from the killing."

It all sounded reasonable to me at the time. Figured both men for better trackers than I would probably ever be, and no doubt existed in my mind that Harry Tate could outguess the vicious sons of bitches no matter what they did to try and throw us off the scent. But Lucius was right. The killers took their time and left a trail a hymn-singing near-blind Ohio spinster could have followed.

We caught up with them east of Chickasha out on the Washita about a week later. Unfortunately, by then, we'd got kind of sloppy in our tracking and stumbled right into their camp. Harry had the lead, and I still don't know to this day whether he went to sleep or just missed some sign that would've kept us from ending up in a situation none of us would have wished on anybody. Whatever the reason, we made a simple mistake—simple and deadly.

The way it happened is still a bit muddy in my brain. I remember Gunpowder and me brought up the rear right behind Lucius. All of a sudden he stopped and, before I knew what had happened, we were facing at least eight men milling around a campfire right in the middle of the trail. Lucius pulled up on Harry's left. I went to the right. We moved as far away from each other as the cramped tree-lined pathway allowed, but that still left us much too close to each other for my taste. Made awful good targets all bunched up like that.

The appearance of three heavily armed men wearing

badges had a sobering effect on that gathering of Satan's students. Tin plates clattered to the ground, coffee got pitched into the bushes, cups rattled off rocks, and things tensed up real fast. Pretty soon, quiet dropped over the whole shindig like a wet blanket saturated in the aroma of bad coffee, sweat, and horse manure. For a second or so I thought for sure I could hear earthworms breathing. Fingers twitched over pistol butts, and everyone got to blinking like a hot wind from hell was swirling around all of us.

Harry kind of turned toward me. I could see the worry in his eyes, but he didn't waste any time with the killers when he zeroed back in less than a second later and said, "About a week ago we buried a cowboy named Diggs over near Willard Rump's place on Mill Creek in the Choctaw Nation. Some of you men killed him."

A feller with a hooked nose and dank stringy hair squatted by their fire, and didn't sound a bit perturbed when he spat tobacco juice into the smoldering coals and said, "Well, now, is that a fact?" He took his hat off and wiped the brim out with a dirty blue-and-white bandanna snatched from his hip pocket.

Lucius urged Hateful up about half a step ahead of Harry, and propped his left arm on the pommel of his saddle. He leaned over slightly to cover the fact that his right hand slid to the grips of the cross-draw gun resting against his belly. Harry already had himself cinched up for the fight, and since I usually rode with the Winchester across my saddle, it wasn't much of a trick to bring it to the ready.

The lawdog from Texas jumped right into the middle

of the hooked-nosed man with, "That's a fact, Brutus. And here's another one for you back-shootin' sons of bitches. We'll take all those willing to Fort Smith after you've buried the ones that don't want to go." His outburst just about snapped everyone's garters. Didn't know at the time why he popped off like that, but it was done, and he couldn't call it back. Besides, he'd just managed to say it before Harry or me could.

One he called Brutus looked surprised, and gave the Ranger a long careful eyeballing, then spat in the fire again. "Ah, we're in the company of the famous Texas lawman Lucius Dodge, boys. You're a long way from home aren't you, Lucius? Folks round Fort Worth will probably get to missin' you if you don't get back home soon." The man's voice rasped through his words like a crosscut saw.

Our Ranger friend didn't even blink. "Hayden, I want you and Handsome Harry to meet the one and only Brutus Sneed. So many people in Texas have posters out on this ugly son of a bitch, you could wallpaper every day parlor in Fort Worth with his ugly face. If he ain't raped it, killed it, or set it on fire, God's a possum, preaches services in the Alamo every Sunday, and Saint Peter leads the hymn singing."

Sneed brought himself painfully to a standing position in much the same way you'd expect of a man whose spine was kinked up because age, rheumatism, and gunshot wounds had turned it into something like a rusted chain attached to a boat anchor.

He motioned to the men standing on either side of him. "Looks to me like you and your friends are slightly outnumbered here, Dodge. Why don't you do-

rights back off, and we'll pack up and go on our way."
I could tell he didn't like the proximity of all the guns
sitting on the horses less than twenty feet from him.

"Sorry, Mr. Sneed," I added, "but Texas Ranger By
God Lucius Dodge is right. Someone's gonna either
swing in Fort Smith or die right here for what happened to Jeff Diggs. One way or another, some of you
men are gonna pay for what you did. Might not have
been any law there when you killed him, but it's here
now—and we're it." By the time I got to the end of
that speech, my voice had dropped to the colder-than-
Montana-in-January stage.

Guess Lucius had talked all he wanted and listened
to all he cared to hear. Both his hands filled with fire-
belching pistols and, in half the time it'd take to blow
out a candle, he'd dropped at least two of those yellow
bellies. Bullets whizzed all around me, but none of
those poor boys were a match for the three of us. Way
I've got it figured today, if you'd have been able to
take all the gunfighting skills of every man in the
bunch and lump 'em up together in one man, he
wouldn't have stood a chance against any of our party.
Especially Handsome Harry Tate. But hell, don't ever
let anyone tell you different, being lucky's always better'n being good. The truth of it all is when it comes
right down to the nut-cutting, the least little thing can
render all the experience and talent you have to the
not-worth-spit level. And be goddamned, that morning
when the best man there had his luck run out so fast,
it was like watching lightning hit a hundred-foot-tall
oak on a hill.

•   •   •

For a about a minute I couldn't talk anymore. Franklin J. Lightfoot, Jr., stared off into the space above the ceiling fan, and then started tapping his pencil against the top of the yellow notepad.

"You okay, Hayden?" He leaned over and patted the side of my left thigh. Shook my leg like he wanted to wake me up or something.

Had my elbows on my knees and my head propped in my hands. Couldn't believe after all those years the memory of that dreadful, deadly day still had the power to affect me the way it did.

"Them low-life scum-sucking bastards killed Handsome Harry, Junior." My revelation came from between fingers, like I was trying to hide the horror of it from him and the words just managed to escape.

"What? What did you just say?" Don't know who was more astonished—him or me.

When I looked up, I could see the shock in his eyes. Guess the tears on my cheeks surprised him. Hell, they surprised me. Always did. "They killed Harry. Those sorry bastards Lucius didn't knock down in the first volley, and who managed to get a gun up, must have all fired at ole Handsome at the same time. That monster Sneed led it all. Never understood how it happened, but I think it was because Harry was in the middle and easiest to get a bead on. Kinda like me and Thunder at Drinkwater's Store."

Junior slumped back in his chair and rubbed his brow with the tips of his fingers. "Sweet Jesus." He sounded like a man who'd just lost a good friend.

"Exactly the way I felt at the time, Junior. They peppered him pretty good. Just like Jeff Diggs. His falling horse brought Gunpowder and me down at the same time. Over the years I've come to believe if man and horse hadn't pushed us aside when they tumbled, Sneed's bunch would've killed me too."

Silence dropped between us the way night sounds vanish when something dangerous prowls around in the dark. I'd known from the very beginning of our little talks there would be a lot of pain bubbling up to the surface if we went on long enough. Hell, Harry Tate was the leading edge of an iceberg made from a lifetime of grief.

"You already know by then I'd killed my share of men, Junior. Rubbed out some because I had to. Others got snuffed because they deserved it. And even shot hell out of my share because Judge Parker secretly wanted them dead. When Gunpowder and I got bumped, it caused me to miss at least two shots, maybe three. Didn't matter a whole lot. Ole Lucius must have fired every round he had from those pistols hanging on that wiry mustang of his. But you know, that hook-nosed son of a bitch vanished like fog burned off by the morning sun."

"Damnation, Hayden. You mean to tell me Brutus Sneed got away?"

"Don't know how, Junior, but he did it and took one of his sorry trail mates with him. After Harry went down, Lucius rushed the rest of those ole boys and blew craters in anything what moved. If you've never seen a skilled Indian fighter practice his trade, you've missed something close to a work of living art. Those Texas boys had been killing Comanches for so long, they tended to take the fight right to anybody who came at them in a group the way Sneed and his bunch did."

I had to stop for a minute and get my breath back. "What's that old saying, Junior? Something like, life's hard and then you die? Well, dying can be hard too. Mostly for those who have to watch it happen, then get left behind, I think. Harry had a tough time of it— quick, but tougher than swallowing thumbtacks. He saw death coming and faced it a lot better than most."

"Well, hell. They didn't kill him outright?"

"No. I crawled over to where he fell and dragged him to the base of a gnarled-up oak tree. He had a nasty wound in his right cheek just under the eye. A lot of bone and stuff got pushed into his skull. At least two more perforated his vest on the left side, and the holes drilled through the garment still smoked. Don't know how he held on to the gun in his right hand. The way his wrist was shattered, he never would have drawn a pistol with any kind of authority again."

Lightfoot's amazement deepened. "He managed to live for a bit? God Almighty, that's just incredible."

"Yep, but ole Harry's being able to survive getting shot to hell didn't even come close to the oddest thing that happened right then."

"What do you mean?"

"Well, I rested his head in my lap and had my right hand over the holes in his chest trying to stop the sucking and frothing from the wound. He didn't appear conscious. His face twisted up from the pain and his breathing came in ragged bloody gasps. He coughed one time, and a couple of his teeth landed in a gory wad on his chest. And then, Old Bear kind of appeared right at Harry's feet. I never did get used to the way he could show up like smoke that took living form. Some people in the past have said I've exaggerated his ability to go invisible and then reappear like he did, but—with God as my witness—he could do it."

My old would-be Indian friend dropped to one knee, placed his hand on my shoulder, and said, "Let me see his wounds, Tilden."

We moved Harry into a semi-sitting position against the tree, but I felt pretty certain he didn't have a chance in hell of making it. Then again, anything was possible, especially when you had a man who could make himself invisible trying to keep you alive.

Old Bear gave Harry a quick going-over, reached into the fringed and beaded pouch that always hung against his hip, and pulled out a piece of what looked like pond reed about four inches long. Then he whipped out that big bowie and cut a hole in Harry's throat so fast I almost passed out watching it. Blood spurted all over the front of our wounded friend's shirt as the old man shoved the reed into the hole, then quickly punched some wads of cloth into the chest wounds. Harry seemed to kind of inflate like a kid's carnival balloon. His eyes popped open and he started trying to talk, but nothing came out for several seconds. Finally, he made this tiny motion with a finger of his left hand for me to lean closer.

Bent over as near as I could, and barely heard what he whispered in my ear. "Hayden." Bloody foam bubbled from his lips.

"You shouldn't talk, Harry."

Old Bear tugged at my sleeve. "Let him say his piece." He turned away and said under his breath, "He won't have another chance."

Harry's liquid words came slowly, between ragged gasps for air. "Hayden . . . letter . . . inside pocket . . . write my father . . . tell . . . how . . . I died. Tell him . . . sorry . . . he'll understand. Good friend . . . pistols . . . you take them . . . saddle and traps . . . for Billy Bird . . . horse for Old Bear . . . you'll see to it . . . won't you?"

I pulled the bloodstained envelope from his breast pocket and said, "I'll take care of everything, Harry." Not since the murders of my family had anyone's death affected me so profoundly. It reminded me of Travis Teel's killing out on the Muddy Boggy and the way Harry and Billy wept for the man when they buried him. I hadn't known Travis that well, but memories of the way they mourned the loss of their good friend suddenly swept over me in a wave of emotion like I'd never experienced.

Harry had helped me save Elizabeth from Saginaw Bob, and almost died when Tollman Pike shot him out of the saddle on the trail to Dallas. We'd fought side by side in gun battles from the Nations to the wilds of North Texas and even Dodge City. We froze in the winter, burnt up in the summer, and did it all together. I loved the man, and now his life drained into the mossy bed below him, and I couldn't do a goddamn thing to stop it. Let me tell you something. There's nothing in this life can compare to the hopelessness of watching Death reach into the chest of someone you love and steal them away from you right before your unbelieving eyes. It's theft of the most extreme kind.

Harry came back around long enough for one last run at the world. "Hayden . . . there's a woman . . . Fort Smith . . . Nancy Childress . . . find her . . . tell her . . ." His voice faded, and his head fell to one side. A single, tortured, blood-soaked breath escaped his lips, and un-blinking, tear-filled eyes fixed on mine as he passed.

When I finally looked up at Old Bear, Lucius stood behind him holding the reins of his horse in one hand, his hat in the other. For several minutes I couldn't move. Wanted to stand, but my legs didn't seem attached to the rest of my body. Old Bear leaned over and pulled me to my feet.

Everything got so quiet for a while. The drifting smell of gun smoke and death hung over us, but as I looked away from what had been my friend, my eye landed on a patch of yellow wildflowers a few steps away from his feet. Their beauty and fragrance overwhelmed my senses. Then I noticed the sprayed specks of Harry's blood that decorated many of those pale petals. Still believe it was a sign from his departing spirit.

For a second or so, it seemed like I really needed to be away from that dreadful spot. Turned and started toward Gunpowder. Felt like a blindfolded circus performer on a tightrope. My balance left me. Must have staggered some. Old Bear grabbed me on one side, Lucius on the other. Could tell they were concerned. But eventually that helpless, drunken feeling passed, along with the nauseous wave of loss which accompanied it.

Took us a bit to dig a suitable hole in that piece of

rough, isolated soil. The thing I remember most was how red that dirt was—red to the orange side. And so dark my good friend Harry Tate's life bled into it almost unnoticed. We put him in the ground under the oak where he drew his last breath, and laid him out so he rested with that clump of yellow wildflowers at his feet.

Once we got him properly covered, I picked out a passage of Shakespeare for him. *Hamlet*, Act One, Scene Three. And although it was a father's advice to his son as he left home for the first time, I felt it described my feelings for Harry better than anything else I could have found—even if I'd spent years in the search.

"As Polonius said to his son Laertes upon his departure for college, 'Those friends thou hast, and their adoption tried, grapple them to thy soul with hoops of steel.'" Afraid that was all I could get out. Just couldn't read anymore. Wanted to, but couldn't do it.

And even now, with more than half a century past that grisly day behind me, I can close my eyes and describe every rock, blade of grass, and the leaves that decorated all the trees around us. I remember how Lucius stood with his hat in his hand, bent slightly at the waist and staring at the grave like a man who understood an anonymous spot like Harry's very likely awaited him in some barren godforsaken piece of unexplored country where no one knew him or cared when he'd left this life.

Can still see Old Bear as he held his arms aloft and sang a painfully beautiful song I couldn't understand to a cloud-covered piece of heaven that suddenly opened up and drenched us with tears.

And perhaps oddest of all, a stocky Indian man appeared behind Old Bear. He was a head and a half shorter than his companion, wore a dark blue shirt, wheat-colored vest, a breechcloth over leather leggings, and moccasins. His braided hair hung in tails down each side of his head. He'd tied them off with blood-red ribbons. The only other flash to the man was some silver hoop-shaped earrings that sparkled when the light hit them.

Both of them sang totally different songs, which seemed to blend together in one sad, sonorous series of notes that climbed the limbs of the surrounding trees and floated to the weeping clouds like gifts offered up as bribes in an effort to get the Great Spirit to give our friend back to us. But if I've learned only one thing in this life, it's that you can't bribe God. Indian or not, the dead are simply dead, and the grief of every person in the world never brought anyone back from the other side.

Guess I'd been standing there for fifteen or twenty minutes when Lucius leaned over and said, "What do you want to do now, Hayden? You've just got an ice-water-clear lesson on how dangerous Brutus Sneed is. He won't let us bring him back alive, if we can catch him. But you name it, and we'll do it together. I'll walk into hell's vestibule with you, and we'll kill the devil together." It sounded like something Harry or Billy would have said. You can't buy trail mates like that. Not with all of Croesus' gold. Only hardship and death guarantee such friends.

My response must have barely come out as not much more than a whisper. "Well, then, we'll ride these sons of bitches into the ground, kill 'em both, and anyone else who happens to be with them."

After I inked all the dead men's hands and pressed them to the backs of John Doe warrants for identification, he had to run to catch up with me as I jumped on Gunpowder and kicked him away from that gory scene. He yelled something about burying the six dead outlaws. I hollered back they could rot where they fell as far as I was concerned. He shook his head, leaped into the saddle, and followed. Sometimes the best thing to do with death and loss is simply get away from it, as quick as you can.

Old Bear and his friend were already ahead of us scouting the trail behind Caesar. Couldn't help but think that maybe if Bear had been with me, Harry wouldn't have died the way he did. Guess Bear must have felt some guilt himself, because he went at the job like some kind of possessed fiend. We had a hell of a time keeping up. The trail went west and a bit north into the foothills of the Arbuckle Mountains. Stayed with it the first day till dark set in and we couldn't see much of anything. Old Bear and his friend lit pine-knot torches and tried to keep going, but things got to the point where even they had to wait for the light to come back.

That night we sat around a cold camp. I needed something to move my mind away from what had happened to Harry, and took it as my first opportunity to find out what I could about our newest addition. Think, with some good reason, it had begun to seem to me as though everywhere Old Bear went, I ended up with another orphan following me around. First there was Caesar, then Daniel Old Bear, and now a real honest-to-God Indian for crying out loud.

"Who's our new friend, Daniel?" Tended to call him by his Christian name when I wanted him to really pay attention.

Couldn't see all of his face in the moonlight, but I would have bet money he smiled as he chewed his beef jerky and said, "An old Kiowa friend. Name is Charlie Three Bones. Got word two moons back. Charlie needed help. Had to go check on him."

"What kind of aid and comfort could a Kiowa named Charlie Three Bones need that would put you on the trail to lend a hand? I've never heard you mention the man by name before."

"Back when the Cheyenne took me from my white family, started out living with them. Then, for a while, I went with some Cherokee people. Eventually spent a good deal of time with Kiowa folks. That's where I met Charlie. He loved to roam the world before the government got him. Being cooped up in the Territories has been hard on ole Charlie. Man used to be a soldier. Wore the red sash of the Kaitsenko—the Society of the Ten Bravest. Been struggling with his loss of freedom ever since the government first moved his people. Guess it got the best of him. Started drinking. Whiskey no good for Indians like Charlie. His friends were mighty concerned. Sent me word to come quick as double-greased lightning. Had to make a fast trip over to the Wichita Mountains and see for myself. Figured I'd bring him with me to keep him away from the jug. He's a good man, Hayden, and when we catch up with them fellers who killed Handsome Harry, we might need him. We're headed right into Charlie's regular stomping grounds. By tomorrow morning he'll recognize every blade of grass we step over."

He leaned into his bedding. I took the hint and left him to his own thoughts. Lucius stirred in his spot, sat up, and pawed around under his blanket. When he finally found what he was after, he cursed the offense to his comfort and flung it into the darkness.

"You know anything about Brutus Sneed, Tilden?" He slapped at his blanket, rearranged his saddle, then fell back into his newly made bed.

"Never heard of the man before you called him out today."

"Well, he's a bad 'un. First time I ran across him was five years ago down on the Clear Fork of the Trinity 'bout sixty miles west of Fort Worth. He and some of his friends were borrowing cattle and horses from everyone in north Texas. Sylvis Bond and me caught the thieving bastard in the act of changing brands on some stock he and his friends had appropriated. They didn't stay caught long, though. Before we could put the shackles on 'em, Brutus came up with a .32-caliber Colt's pocket gun. Guess Sylvis must have missed it when he searched the man. Sneed put at least three slugs in Sylvis and got away, while I tried to keep my friend from dying by plugging up the holes in his leg with my fingers."

It all sounded so familiar. Lawmen all over the West who managed to survive for more'n a few months on the job could probably have told similar stories. So many of us died back then—so many good men taken away.

"Did your friend make it?"

"He made it, but he never walked the same way after that little skirmish. One of Sneed's slugs caught him in his upper left thigh and blew a hell of a hole in the meaty part of his leg. Feared for a while we might have to take it off him."

"You've evidently run across Sneed more than once."

"Yep. And every time it came out bad. Like this last one with Harry. Sneed's always managed to weasel out of whatever trap we put down for him. Hell, one time me'n a posse set up in the trees along the north side of Little Mary's Creek. He and his brother, Conner, came riding up on the south side. We poured the lead to 'em. Conner got hit right off and went down pretty quick. Somebody managed to lodge at least one in Brutus. That put him afoot. But, hell, he pulled his rifle and went to pumpin' blue whistlers into those trees so fast, my posse panicked and ran like scalded dogs. Then he picked Conner up, threw him on a horse, jumped up behind, and lit out like lightning. Found Conner on the trail a day or so later. He'd been shot through at least five times. Don't know how he made it as far as he did. Didn't matter anyhow. Brutus got away again. Hadn't heard anything from him in better than a year. Hoped maybe someone had sent him to the fiery pit where he belongs. Guess we'll have to do that tomorrow, Tilden. But be aware, the man is slippery, dangerous, and will kill us all if we give him a chance."

Let that one lay there for a minute before I said, "Don't worry, Lucius. He's not gonna live too much longer, if I have anything to say about it. He might not have been the one that killed Handsome Harry, but he caused it, and I aim to see him dead for it before the sun goes down tomorrow."

The Ranger from Texas pulled his hat down over his face. It muffled his voice, but I heard him say, "Good. Glad you see it my way."

6

"Been a Bane to My Existence"

DANIEL OLD BEAR probably should have been declared a prophet. Next morning, about twenty miles south of a hole in the ground people call Purdy these days, we came upon a Chickasaw feller and his family in a spring wagon. Old Bear and Charlie Three Bones talked with the jittery Indian. His wife sat next to him on the seat, but kept her head down and wouldn't look at us. Several ragged children hid behind their fidgety father and peeked over his shoulder. He spoke hardly any English. Old Bear had to translate.

"His name is Matthew Broken Hand. Says men came to his house—this morning—early. Three men. They took over. Forced him and his family out. Barricaded themselves inside. Seemed ready for a fight. Says the men had lots of guns and sacks of cartridges."

He turned to me. "You want to ask him anything, Tilden?"

"Is he sure about how many men there were?"

"Already questioned him over that piece of information. Twice. Says he's deadly certain. There's three of 'em now."

"Where'd the third one come from?" Lucius sounded some perturbed as he pulled one of his cigars from the pocket of shirt and fired it up.

Old Bear shrugged. "Don't know. Could've met along the trail. Likely came across him up ahead of us somewhere. Could be they were waiting on this third man when you boys ran into them back where Harry bought it. We'll probably find our new man's tracks between here and the house. Broken Hand says his place is about ten miles north of here. In a little valley. Says he chopped out just enough trees for the house."

We hadn't managed to go but about another mile when Charlie Three Bones located the spot where the third man's tracks crossed the other two. The Kiowa warrior slipped off his horse. He studied the sign left by the passing killers, then pointed off in the distance.

Old Bear acted as his friend's interpreter. "Big man. Riding a mule. Huge animal. Stopped here. Man spit a lot of tobacco juice all over. Talked with the men we've been following. They rode off that way." The right arm of Charlie Three Bones came up again. He and Old Bear pointed in the general direction of where we were already headed.

Lucius made a moaning sound, pushed his hat back on his head, and ran his hand from his forehead to his chin several times.

"What's the matter?" I figured if he had more bad news, we might as well get it all out in the open.

"Well, there's no way to be certain, but Brutus has a friend who sometimes travels with him. Rides a mule. Sure as hell don't need to hear he was anywhere around right now."

Old Bear reined up beside us. "Big man? Weighs two hundred fifty or three hundred pounds? Maybe more? Walks funny? Feet all turned in?" He held his hands out, palms down, and turned the tips of his fingers inward. "What you call pigeon-toed."

Lucius slapped his leg with the leather quirt hanging from his wrist. "Sweet Jesus. Sure 'nuff sounds like him. Dynamite Dave McNutt."

"Good God, Lucius, how many more of these Texas bandits do you think we'll run across out here before this all shakes out?" I stood in the stirrups to emphasize how irritating the whole thing had become.

He looked puzzled for a moment, then grinned and said, "Damn, Hayden, I didn't bring 'em." He sucked a piece of tobacco from his teeth and spat it between Hateful's ears. The horse snapped its head around and tried to bite him on the leg just above his boot top. "The only one I suspected might be around these parts was W. J. McCabe. But I'll tell you this, if Dynamite Dave is with Brutus, we've got a whole new snake to stomp and he's mean as hell on a pitchfork." He scratched another lucifer on the butt of his belly gun and tried to puff his dead smoke back to life.

Have to admit here I've always hated the nicknames some of those viciously evil sons of bitches often gave themselves. Most of the time the name was just another

way to intimidate folks. But, hell, those florid monikers
were often accurate in their symbolic assessment of the
no-account's personality—peculiar or otherwise. If
people called some homicidal brute Black Bart, Mys-
terious Tom, Deadeye Dick, or anything else angry and
descriptive, most times they had a good reason for it.
But it didn't make their extravagant handles any easier
to stomach. Just seemed like self-serving bilge to me.
Especially when you found out later those ole boys'
real names were Bob Johnson, Mortimer Thomas, or
Richard Fudge. Now we had the prospects of meeting
up with Dynamite Dave. Didn't sound like a good time
at an afternoon church social to me.

Went to sleep that night listening to Old Bear and
Charlie Three Bones whisper back and forth to one
another. Couldn't understand what was said, but figured Daniel wanted to keep his friend's mind occupied
so he wouldn't get to thinking about the jug again.

Early the next morning, we pushed deeper into the
thickening forest. By the time we finally got to Matthew Broken Hand's house, the trees had closed in on
us so tight, Old Bear and Charlie Three Bones made it
pretty clear they had the distinct feeling of being
hemmed in and weren't at all comfortable with the situation.

But then we hit this spot in the woods where it all
opened up. Broken Hand had taken down every tree
on something like three or four acres of land and built
his house right in the middle of the cleared field—a
two-story rough plank structure that looked to be an
earnest effort to copy the houses of white people somewhere out on the East Coast. Rarely saw a house sitting

on piers out in the Nations, but the four corners and middle of his rested on what appeared to be carefully selected flat rocks as good as, or maybe better than, any made of brick back in Fort Smith.

As you viewed the house from the front, a rail corral stood to the right, or east side, with a shelter built against that end of the house to protect his animals from bad weather. On the other side and slightly behind the rough building, chickens clucked and complained in their wire-wrapped shelter. An outbuilding stood some distance back of the place in a spot so far away from the house it almost hid itself in the dense woods.

Old Bear said something to Charlie Three Bones and both men laughed behind their hands. Lucius wanted to know what was so funny. "I just pointed out that when the weather gets real bad, there must be a lot of business done between the back door of the house and the outbuilding. Charlie Three Bones noted as how Matthew Broken Hand might well be the only Indian feller in the Nations with a real honest-to-God outhouse." It always proved a marvel to me how he could swing back and forth from a fractured, halting form of English to the expression of complex thoughts you wouldn't have believed him capable of putting across. He might have dressed like a refugee from several of the Plains tribes, but beneath the aboriginal exterior resided a mind sharper than the business end of a Mexican hornet.

We sat back in the darkness of the tree line and gave the whole place a good looking-over. Old Bear came up with something I never would have thought of.

"Broken Hand must have made one of those trips to Washington. Probably owns a blue and gold ribbon with a brass medal with the Great White Father's face on it. His house sure doesn't look like anything else you can find most Indian folk living in around here. 'Cept maybe Quanah Parker's place over in the Comanche Nation."

Lucius smiled, sucked at something between his front teeth, and pulled his rifle from the scabbard. "Yep, be willing to bet he worked a year sawing logs into all those boards, and here we are about to shoot the everlasting hell out of the place."

I didn't want a repeat of Drinkwater's Store, so we talked it over and decided to surround the rough dwelling and get in as close as we could before making our presence known. A dry creek bed twelve or fifteen feet across and six feet deep, with a rough bridge over it, slashed from one corner of the plot to the other about sixty feet from Broken Hand's front door. Stumps still jutted out of the ground everywhere. We actually had plenty of cover.

Old Bear talked it over with Charlie Three Bones so there wouldn't be any misunderstandings. The rugged-looking Kiowa brave nodded like he understood, took his rifle, and headed for the west side. Lucius circled around to the back. Old Bear to the east. I elected to move in on them from the front again, and set up in the creek near the far end of the rickety bridge.

The dusty creek bed was deep enough for me to stand upright and have my head above the banks so I could see almost everything around the house. Waited for my posse to get situated before I opened up the discussion. A few seconds before calling out to the house, I remember thinking that Carlton's wagon full of dynamite and that cannon sure would've been nice to have along for the dance.

Had barely managed to stand completely upright so I could yell out when a skinny runt carrying a galvanized bucket full of some kind of slops stepped onto the front porch and tossed the contents into the rough yard. He must have seen something. Maybe he spotted my hat sticking up over the ditch bank, or maybe he had a second sense of some kind about those things. Anyway, he stood there holding the bucket in both hands for a second or so like he was sniffing the air. Then he dropped it and went for his gun. Hell, he didn't give me much of a chance to think it over, and I couldn't waste any time. In about a split second I figured he was as good a way as any to start the ball rolling. Jerked the Winchester up and blew him back into the open doorway.

A lot of yelling and screaming from inside followed my blast. After a bit, it finally quieted down again and I yelled, "Brutus Sneed, come out here and give yourself up for arrest. You will be taken to Fort Smith to stand trial in Judge Parker's court for the murder of Deputy U.S. Marshal Harry Tate—or you can fight—and I guarantee we'll see you dead before the day's out."

A booming voice from inside the house screeched, "You shot Albino Bob, you son of a bitch! Whoever you are, you can go straight to hell!" From what he said, it sounded like I hadn't managed to kill Albino Bob. Didn't usually miss that much on a shot that close. Hunkered down in the ditch, checked the sights on my rifle, and wondered how I'd managed to let him get away.

"You're talking to a deputy United States marshal who is in possession of a warrant for your arrest, Sneed. My name is Hayden Tilden, and you've got exactly one minute to come out of Matthew Broken Hand's house and surrender—or my posse has been instructed to kill you where you stand."

Some real hot discussion flared up inside the house. Men yelled back and forth at each other again. Could only make out snatches of what got said from where I stood. From the tone of it, I gathered one of them didn't like their prospects and wanted to give it up. Another one shouted him down. Squeaky voice I took to be Albino Bob's dying effort to contribute didn't sound very enthusiastic about any of it. Got quiet for a second or two. Then all hell broke loose.

Guess the two who could still move around stayed in a dead run from window to window for the next twenty minutes or so. Sprayed bullets at anything and everything that moved. Then all their guns turned my way long enough to pin me down for a few seconds. While I tried to keep my head from having windows put in it, that fat bastard must have stepped out on the porch and tossed a stick of his favorite explosive my direction. He came up short by about twenty feet, but the ground bucked, snorted, and threw clods, horse manure, and chicken shit all over me. He followed the first one with another. It came a lot closer, and set my ears to ringing like church bells on Easter Sunday.

Put the rifle aside and pulled my pistols, Harry's

ivory-handled scroll-engraved Colts, and held them over the lip of the ditch. Couldn't see a damn thing for the smoke and dust, but ripped off six or eight shots real quick. That stopped the blasting on my side. But they must have run to the back and pitched a few at Lucius to get his undivided attention. Heard his rifle go off several times between the explosions.

When I managed to get a peek over the lip of my creek bed, saw Charlie Three Bones lying on the ground underneath the corner of the front porch. Watched as he crawled further under the house till I couldn't see him anymore. Then, guess he started rolling around and shooting up through the floor planks. Heard yelping and gunfire from inside the house, none of it directed at the outside. Gave me a chance to get reloaded, scramble out of the ditch, and land between the front window and the porch in a blind spot where they couldn't have seen me unless they were outside looking back at the house.

Old Bear and Lucius had made it to the rough building too. We all started pouring lead through whatever window we could reach. Heard heavy feet stomp up the stairs and quicker'n a turpentined cat, they were firing down on us from the windows above. Only safe place was under the house or the first floor. Lucius and me hit both doors at about the same time. Old Bear followed Lucius. Charlie Three Bones snugged up behind me.

Soon as we got inside, I almost tripped over Albino Bob. Opening round I pitched in his direction must've caught him about three fingers below the heart. Guess he lived about long enough to contribute to the initial disagreement before God tore his ticket for the great beyond.

Lucius made a motion at the ceiling, and we all started firing at the same time. The four of us must have put close to fifty shots up their britches legs before we had to stop and reload. Then I heard this odd thumping noise outside, and got back to the front porch in time to see Brutus Sneed hobbling for the wooded area where we'd staked our animals. Lucius and I both sent lead after him, but he managed to make the curtain of trees before we could get him lined up in our sights.

Levered a round into my rifle and started for the horses. "Check upstairs, Lucius. Make sure Dynamite Dave is no longer with us." Carefully made my way from stump to stump till I got to the trees. Turned out not to be a problem. Found Brutus Sneed lying spread-eagled flat on his back about ten feet from where the horses stood. His head was all caved in. Squatted down to check him over a bit closer, and heard a single gunshot back at the house. A few minutes later my friends all snaked their way up to Sneed's body.

Looked from face to face as they scratched their chins and walked around the fallen outlaw. "Can't figure it out, Lucius. You got any ideas, Old Bear? He seems to have made it to here just fine, but something happened and he ended up with a busted skull." I grabbed the man's chin and pulled it to one side so they had a better view of his sunken forehead.

Lucius scratched his jaw, looked from the horses to the body, and started laughing. He dropped his rifle on the ground, placed both hands on his knees, and went at it like someone had loaded the biggest heap of hilarity on him he'd ever heard. He jerked his hat off and started slapping his crusty thigh with it. Dust flew in all directions.

I stood and faced him, but he couldn't seem to get hold of himself. "What the hell's so funny? Is this some kind of joke only half-witted Texicans can understand?"

He grinned and wiped the tears from his eyes. "Oh, hell, no, Tilden. I think almost any of you Arkansas clod-kickers can get this one." He swabbed his face with a bandanna and stuffed his hat back on. "Our dearly departed friend Mr. Sneed has been the victim of God's own personal brand of swiftly applied justice—meted out by one of his favorite creatures. Ole Brutus made the singular mistake of trying to walk up behind Hateful. I think she kicked the hell out of him." He peeked at me from under the brim of his Texas sombrero, and a wide, toothy grin lit up his face again. "Seems fitting, don't you think? God came down here and used my horse to take care of the man who killed Handsome Harry Tate. Honest, Tilden, if Providence got any better, I couldn't stand it and the law wouldn't allow it. An outcome like this one is what a south Texas rancher would refer to as larrupin' good. Sweet Jesus, it just can't get much better than this."

Old Bear absolutely loved the cosmic implications of our Texas Ranger friend's philosophical meanderings about Brutus Sneed's exit from this life. He got to mumbling stuff about the Great Spirit and a whole heap of other mumbo jumbo I couldn't understand. Hell, it was just an accident as far as I was concerned.

"Well, Lucius, there is one glaring problem with this whole thing."

"And what would that be, Marshal Tilden?"

"Call it God's hand in the matter or fate or luck or whatever else you want. But the simple fact is your horse cheated me out of an opportunity to even the score with the ever-lovely Mr. Sneed. Personally, I wanted to put a few chunks of lead into the murderin' bastard before he departed this life." Pushed at the corpse with the toe of my boot. "Hell, he never knew what hit him. Hateful did Sneed a huge favor as far as I'm concerned. If I'd caught him alive, it would've been tempting to pull a Saginaw Bob, Minco Springs song and dance on his sorry behind."

Lucius led Hateful away from his stake and stroked the beast's neck. "Who the hell's Saginaw Bob, and where's Minco Springs?"

"Hell, I'll tell you later. What happened to Dynamite Dave?"

Old Bear stepped up, let the hammer down on his Winchester, and said, "We wounded Mr. Dynamite. Several times. But he could still walk. When we got to the second floor, he tried to climb out the window behind his friend. Charlie Three Bones and I shot him in the right leg at the same time. Could have broken the other one when he hit the ground. Don't think he'll be going far from where we left him."

Holstered my pistols, pulled my own bandanna, and wiped all the sweat and grit off the back of my neck. "He's still alive?"

Old Bear and Charlie Three Bones grinned. "Was the last time we saw him." He nudged his companion and said something in Kiowa. They both laughed. Charlie Three Bones spoke and made broad motions as Old Bear interpreted. "My friend says he'll be glad to kill the big man for you. Wants the scalp. Been so long since he's taken one he'd be right grateful. Might put him back in touch with the past and his ancestors."

Lucius got all puffed up and started blowing steam. "Ain't gonna be no scalpin' done as long as I'm around. Hell, I've seen enough of that kind of stuff from years of fighting the Comanche down in Tejas to do me. So the two of you, and any of your 'ancestors' that may be floating around in the air hereabouts, can forget about taking a knife to Dynamite Dave's hair."

"Can he talk?" Figured I might as well see what could be learned from the man if he was still alive.

Old Bear shrugged and winked at Charlie Three Bones. "We shot him. Didn't try to talk to him."

Well, Dynamite Dave turned out to be a lot more man than any of us expected. By the time we got back to the house, he'd crawled all the way to the dry creek bed and was lying under the bridge in almost the same spot I used when the dance started. He attempted some more-than-worthless defensive shooting as soon as he heard us coming in from the trees, but couldn't do much damage lying on his back, punching holes in clouds. Once we'd flanked him, by crawling up on either side and pumping a few more in on him, he gave up pretty quick. But I've got to hand it to Dynamite Dave—he was one tough ole bird to have made it as far as he did with all those leaking holes in him.

Took all four of us to pull the bastard from his hidey-hole. We got him out into the ditch and propped him up. Our randomly placed shots up through Broken Hand's second-story floor had shattered his left arm above the elbow. Several others had burned trenches up his front and backside. The top of one of his ears sported a nice new notch, but I can't remember which one. One round had blasted most of his left heel away. His left leg was broken, and Old Bear's shot, which knocked him out the window, had shattered the big bone in his upper right thigh below his hip socket. The man was a hell of a mess, and to this day, I can't imagine how he managed to live as long or crawl as far as he did in what had to have been an incredibly painful attempt to get away.

At first blush we all offered up opinions that none of his wounds were life-threatening when viewed separately. But on closer examination we decided that given the number of them, and his loss of blood, he didn't have much time left. So we got him in as close to a sitting position as we could and poured some water down his throat.

He gagged and spat up all over his chest, reached around, pulled his vest aside, and exposed another hole below his rib cage and a few inches above his belt. "You . . . badge-wearin' . . . bastards done put a . . . lot of lead in me . . . today. Swear . . . to an everlastin' . . . God . . . your type . . . has been a bane to my existence . . . since the . . . day my sainted . . . mother gave birth to me." His breathing came in ragged gasps, and it took a great deal of effort to force his words past split bloody lips.

He grabbed a spot above the hole in his belly and groaned. Near as I could make out, if that one came up through the floor, it had probably punched a hole down low, then spurted upward and lodged somewhere in his chest. Pretty soon he started spitting up a lot of blood. From then on we knew he wouldn't make it too much longer.

"Hell, this . . . wasn't even . . . my fight. Still don't know . . . why . . . you boys . . . wuz a-chasin' Brutus . . . to begin with. Didn't have . . . time . . . to find out . . . much before the shooting commenced. Acorse . . . don't guess it . . . woulda mattered. Hate you . . . sons of bitches so much . . . I couldn't . . . pass up . . . a chance to kill a few of you." His head fell back, his eyes rolled around, and for a moment we thought he'd bought it. Then, damned if he didn't come back to life again.

Lucius poured some more water down him. Didn't help any. Think it actually made his situation worse, but he kept calling for it and given he was on his last few minutes of life, no one objected.

"Guess you . . . can collect some . . . money on me, boys. They's posters out . . . all over Texas. You'll get . . . to split a nice little sum . . . for puttin' an end . . . to Brutus and me. May even . . . get something . . . for Albino Bob's . . . nasty, stinking hide." His words came out slow, painful, and bloody. "Bob . . . had only been . . . with Brutus . . . a few weeks. Think he . . . came in from Mississippi . . . or Louisiana. Lot of fog . . . in my brain . . . right now, you know. Just . . . can't remember . . . for sure."

He faded off on us again for a minute or so, and I got to thinking he'd finally made it to his personal spot in line shoveling coal for that forked-tailed fellow's furnaces in hell. But then his droopy eyes snapped open again, and he took one final run at the world before he checked out.

"There's . . . a letter . . . in my inside . . . jacket pocket. Addressed . . . to my mother . . . in Uvalde, Texas. Appreciate it . . . if one of you boys . . . could post it. She always knowed . . . I'd go out . . . like this . . . sooner or later. Just . . . to let her know . . . I'm dead. So she won't . . . spend a lot of time . . . wondering what happened to me."

By the time he got that far along, his speech had slurred down to the point where I could barely understand him. Then his head kind of flopped over to one side and his eyes froze open like he'd just seen something that surprised the hell out of him. Didn't relish carrying his letter around next to Harry's, but it's awful hard to deny a man much of anything when he's about to meet his Maker.

Clear as an icy cold morning in February, that dead man said, "Wish I'd never left Texas. You can rob anybody you want down there." He mumbled something about someone named Ramona, and was finally deader'n a can of corned beef.

Lucius leaned over to make sure the big man had gone to the Maker for certain. "Damned if that ain't about the most touching scene I've had to witness in an Arkansas coon's age." You couldn't have cut the sarcasm from his mocking line with a barber's razor.

Well, leaving a bunch of bodies out in the middle of nowhere was one thing, but we couldn't ride away from Broken Hand's house with dead men all over his property. So we stayed around another day to clean up our mess, as best we could. He and his family came back about the time we threw the last shovel of dirt on the three killers. Always felt those terrified folks had been watching us from a distance and waited till it looked safe enough before coming back in for a good look.

Broken Hand's wife pitched a hellacious purple screamer of a fit when she got inside and saw what had happened to her house. Felt so bad about all of it I gave them twenty dollars out of my own pocket to start repairs, and promised I'd send some more from any rewards we managed to collect. The gesture seemed to take some of the edge off the whole thing. Filed a claim for the damages with the court, and when everything finally shook out, was able to send them another two hundred dollars. Several years later, I served a warrant on one of his neighbors, fellow named John Shoots at the Moon Moses. Went by to check on the place. It was as nice as any house in Fort Smith.

Soon as we got all that sorted out, I headed everyone north for Big Cougar Bluff. Took us another week. When we finally arrived, Billy and Carlton were nowhere to be seen, and according to Old Bear hadn't been there. So we squatted and waited. Hell, when those boys showed up a few days later, they had a tale to tell that trumped ours like an ace-high flush.

Lightfoot squirmed in his chair, dropped his pad on the floor, stretched, and stared at me from under hooded eyelids.

"Hayden, you're gonna have to tell me that one tomorrow. I'm about worn down to the proverbial nub today and need to take a break. Do you think we could start this up at about ten o'clock tomorrow morning? You can tell me Carlton's tale then."

"Well, yes, Junior, we *could* do that. But the absolute truth of the thing is it'd be a whole bunch better if you got Carlton to enlighten you about his particular piece of Smilin' Jack Paine's story."

"Carlton? Hell, Carlton has tried to die on us at least twice since I've started coming here. He's spent the last few days in an all-out effort to do a jackknife into the great beyond, and on top of that, he doesn't even seem to know where he is about half the time. Do you really believe the man has the residual mental capacity to keep his mind on and tell such a story if he can recover from this latest episode?"

"Oh, hell, yes. This kind of stuff happens two or three times a month. Back a couple of years ago, he had one of these spells at least once a week for months. Most people would be slobbering vegetables by now if they'd experienced all the unfortunate crap that falls on ole Carlton. Believe me on this one, Frank. Carlton J. Cecil's tougher than a deep-fried cavalry saddle. God's been trying to carry him away about every other day now for almost five years, and that crazy old jaybird keeps fighting him off. You take a break and come back in two or three days, my friend. I guarantee you Carlton J. Cecil will recover."

He slumped in his chair, stared at me for a minute, winked, forced himself to his feet, and headed for the door like a man pulling a plow. Remember thinking, well, hell, I've done it now. If Carlton can't make it back onto his wheeled throne pretty quick, I'm gonna look about as smart as a guy who'd use a shotgun to hunt flying fish.

So, I ambled down to the old fart's room and pulled a chair up beside his bed. Figured it wouldn't hurt to buy myself a little insurance just in case he actually passed on this time. Nurses had him hooked up to three or four different kinds of liquid. Usually had to rehydrate his desiccated old carcass for a couple of days, then fill him full of all kinds of other stuff before he made it back from the other side.

He must have heard me, because his eyes fluttered open like broken window shades flipping around. Stared at me for almost a minute before full recognition flittered across his face. Then he smiled and said, "What the hell's going on, Hayden? Think we'll have to blast our way out of here?"

Guess he lost that thread and picked up on another pretty quick. "Any of them dancin' girls still around? I really like that 'un named Ruth. Blond-headed gal looks awful good in that white thing she wears. Heddy's better-looking, though. Actually like her better'n Ruth. Course Marty's a real juicy little thing, but she's only here one day a week."

Pulled on the sleeve of his pajamas to get his attention. "Carlton, I need you to do something for me."

He cupped his hand over his ear and started to play hard of hearing on me again. I wasn't having any of it. "Don't you dare drag out that ole 'I'm so deaf Gabriel's horn would sound like a tin whistle' stuff on me today. We don't have time for it right now."

A devilish grin crooked its way across his face. He

dropped the hand back onto the bed. "Oh, really?" Fumbled around under the bedcovers for a bit, and went to complaining. "Don't know where they hid my pistols, but I'll put windows and doors in whoever you want. Just point 'em out and aim me in the right direction."

Carlton brought his gnarled fingers out of the sheets like guns and started waving them at the ghosts who danced around his bed and shot back at him. "Damn you, sorry bastards. Hold still, for cryin' out loud. Sweet Jesus on a handcart! Hard to hit 'em when they move that fast, ain't it, Hayden."

I pulled his right arm back down to the bed and held it there. "Need you to concentrate, old man. Want you to talk to Lightfoot in a couple of days. You're gonna tell him about the time you and Billy pulled the cannon from McAlester's Store up to Big Cougar Bluff."

His head turned toward me like something mounted on a rusted swivel. For about a minute he didn't say anything—laid there staring at me like I'd come from some faraway place he didn't believe existed. Then, his eyes lit up again and he smiled.

"Long time ago. Almost forgot that one, Hayden. Hard to believe anyone could forget something like that, ain't it? Hellfire-and-brimstone fight like that'n ought to stay with a man right up till the time he has to quit this life and give up his spurs."

"Well, you work on it for a couple of days and we'll sit down with the boy and see how much you can scratch out of that lump you call a brain. Okay?"

He scratched at the one or two remaining hairs on

his freckled head, then examined his finger like he expected to find something. "Oh, you bet. I'll work on it. We'll have a fine time with Junior."

"Now listen, old man, don't polish this stuff up too much. I'm gonna be right there listening, and don't want you to put a whole bunch of fancy embroidery on it."

He squinted and looked disappointed. "Oh, come on, Hayden, cain't we pull his skinny legs a smidgen here and there as we go along?"

Had to laugh. "Okay, a smidgen. But don't get carried away. We want enough of the truth to keep him coming back for more. If you start colorin' this up redder'n a Navajo blanket, we might lose him and you wouldn't want the boy to stop coming to see us, would you?"

The next day I went down to the nurse's station and called Junior. He'd left me a fancy-looking embossed business card with his office number on it.

Phone barely got a chance to ring. "Features desk, Franklin J. Lightfoot, Jr." Boy had a real superior, officious-sounding demeanor on the squawker.

"Junior, this is Tilden."

"Why, Marshal Tilden, what a pleasant surprise. What can I do for you?"

"Need you to bring a sack of lemon drops when you come back out tomorrow."

"Lemon drops?"

"Yeah. And if you can get 'em, bring the kind they sell down at Walgreen's Drug Store."

"Walgreen's? Why Walgreen's?"

"Carlton J. Cecil is a connoisseur of finely aged

lemon-drop candy. Can't testify to the thing myself, but he claims Walgreen's Drugs lays out the best you can put in your mouth. Bring some, and I can guarantee you'll make a friend for life. Course I'm talking his life here, not yours."

A fairly pregnant silence came to me from the other end of the line before he finally said, "How big a bag should I buy?"

"The bigger, the better. Might even be a good idea to bring two, but we'll have to parcel them out to him a few at a time. Understand?"

"Hell, no, I don't understand, but of course I'll do it because I know you have a sound reason for asking."

"You're a good boy, Frank. It don't take much to make an antique killer happy, just a few chunks of flavored sugar. You're gonna be surprised what you get for that fifty-cent investment. See you in the morning."

"I'll be there," he said, and hung up on his end.

Way I had it figured, if everything went just by-God perfect, Franklin J. was in for a real treat.

7

"A Tart-Tongued Woman With an Ax to Grind"

FRANKLIN J. LIGHTFOOT showed up the next day sporting a toothy grin and carrying what looked like a five-pound bag of lemon drops. Nurse Heddy and me already had all the chairs and tables arranged out on the sun porch, but I wanted to wait and check everything over with Carlton before wheeling him out for his big debut performance.

I said, "Sweet Jesus, Junior. Did you buy up everything Walgreen's had? We don't want the old fart to go into diabetic shock—least not right away. Take a handful of those little weasels and give me the rest. I'll hide 'em. We'll dribble him out a few at a time. He's like a hungry dog. You give him this whole bag and he won't quit gobbling them down till it's completely empty."

Stopped at my room and squirreled all the leftover

goodies in a spot under my socks, and hurried on over to Carlton's room. Nurse Ruth Willett had checked on him and entertained the crazed coot most of the morning while I got everything ready for his entrance.

Whizzed over to him—least I did as much whizzin' as a man my age could—grabbed the grips of his chair, and started rolling him toward the porch. But I'd gone only a few steps when Heddy had to take over for me. Huffed and puffed along beside him.

"You ready, Carlton?"

"Hell, yes. Was born ready." His voice sounded like a rat-tailed file ripping through the teeth on a handsaw.

"You remember everything we talked about? All the stuff from yesterday and the day before?"

"Yeah. Well, most of it. You said Junior might bring me some candy."

"What else?"

"Whattaya mean, what else?"

"Dammit, old man, don't mess with me this morning. I'm doing my best to give you a chance at immortality here. You've got a sterling opportunity to live forever on the printed page. You could end up being as famous as Heck Thomas or Bill Tilghman— if you play your cards right. So, cinch it up tight and put on a good show."

He threw his head back and laughed. "Knew that'd get yore goat, Hayden. Really jerks yore longjohns up in a knot when I play deaf or dumb. Don't fret about it. Won't let you down. Just point me at Franklin J. 'Whistle Britches' Lightfoot. He'll never know what hit him when I get through with that wet-behind-the-ears puppy." He giggled again, shook all over, and twisted his head my direction. "Hell, Hayden, no one knows who Heck Thomas was, or Bill Tilghman for that matter. You three boys might have been the most famous marshals ever come out of Parker's traveling band of do-rights. But I'd bet everything I ever owned our friend Franklin J. Junior could go to downtown Little Rock and stop the first fifty people he met and not a damned one of them would know who any one of you was. Well, maybe some would recognize you now because of *Lawdog*."

He might have been fake deaf, a lot oversexed for a man his age, and a little bit crazy, but he was right as rain about that one.

Lightfoot stood and offered his hand as we rolled to a stop in front of his chair. He almost yelled, "Morning, Mr. Cecil. How're you doing today?"

"No need to scream, boy. I can hear fine today. I'm not bad. Not bad at all. Yourself?"

The boy looked a bit puzzled. "Fair to middlin', Mr. Cecil."

Heddy locked the wheelchair into position. Lightfoot and I got ourselves situated in our respective wallows, while Carlton counted the sugary yellow treats the boy dropped in his hands. Most times we'd have moved him out of the wheelchair, but Nurse Ruthie had already passed dead-certain judgment and declared it would be a better idea to keep him in it just in case we had to get him back to his room real fast. With all that candy in his trembling fist, he didn't care much where he sat anyway. Personal comfort took a backseat to a sweet tooth the size of a poorhouse soup dish. Personally believe we could have set his toes on fire and he wouldn't have noticed till his shorts flamed up.

Junior pulled his pad out, scratched around for a minute, then looked up like a man about to hear something monumental. "Your hammer cocked there, Mr. Cecil?" The boy smiled at his own joke. Thought there for a minute he might bust out laughing.

"Hell, yes. My hammer's always cocked. Along with several other things." He smiled, and I could see the candy sitting on top of his wiggling tongue.

"Mr. Tilden told me that when the two of you went out after Smilin' Jack Paine he left you with Billy Bird at McAlester's Store. Is that correct?"

"Yep. We stayed at McAlester's Store fer a bit."

He smacked his lips and rolled the candy around in his mouth, but didn't say another word for about a minute. "Always liked Billy Bird. Enjoyed his company. Felt safe with a man who could handle a brace of pistols the way he did. Anyone would."

"Tell us what happened after Hayden left the two of you. Can you remember that?"

"Most of it. I've lost some along the way. But I think I can remember most of it." He leaned over in his chair and nailed the boy with a look that sizzled from the power he'd known in the past. "But let's get one thing straight 'fore we get started. Things I'm gonna tell you here today have been a secret for over sixty years. Me'n Hayden are the only ones what can tell the whole story, and we've kept it to ourselves all this time."

He threw me a conspiratorial glance and winked. Well, he kind of winked. Carlton had a way of closing his right eye real slow. It was something like a wink, but a real strange one.

He snuggled back against his chair, closed his watery sagging eyes like the world had fallen on him, and for a moment I thought he'd dozed off. But then it started, and—honest to God—the man performed like a classically trained Shakespearean actor. It has to go down as one of the most amazing things I'd seen him pull off in years. And, hey, I've seen him get away with some doozies.

My ancient friend started slow. At times it seemed like he had to really stretch to find the right thoughts and attach them to the correct words. Then, his rheumy eyes would brighten up and he'd go at it like a long-legged, thoroughbred Kentucky racehorse that hadn't been let out to run in a coon's age. And just like I'd hoped he would, once he got moving in the right direction, the memories of who he'd been and what he'd done took over the situation, and it all came pouring out. Funny, but for the first time in months he didn't bother to do his "I'm deafer than a post" act—tricky son of a bitch. Always knew he faked it.

Hell, I'd bet anything his hard-of-hearing trick was just another deception designed to get them pretty young nurses and other less than cautious females to lean over close when he talked to them so he could look down their blouses. Good thing the randy old goat couldn't get around any better than he did.

Well, there we was—dressed up pretty and not much of any place to go. Had that cannon hooked up behind. All the ammunition we could possibly ever need. We was on our way to Martin Luther Big Eagle's nest up on the Canadian. Then, this plow-pusher come up and said he'd found some poor murdered feller in the creek behind his house. Hayden, Harry, and Lucius Dodge struck off looking to help him out. Me'n Billy headed due west for the Canadian. Warn't nothing unusual 'bout such events, though. Hell, I tried last night, and couldn't bring to mind a single time things actually worked out the way we wanted them to when we started on one of those raids. Hayden can tell you the same thing.

We took our time, but hit at it pretty steady. Managed to get over there in the Chickasaw Nation 'tween the Muddy and the Clear Boggy. Billy had the reins that day. I'd managed to doze off for a while when he punched me on the arm.

"Whaddaya make of that, Carlton?"

He had us stopped on a pine-covered hill what looked down on a grassy glade. Appeared to be a fine place for a camp. Guess some other folks thought so too. Their wagon smoldered and sputtered down below us. Must have been burning for a spell 'fore we showed up. Flames had died down. Warn't nothing but ugly black smoke coming off the wreck. Steady breeze brought the odor all the way to where we'd stopped. You know, the burnt-up smell that causes your eyes to water and your nose to scrunch up. Comes from wood, clothing, and all the other stuff that makes up what normally goes in a house. Overpowered everything there.

During my time out on the trail, I noticed as how killers and thieves often liked to set fire to everything in the hope they could somehow manage to cover up their most brutal crimes. Seldom worked—if it ever did. Come to think of it, cain't remember a time it even came close to accomplishing what they intended. Every instance I can bring to mind ended with the perpetrators being caught, jailed, tried, and their sorry necks stretched for their no-account misdeeds.

Climbed off our rig, got our rifles out, and ventured down the hill to see what might have transpired. Billy went at it from the left. I covered his back, and kinda trickled down on the right. Pots, pans, clothing, and all other forms of personal belongings decorated the grass-covered ground like hell its very self had rained down from above onto those poor folks.

Here and there, larger items like a trunk or leather valise had been ripped open and emptied in an effort to find something valuable. So much stuff in the grass you had to wade through it. Found three bodies. Man, woman, and a youngster. Folks died some horrible deaths. Woman was laid out on her back with her dress bunched up over her head. Her death was bad enough, but their combined departures from this life—and everything else—made for an awful sight. Never seen Billy Bird that mad afore.

"God damn the bastards that did this." He stood over what had been a fine-looking little boy about five or six. Tears rolled down Billy's cheeks and hissed when they dropped into the smoldering ashes near the body. Kept shaking his head like couldn't believe his own eyes. Said the same thing over the man and his wife.

But, hell, we both knew things like that happened all the time out there in the Territories. So many murderers was running loose in the Nations, anyone caught in the boonies alone was shootin' craps with their lives.

But them killings seemed to have had a deeper effect on Billy than others we'd come across together. Still don't know why.

We'd been investigatin' and scratchin' around for about an hour. Got the corpses together and under the only piece of tarp not blackened by the fire. Gathered up most of the stuff scattered around on the ground. I happened to glance over Billy's shoulder while we were sharing a sip from one of our canteens. Had to give it a serious effort to see what was really there. A girl who looked about seventeen stared at us from the safety of the tree line. The color of her clothing and the way she hunkered down and eyeballed us over her knees turned her into a living rock. Even someone as sharp-eyed as I was back then could have barely made her out as human. Something catlike about those eyes of hers.

Whispered, "Billy, there's someone watching from the woods directly behind you."

"Can you make out more than the one?" His eyes narrowed down under scrunched-up brows, and his hands dropped to the buckle of his gunbelt before easing to the grips of his pistols.

"Don't look like but one to me. Young girl. 'Bout sixteen or seventeen from all appearances."

"Can't see any others?"

"Nope. Just the one."

His hand came up, and he pushed his hat onto the back of his head. "What we gonna do, Carlton? Make the wrong move and she'll probably run like a turpentined wildcat. Hell, can't really blame her if she did."

Well, we cooked it up that he'd stay with the dead

folks. I'd sashay back to the tumbleweed and then circle around behind our ree-luctant observer. Everything
went pretty good till I got just a few feet from the girl.
Could see she was shaking all over. Fear can do that
to you. Seen it lots of times. People tremble like it's
fifty below and there's a heavy wind from the north.
Had my arms stretched out and was about a step and
a half away when she jumped up and started screaming
like the lunch whistle at a sawmill. Don't know what
possessed her. She turned and tried to run straight over
me.

Heard Billy yell, "Hang onto her, Carlton. I'm coming as quick as I can."

Black-haired gal fought like a branded bobcat. Hell,
she put scratches all over me. Found one a couple of
days later on my shin down inside my boot. More'n
sixty years later, this very day, and I still haven't been
able to figure out how she managed to do it.

"I've got her now!" Billy grabbed our phantom by
the arms above her elbows. He had his grip from behind, and you'd of thought she didn't have much of a
chance at getting away from him.

Hell, she broke loose and put a set of marks on his
face that looked like a Chicago street map. He went to
yelping and hopping around like she'd filled him full
of pistol balls. Ended up chasing her all over the clear-
ing and half the woods around it before we finally
brought her down the last time. She just kinda played
out and couldn't go anymore.

Tell you this for damn sure, we were both gladder'n
hell when she finally gave up the fight. Between the
bushes, brambles, and her fingernails, we looked like

someone had beat the unmerciful bejabbers out of us with a nine-tailed whip.

Later, Billy kind of gingerly handed her a canteen and said, "Do you have a name, little girl?" Have to admit, he sounded a mite sarcastic.

She snapped at him like a stomped-on diamondback rattler. "Don't be callin' me your little girl, you smart-mouthed bastard."

I sat beside her in a rocker we'd hauled out of the wreckage, and couldn't help but grin when he pulled back like she'd slapped him again. Figured I'd try and help him out. Made a kind of back-door effort to ease in on her. Talked low and like we might know each other.

"Look, miss. You ain't got nothing to fear from us. We're deputy U.S. marshals from Fort Smith. We're here to help."

Gal nailed me to that chair with a look what made me believe she coulda took an anvil apart with a tooth-pick. "That's rich. That's exactly what the leader of the bunch that killed my ma, pa, and Winslow said when they rode up yesterday."

Billy slapped his thigh with his hat and kicked out at a wooden bucket most likely dropped by the killers when they made their exit. "Well, now—there's a new wrinkle, Carlton. Never heard of anyone claiming to be a marshal in these parts without actually being one. Maybe some kind of raggedy-assed Arkansas town law, but not one of Parker's deputy marshals."

Few days before we'd struck out from Fort Smith with Hayden, I'd heard of another posse of the court's lawdogs what moseyed in from a fairly profitable raid and told a similar story. "Billy, you missed Louis Poteet when he and his bunch came back 'bout ten days ago. Think you were in Vinita pickin' up a prisoner at the time. Anyhow, they happened upon a house over on the Chickasaw-Seminole line where a feller named Johnson Pratt told 'em about a passel of yahoos that sounded almost exactly like these ole boys."

"The hell you say. Did Pratt recognize any of them?"

"Said their leader was that ever-lovely gentleman we both know and love so much, an African-Seminole breed named Wilson Bowlegs. Two of his party looked like renegade cowboys. The other two were most likely Wilson's good friends and running buddies Bully May and Loftis Green Grass."

"Sweet Jesus, Carlton. What a bunch for a dirt farmer to have to try and deal with."

"Yep. They're about as bad a crew as we could find out here. Anyway, they all showed up at Pratt's house, wore badges, and claimed to have a warrant for his arrest on a cattle-theft charge. He resisted when a couple of them grabbed him. They beat the tar out of him and then started on his wife. By the time they'd finished, the whole damnable bunch took a turn with Mary Bushyfoot Pratt. At least in that instance, thanks to a merciful God, they didn't manage to kill anybody, though. If what we've found here is any indication of what you'd just about have to suspect, seems they're graduated from assault and rape to murder."

"There was five of them bastards got my parents too," the girl blurted out. The bile in her voice bubbled up like boiling acid and could have burned through the barrel on Hayden's monster Winchester. "Leader of that pack of animals was a big black feller, for sure. Heard at least one of his people call him Wilson. He took off his coat and shirt when he jumped on my mother. I could see an ugly scar that ran from the left side of his neck all the way down his chest almost to the waist of his pants. Couldn't miss it. Looked like somebody tried to cut his arm off."

She flummoxed Billy to the point where he jumped up, stomped around our hastily made outdoor office, and went to kicking at anything in his way. "Goddammit, Carlton. Can you believe that? This job's hard enough as it is. Most folks roughing around out here are the worst kind of riffraff wearing boots, and now we've got to deal with a bunch of thugs claiming to be us. If that ain't one hell of a development, I'll eat one of them trunks over yonder and not use any salt or pepper."

Couldn't have agreed with him more. "Marshal Bird and I have both had dealings with Bowlegs and his bunch before. Turkey Creek Jim Painter carved that scar you saw into his sorry hide. Bowlegs and Painter got into a scorching disagreement over napkin-folding, the use of appropriate silverware, tea cakes, or some such thing over in Jamie Stark's nasty dive one night several years ago. Turkey Creek Jim almost cut ole Wilson in half with an abbreviated ax he calls a bowie knife. Too bad he didn't finish the job."

Guess the girl hadn't completely lost her sense of humor. She shot a glance at Billy. He was still stomping around snorting like a range-crazed steer at a church social. She said, "You gonna kick the hell out of everything left on the ground before you eat it?"

I tried to calm him down a bit myself 'cause I knew he could be real hard to handle when in a fighting mood. "Take it easy, Billy, don't get yourself all wall-eyed and bow-necked just yet."

"Well goddammit, Carlton, we've both run into that peckerwood Wilson Bowlegs. Hell, he and his father Simon have bonded out on everything from stealing other people's horses to murder. And honest to God, every time I think they've finally gone just one step too far, another silver-tongued lawyer manages to keep them from getting what they deserve. Remember last year about this time, Barnes Reed jerked Wilson up short for bootlegging, introducing, half a dozen other things illegal, and that slick bastard J. Pinckney Bradford got him off. Wasn't for ole J. Pinckney, Bowlegs would be up in Detroit breaking rocks right now. But is he? Hell, no! He's still running loose out here in the Nations thieving and raping. And now he's gone to killing people."

Whole time he was blowing off that particular cloud of steam he'd stopped dancing, but whacked at a chunk of wood with his bowie knife. Went at it with such devotion for a minute or so, I began to fear he might lop off one of his fingers.

Went back at the girl and tried to take some of the edge off Billy's tirade. "Miss, we really are deputy marshals from Fort Smith. Show her your badge, Billy." He pulled his vest back to expose the rough star covered by a half-moon. But even at that she didn't buy it.

"Them others had badges too. Flashin' that little chunk of tin don't mean spit after what I've had to witness. If'n I coulda got to a gun soon enough, both you crazy yahoos would be dead right now."

She shot that at him like a slug from an old Sharps rifle. He took half a step back before he leaned down toward her again and asked, "Was their badges like this one?" Put his left thumb behind the metal emblem and pushed it forward to give her a better look.

"Not exactly. They wore great big oversized stars. You know, like those five-pointed things you put on your Christmas tree. They didn't have a little hat on top of them like that one."

Then Billy managed to ask the one question that really was burrowing a hole in my brain. "How'd they fail to notice you in this bloody business, miss?"

Gal got a look on her face like she was about to rip something real important off a place on his body she hadn't scratched up in their initial introduction. "Pa sent me off to the woods to look for huckleberries, blackberries, and strawberries. Any kind of berry I could find. He had a real weakness for berry pies. Them evil bastards had just rode up when I got back. I heard and saw it all. Didn't take them long to finish their raping and killing. Had everything ablazing pretty quick afterward. I hid myself in the woods and waited for them to leave. Didn't come out till early this morning. Thought you was the same bunch when I heard you come up. But then saw that cannon and figured you couldn't be run-of-the-mill murderers and thieves. I mean, who in the Indian Nations drags a cannon around the countryside, but the cavalry or the law. Even at that, I didn't necessarily want to have anything to do with you."

Well, she'd opened up plenty enough for me. Jumped in and asked our original question again. "Can you tell us your name, miss?"

If the look she threw me had been made out of volcanic fireballs, she'd of burned me to a crisp. Hell, I'd still be sitting out there in the middle of Nowhere, Oklahoma, smokin' to this very day. Don't think hell coulda been any hotter. We stared at each other for a long time, and eventually tears started to pool up in the corners of those big brown eyes of hers.

Barely heard her when she said, "Judith. My name is Judith Karr. Over there under that nasty tarp is my father Burton, my mother Irene, and brother Winslow."

Then her head dropped into her lap and, with God as my witness, a moan escaped that poor girl's throat from somewhere so deep inside it must have felt like a saw grinding through muscle, gristle, and bone. Don't know why, but even now I can remember thinking men a million years ago must have heard women make sounds like that. Sent gooseflesh crawling all up and down my back and arms. For a long while, me and Billy watched and listened as the horror of witnessed insanity and death flowed out of her on a torrent of tears, accompanied by whispered pleas sent to God from between clenched fingers for help to keep on living. Hell, I almost cried myself.

When it appeared she'd just about finished with her grieving, Billy astonished me when he said, "Don't worry, Miss Karr. Marshal Cecil and I'll catch the men who did this, and see to it they pay for what happened here." The steel in his voice could have been used to make swords for the Union Cavalry for the next fifty years. Even so, he'd surprised the hell out me.

Pulled him aside as quick as I could. "What are you getting us into here, Billy? We've got to move ourselves, and this Confederate ground-shaker here, up to Big Cougar Bluff as soon as we can. Not sure we have time to chase all over hell and yonder after the worthless scum that did this. At least not right now, and as much as I'd like to."

He jerked a pistol, flipped the loading gate back, and set the cylinder to spinning. "We're gonna make time, Carlton. Won't matter if we're a bit late showing up for Hayden's dance. Boy can take care of himself, and besides, Martin Luther Big Eagle ain't going anywhere.

"Dammit all, we're supposed to be out here trying to keep massacres like this from happening, Carlton. Hell, I wouldn't feel like I came anywhere close to earning my pay this month if I let this slide. And besides, I can't imagine how angels in heaven would feel about it if I did. Ain't going to church when we get back to Fort Smith and have to ask God's forgiveness for not doin' what's right. The boys what kilt these folks could go on to even more awful endeavors if we don't stop 'em. You know how their kind is. They're like wild animals, for Christ's sake. They get the taste of blood slathered around on their lips and it just seems to make 'em worse."

It's real damned hard to argue with sound reasoning. Still didn't like the idea any, but knew he'd hit that big ole box nail right square on its ugly head. Made one more feeble effort to discourage him anyway.

"We don't know how long they've been gone or

where they went." Pretty poor attempt to slow him down, but I felt like I had to try.

"Judith said they were here yesterday. If that's the case, finding their trail shouldn't take me more'n a couple of minutes at the most."

Turned around and almost run over the girl. She'd eased up behind me, and I didn't even hear her. She was standing there with her hands on her hips and her chin stuck out like she was about to slap my jaws for the third or fourth time that day.

"I'm goin' with you," she snapped.

Popped my garters so hard, set my eyeteeth to ringing. Hadn't thought about taking her with us. Truth be told, hadn't thought about her much at all 'cept maybe in terms of dropping her off somwheres along the way. Hell, if they was one thing I didn't need on top of a hot-blooded Billy Bird, it had to have been a tart-tongued woman with an ax to grind.

"Miss Judith, we can't—"

"Can't what? Take me with you? Is that what you were gonna say? Well, you can just save it for somebody else. I'm going along on this hunt. I want to be there when those bastards get what's coming to them, by God."

Billy found a splintered piece of oak and whacked himself off a toothpick. Between heavy-duty digs at something in the back of his mouth that must have been about the size of a small calf, he said, "Sorry, Miss Judith, but you'll have to stay here."

God Almighty, but that was the wrong thing to say. Little gal took about ten feet in two steps, and damn near climbed him like a tree. Think she was standing on his feet when she shoved her face right up into his and said, "Just you try and stop me. I don't think you're big enough, by God!"

Took everything I could do to keep from bustin' out laughing. But, hell, didn't want to make her too much madder'n she already was. So I said, "Well, Billy, we can't leave her here. And if we shoot her ourselves, it's gonna look real bad should anyone find out. Judge Parker wouldn't like it much if we started some kind of fashion by rubbin' out little girls who survive massa-crees."

It was enough to get her turned my direction for a second or two. Billy kinda snickered, she grinned and dipped her head. But from under fluttering eyelashes and filled with steel, she said, "You're not changing my mind here, Marshal Cecil. I'm going with you even if it harelips the devil."

Figured there warn't no profit to be had in arguin' with her any further. So I let it go, and started making plans in the back of my brain to drop her off some-wheres along the trail. Hell, there had to be a family nearby that'd take her in. Least that's what I thought at the time.

We scrounged up everything that looked like it might be worth keeping, and piled it all up in one cor-ner of the tumbleweed. The girl fell on a piece of goose-down mattress that managed to survive, and went to sleep like a year-old baby.

She dozed during the whole stretch we worked on her family's grave. Didn't have the time or energy to dig but one hole. Had to put all three of 'em in to-gether. I woke her up when everything was ready, but she stood next to that ugly depression in the ground like a stick of stove wood. Not sure she even blinked while Billy and I both made a pretty sorry effort at saying a few words over those poor unfortunates. Didn't have a good book to read from. Her family Bible must of burnt up in the fire.

Franklin J.'s gaze darted back and forth from Carlton to me. A phenomenon reserved for old, worn-out people surprised both the boy and me. Carlton's head dipped slightly, his chin rested on his chest, and he took himself a deep and much-needed nap.

Our cub reporter snickered and said, "Well, perhaps it's time to make a pit stop anyway. Won't hurt if we slack off for a few minutes." He pushed himself out of his chair, and wobbled off toward the visitors' facilities while I kept an eye on Cecil. Wanted to make sure he hadn't had another of his spells, or even died, and we just didn't notice. Wouldn't have looked good, you know.

'Bout fifteen minutes into the nap his eyes popped open and he went right on like he'd never stopped. By then, Junior'd made it back. I could see the shock on his face when ole Carlton picked up the thread and went on knitting his tale like nothing had happened. Some folks don't believe in such things. Believe me when I tell you, with Carlton J. Cecil, you just never knew where you might end up next once the trip started in earnest.

8

"More Fun Than Fort Smith's Fourth of July Carnival"

GUESS BILLY AND me invested a lot more time putting those poor folks in the ground than it took to find them killers' trail. Lucky for us the evil scum seemed headed in the general direction we were, and didn't make any effort at all to cover their tracks. Same kind of thing almost always happened when murderers felt like they'd done gone and got away with the slaughter of everyone who might be able to follow them.

But boys, honest to God, Deputy U.S. Marshal Billy Bird took one of the horses tied to the wagon and ripped off after that bunch like a bloodhound on a mission. He went at it with so much enthusiasm, I had to spell him as often as I could, and we finally took turns scouting their trail. He'd work it for several hours, then I'd take over for a while.

Don't think Miss Judith Karr so much as twitched for the first two days or so. After her hot-mouthed lecture on coming along with us, I had to really work at keeping her conscious long enough to get some food and water in her.

Billy vowed as how it appeared to him like she'd adopted the vacant-eyed look of someone who'd spent time in an opium den. Guess she suffered from what most folks today might call shock and depression. Suppose watchin' your whole family get viciously rubbed out the way she did could do that. Entire eventuality brought Hayden and Saginaw Bob to memory. After a while, we began to worry she might not come out of her fog at all.

But thanks to a merciful God, third night away from the graves, she finally snapped out of it, and I had to do a serious reevaluation of my thinking up till then. Guess you can get somewheres on the dark side of famished during one of those spells, 'cause, for the first time, she wolfed down everything we could throw her direction. Wouldn't have been a good idea to drop your hat around that black-eyed gal there for a while.

She gnawed on a piece of jerked beef and growled, "God, I can't ever remember being so hungry. This stringy stuff's better'n pork roast." Washed the meat and some corn fritters down with half a pot of coffee, and then started scratching in our food larder for anything she might have missed. Billy fished around in his war bag and came up with a stick of peppermint candy that she went at like it was the last piece of flavored sugar in the world. On top of all that, Judith Karr couldn't wait to talk our ears off.

"My father's brother, Uncle Eli, came down here from Bourbon County, Kansas, and married up with a Chickasaw lady. He always said they'd moved from South Carolina so's he could 'get the hell away from all them goddamn people bent on crampin' my freedoms and sech.' Said he and my father could plant horseshoes and grow horses back there in Spartanburg County. Papa worked a fine spread out on Tyger Creek about thirty miles south of town. But like most men, they was born with itchy feet. So, we moved to Kansas, and almost starved to death."

She stopped for a minute and licked on that peppermint like she might not quit till it was all gone. Sugary red juice dribbled down her chin when she went back to her tale. "My uncle gave up and came down here 'bout a year ago. Papa held on in Kansas for as long as he could. First year, our crops floated away. Next year, they blew away. Then, we had a dry spell. Everything parched up to a crisp. Big storm came through couple of months ago. Lightning started a fire that burned every food crop and blade of grass in our part of Kansas. Watched my father fall down on his knees in the fields and cry like a baby. Thunder boomer broke him, and seein' him snap like a rotten cottonwood limb almost tore the heart right out of my chest. Don't think my mother recovered from it."

Then she stopped again, leaned against the tumbleweed's wheel, and stared out into the dark like she'd lost her thoughts, or didn't want to go any further with remembering all that pain. She wouldn't have got any back-mouth from Billy or me if her story of broken dreams, failure, and death had ended right then. It didn't. But not much more came out. Hell, it musta hurt too much.

"Papa had us on the way to a stay with Uncle Eli till we could get back on our feet again. He and his wife have a farm near Tishomingo. It was the only place he could figure to take us."

Well, that really capped it. Being as Tishomingo was way south of where we'd found her, there was damned little if any chance we could somehow drop her off with her own family anytime soon. 'Specially since Billy had already committed us to running them sorry killers to ground.

Guess she played her string completely out with that last bit of business. Girl dropped into her pallet like a felled oak, and snored so loud I eventually had to move my stuff about fifty feet from the main camp to get away from the noise. Hell, up till that night, I didn't know a tiny woman like her could get to honkin' like that whilst she was asleep. But good God Almighty, that gal snorted like a bull buffalo almost all night long.

Early next morning, I climbed to the top of a hill near where we'd camped to watch the sun bring everything back to life again. Never got tired of seeing nature's most spectacular show. Stood there looking down into the valley, and watched as a blanket of light crept toward me and pushed all the wet reluctant shadows aside. Individual trees popped out of the darkness for a few seconds, and then blended into the overall wash of colors that forced them back into obscurity. I loved to watch God at work.

On the way down the hill, passed a spot of sparkling

clear backwater from the creek near where we'd made
our camp. Heard splashing, and figured maybe Billy
had decided to take himself a bath. We'd been on the
trail for more'n a week by then and, between the two
of us, we smelled about as ripe as a pair of dead armadillos. So, I even entertained thoughts of getting in
for a soaking and rinse myself. But I pulled up short
in the bushes when I realized our newly acquired female ward was the one making all them watery noises.

A narrow shaft of light cut through a spot in the
trees, and dropped on her like God's own fingertip. Up
until that moment, don't think I'd ever seen anything
so beautiful. She stood 'bout knee-deep in ice-cold
creek water and had a piece of rag in her hands. Every
once in a while she'd dip her cloth in the water, hold
it over her head, and wring it out. Kind of like a self-
made waterfall.

I'd been with my share of women of the evening.
We used to call them soiled doves, or if we really
wanted to get insulting, alley bats. Don't think I could
remember actually ever seeing one of them totally,
completely, and absolutely buck-assed nekkid like Judith was that morning. Girl was a study in contrasts.
Her hair sparkled the color of wet coal, and the slick
sheen of her skin glistened like the color of the inside
of a Granny Smith apple covered in dewdrops.

She ran the rough cloth over her body several times,
and pretty soon glowed up all pink and glittery. Knew
my hide-in-the-bushes act was probably wrong, but
hell, I couldn't take my eyes off'n that gal. Time or
two, she seemed to hold her breasts up to the light like
she was so proud of 'em she couldn't hardly stand it.

Hell, I was proud of 'em, and they weren't even mine.

Every few seconds or so, I tried to pull away from her back-to-nature show, but must have watched for almost ten minutes before she finally finished and started for the bank. She'd left her clothes spread out on a rock, and took her time getting dried off, before pulling on a pair of man's pants and a shirt Billy rescued from the ruins of her family's destruction.

Came to the conclusion right there in them Chickasaw Nation woods that when it comes to God's more delightful pastimes, nothing much beats watching a nekkid woman bathe, and then work real hard to wiggle herself into a pair of canvas britches. I'm not gonna get all self-serving here, and come out with a bucket of blather about how I held my hand over my eyes and didn't watch because it was the right, proper, and modest thing to do. Felt like she was a gift sent to me by the Good Lord on a stream of light directly from heaven's front door. Just too beautiful to be ignored by weak-natured sinners like me.

Don't have a single idea how many other ways lust, or passion, or love, or whatever you want to call it, can break down the walls in a man's heart. But do know that after I watched Judith Karr at her twa-let that morning, I had to have her, and no other woman in the world would do. Guess that's something like love at first sight, 'cause up till then I hadn't really seen her. But from then on, any time she happened to be nearby, I couldn't take my eyes off her, and my mind reeled around like a bootleg-addicted drunk on a two-week binge when she spoke to me.

Let her get back to camp ahead of me by about five

minutes—just to make it look right when I strolled in
for breakfast. Billy had fatback and soda biscuits going. Judith sat on her blanket and sopped blackstrap
molasses from a tin plate. Amazing how you can go
for days, or months, or years, and not so much as notice someone. Then, out of the clear blue, they catch
your eye or ear, for one reason or another. Maybe it's
the way their mouths look when they eat a biscuit.
Could be something about how their tongue can
smooth out sounds most people buzz through like a
crosscut saw. Could be that you just didn't pay attention to what they said and, all of a sudden, you realized
this might be one of the more intelligent of God's creatures. Whatever it happens to be, from then on, you
can't see or hear anything or anyone else. Some people
would call it love. I'm still not certain about the thing
myself even now. But good God, I sure thought it was
love. Had trouble with my concentration the rest of the
day.

Billy hit the trail, and left me on the wagon with
Judith, and for most of the morning, I felt like a man
who'd been on a brain-burnin' drunk and couldn't wait
for the next round of shot glasses to hit the table. Got
stupid too. Before I saw that gal nekkid didn't have
any trouble talking to her. Afterwards, got the worst
case of the tongue-tied heebie-jeebies on record since
the beginning of time.

Hell, she even noticed it, 'cause as we bumped along
the trail behind Billy she turned to me and said,
"You're mighty quiet this morning, Mr. Cecil. Did you
sleep well last night?"

All that snortin' and blubberin' she did the night

before had kept me awake most of the night. But I wasn't gonna complain or say anything 'bout that good-looking gal's sleeping habits, now was I? Way I had it figured, constant memories of her sparkling breasts and lush, female shape would probably keep me from my slumber for some time to come.

So, stumbled into: "Ahhh, yes, miss. Very well. Thank you. Couldn't have been better. Wonnerful. Just wonnerful. Slept like a hibernating bear." God Almighty, a hibernating bear. Felt like the stupidest human in the Nations.

She gave me this cockeyed look like I'd lost what little of my mind might have survived after that morning by the creek. But hell, every time I glanced her direction, all I could see was silky black hair and nekkid flesh. Drove me right straight to muddy-minded distraction.

'Bout the time I thought every cell in my brain, and some important parts of my body, would surely explode and turn me into a pile of quivering goo, Billy thundered up. Dust and dirt clods flew in every direction as he jumped from his heavily lathered animal and tied it to the back of the wagon.

He hopped up on a spoke in the tumbleweed's front wheel on my side just below the jockey box. "How'd you like to try out that big ole popgun of yours, Carl? Maybe some much-needed practice before we get to Big Eagle's place. You know, kinda zero it in, make sure it's shooting straight."

"Jesus, Billy, what in the blue-eyed hell are you rambling on about?"

He pointed off into the woods ahead of us. "Think

I've found our desperadoes. They're holed up in a cabin five miles from here about a hundred yards off the Canadian, right where it turns almost due north. Won't be easy to get at 'em, so I figured we could blast 'em out with your heavy artillery."

Even Judith recognized the real plan he had buried underneath all those bull feathers. "Sounds to me as though you'd like to be the one who tries that big shooter out, Marshal Bird." A conspiratorial grin spread across her face as she added, "And I'm just the one to help you with it."

He loved her plan. Grabbed his hat off his head and slapped it against his leg. "By Godfrey, that sounds like a capital idea, Miss Karr. Just capital. I've wanted to put a match to that fire-breathin' beast ever since Carlton and Hayden dragged it to Fort Smith and left it sitting in the street. What do you think, Carl? Reckon you might let me shoot her? You know, just a time or two, or three, or four. Bet I can put one in Bowlegs's coat pocket within three tries. Whatcha' say?"

Didn't have to think about it long. We had time on our hands, plenty of powder, and bad men who needed a lesson the likes of which they could never have expected. "You bet, Billy. We've got fifty cartridges back there in the ammo box. Don't guess it'll hurt any to throw four or five rounds at those egg-sucking snakes."

Well, we did our best to creep up on that bunch of killers. They'd taken up residence in an abandoned shack on top of a barren knoll not far from the river. It wasn't what anyone would have called a fortress, like the one we expected in Red Rock Canyon, by any stretch of your most vivid imagination. From a couple of hundred yards away, I used my long glass, and decided we could probably smoke them out by pumping enough rifle and pistol lead their direction.

The muddy gray buck and battened walls of the ramshackle house had dried up, and shrunk to the point where you could see cracks in every flat stretch more'n a few feet across. All the windows, especially those on either side of the front door, looked to have once been covered by dried skins of some kind. But harsh weather had blasted them to shreds that fluttered and snapped against their frames, and they were now open to whatever happened along in the way of weather, insects, wandering animals—and desperate men.

Billy lay on his back beside me, picked at his fingernails with the seven-inch bowie he carried in his boot, and gazed at black-bottomed clouds floating over our heads. "You know, Carlton, this is gonna be more fun than Fort Smith's annual Fourth of July Carnival where they put on that Wild West show. 'Member last year when they had Judge Parker ride in the stage, and Belle Starr and them other ole boys flagged it down and robbed the Judge? Hot damn, now that was a good 'un. But it ain't gonna hold a candle to the fun we're about to have at the expense of Mr. Wilson Bowlegs today."

I'd been studyin' on our situation for about twenty minutes at the time. Tried to reckon where we could set up the cannon, and get a good shot or two at 'em. Way I finally had it sorted out, it wouldn't take but a few good blasts from that big ole gun to put them bad boys to giving some serious thought 'bout cashing in their chips.

Spotted a fairly flat piece of ground about two hundred yards from the shack, and behind a clump of trees. "See that place over yonder, Billy. Let's drag her over there, set up back of that big rock." He eyeballed the whole situation for a second or two, grinned, and scampered back to where we'd left Judith and the cannon.

When I caught up with him, thought at first he'd got paralyzed or something. He stood to one side and kinda behind Cletis Broadbent's plaything like a statue carved out of marble. Stared down at a point out of my view, so I ambled over to see what he'd spotted. Pulled one my pistols, 'cause I got to figgerin' maybe he'd stepped on a copperhead or something. Kinda tiptoed around the ammo box and saw Judith bent over next to the barrel. Billy turned his palms up, and kinda shrugged. Had an odd, quizzical look on his face as though what he watched went way beyond his poor ability to understand. That could have just been his typical reaction, though. The man absolutely knew less of women, and feared them more, than anyone I've ever come across.

"Sweet jumpin' Jesus, girl, what in the rambunctious hell are you doin'?" It just kinda spurted out of me like a mouthful of bad chewin' tobacco. She'd opened a small place on her left arm with a knife, and in her very own blood used a finger to scrawl the name IRENE in ragged sloppy letters across a foot-long spot right below the gun's touchhole.

Tears ran down her cheeks when she turned to me and said, "Those motherless sons of Satan are gonna get a message from the bottom of that grave you dug. Take dead aim, Marshal Cecil. Show these boys what it means to kill folks better'n they'll ever be."

Then she got herself upright again, marched over, pulled me down to her size, and kissed me on the cheek. In a voice that sounded like it came from someplace I'd never visited, she whispered, "Do the right thing, Carl."

God Almighty, felt like I'd just got a calling from the great beyond. That black-haired gal infused me with some kind of unearthly power, you know. Well, I guess you couldn't know, but she did it. Think I'd of wrestled Satan himself, best two out of three falls, if she'd asked me to right then. As it was, all she wanted was Wilson Bowlegs and his bunch. Hell, I figured that one was a snap.

Anyway, I didn't have the heart to tell her Cletis Broadbent had already named the gun Beulah. Besides, he hadn't bothered to put that moniker anywhere on the weapon that I'd noticed, so I let it go. Figured I could wash Judith's blood off pretty easy before I had to take the thing back to Cletis. And to tell the truth, I kinda liked the name Irene. Seemed completely fitting given the circumstances Bowlegs, Bully May, and Loftis Green Grass had created by murdering the girl's family.

Billy and me took our time moving everything into place. I gave him some intense instruction in the entire and complete Cletis Broadbent loading method several times before we got the whole contraption set up and ready to fire. Demonstrated the thing by charging the first round myself, and explained—in excruciating detail—why you had to be *extremely* careful 'bout swabbing the barrel out with a wet sponge lest you shoot your ownself. Didn't tell him I'd almost shot myself with the damned thing. No point setting him off on a laughing fit.

We got it eyeballed in and, when everything looked like our first shot should fall right on the front door of the shack, I lit a piece of fuse with a match, and told Billy to wait for my signal before he put fire to powder. Tried to make Judith sit under the wagon, but she wasn't having any of it. Said she'd help Billy reload if the first shot missed. Girl stood there all bowed up at me with her hands on her hips. Knew there warn't no need in arguing the point, so I left the two of 'em to their business, and climbed up the knoll to a spot within shoutin' distance of those three sorry pieces of human debris.

Got behind a nice thick piece of oak tree and yelled, "Wilson Bowlegs, this is Deputy Marshal Carlton J. Cecil speaking. A posse of marshals from Fort Smith has you and your accomplices surrounded. Throw your weapons out the door one at a time and come out of there with your hands in the air! You are under arrest for the murder of Burton Karr, his wife, and young son!"

I'd learned my lesson. My mama might not have raised a pretty boy, but she didn't raise a dummy neither. 'Bout a year before that, my friend Willard Ayers hit the Nations with an arrest warrant for Manuel Peterson on a charge of larceny. Willard, being a damned fine deputy, located the miscreant pretty quick, marched up to his hidey-hole, and started beatin' on the door. "Open up, you son of a bitch," he bellowed. Kept that hammering and screaming up for a minute or so. Then he yelled, "Open up, God damn you!" Hell, it was just a routine arrest. Manuel probably wouldn't have served more'n six months up in Detroit for his thievery. But he must have been pretty nerved up that day. He fired three shots from a Winchester rifle through the door. One of 'em hit Willard in the heart. Killed him deader'n a rotten stump. Manuel was still running loose the afternoon I called Bowlegs out.

It was mighty quiet inside that crumbling shack for about a minute after I sent my challenge up to them. Then, someone yelled back, "You can go to hell, you badge-totin' piece of cow dung. We ain't going nowhere but right here. Just you come on up and see if'n you can take us!"

Couldn't help but laugh. Between guffaws that almost choked me down to a whisper, I shot back, "Wilson, you and Bully and Loftis have exactly one minute, according to the second hand on my genuine two-dollar railroader's pocket watch, to throw your weapons out, and give yourselves over to me for arrest on a charge of murder. If you are not in my custody in one minute and one second, members of my posse will blast you to kingdom come."

A different, and gruffer, voice I took to be that of Loftis Green Grass snorted down the hill, "You can stuff that warrant up your dumb Arkansas ass. You lawdogs ain't so tough as to think you can take us. You boys try and get close enough to blast anything, and we'll send you straight to hell on a outhouse door."

Turned and looked down the hill at Billy. Boy danced around our big popper like a three-year-old kid. My oak tree might have been over a hundred and fifty yards away from him, but he smiled so as I could see almost every tooth in his head. Tried three times to get those boys to come out, but they just laughed and cussed me some more. Language from that place got so hot, I felt embarrassed Judith had to listen to it. Then, I remembered she had a pretty feisty mouth of her very own when things didn't go her way.

Well, their time ran out. Yelled at 'em every fifteen seconds to give themselves up. When I signaled Billy to set her off, that bunch was laughing so hard I could barely stand it. All their levity came to a screeching halt when Irene belched four feet of flame and spit the first six-pound ball their direction. Whole valley rumbled and shook like God was driving a chariot through the place. Watched as that iron pellet flew past me like a fat black bird tied to a rocket. Big sucker hit the ground about thirty feet from the cabin, bounced three times, and went through the front door; knocked down several walls, and departed through the back as easy as punchin' holes in a piece of dried buffalo hide with an ice pick.

Great God Almighty, you ain't never heard such screaming. Found out later Bully May, who'd spent most of his life preying on the meek and powerless, wilted like a pansy on a hot afternoon. He said Loftis Green Grass's and Wilson Bowlegs's eyes got bigger'n coffee saucers.

Down below, Billy and Judith ran back and forth to the ammo box. Smoke and dust was so thick around them, for a minute or so, I could barely make them out. But I could tell Billy was having the time of his life. Didn't take but two or three minutes for 'em to charge the gun again. He waved after they got her elevated a smidgen and had everything ready for another shot.

"Wilson," I yelled, "would you like to reconsider your previous answer? You have exactly one more minute to think it over. Then my friend, at the bottom of the hill, is gonna lay one right in your lap!"

"Damn you!" he screamed back. "When did you Fort Smith lawmen start bringing cannons out here? Dammit all to hell, it's hard enough makin' a livin' in this godforsaken piece of perdition 'thout you sons of bitches shooting at us with cannons! Shit, all we do is a little cow stealing and a killing every once in a while. Why cain't you boys leave us alone?"

Loftis added his two bits' worth with: "I'm gonna kill you, Cecil. Then I'm gonna cut yore heart out, cook it in a pot of navy beans, and have it for supper!"

"You've used your time up again, boys." Pointed to Billy and motioned for him to deliver our next black-iron love note. Saw him shove the match onto the top of the barrel. Think he may have put a bit too much powder in her that time around. Sounded like the wrath of a vengeful Lord had descended on us and heaven was about to suck up everything for miles around. Shock wave spurted up that hill like the Mississippi River being pushed though a thimble.

His first shot could best be described as a kind of lob that arched up, hit, and then ran at 'em. That second one looked like a score chip on the wire over a snooker table. Went by me in a straight line. Hit a spot below the window on the right of the empty doorway and punched a hole in the wall the size of a number-ten washtub.

That'n was the one what killed Loftis Green Grass. Guess he thought he was hid. But Billy's inspired marksmanship delivered that ball directly to ole Loftis's noggin. There warn't nothing left of his head but a greasy spot on the ground about fifty feet behind the house. Wilson and Bully musta got religion about a spit second after Loftis's unheaded body went to flopping around the house and a-spurtin' almost a gallon of blood all over the place.

They both tried to get out the door at the same time, and for a second or so, got jammed up together in the frame. Threw all of their pistols, rifles, knives, and assorted other weapons so far from the doorway, they hit the dirt almost halfway down the hill. Bully May, whose real name was Albert, fell on his knees and cried like a baby.

That no-account, evil gob of spit spent most of the waking moments of his adult life robbin', rapin', and murderin' folks. But he groveled in the dirt and cried like a six-year-old about to get his butt switched for eating green apples.

"Oh, please, Marshal. Please don't shoot me in the head with no cannon. I'll go back to Fort Smith. Won't be no trouble along the way. Just don't let anybody blow my head off with that damnable thing! God Almighty, that's a horrible way to die!"

Billy came up and helped me get them back down to the tumbleweed. Slapped some iron shackles on them villains, and locked 'em to the tail end of the wagon. Then, we found a hole in the ground not far from the cabin. Threw what was left of ole Loftis in it and rolled a sizable rock in on top of him.

Guess I shoulda kept a better eye on Judith than I did, but felt like she'd finally begun to get over the thing when we slammed the steel gate on them boys. Judge Parker woulda hung 'em sure as the cow ate the cabbage. Guess she just couldn't wait. And, in a way, I can't blame her much. Don't see how anyone could.

Two or three days later, while Billy scouted out ahead of us, I let both of the murdering scum get down so they could visit the bushes and see to their private needs. Bully May took care of his business pretty quick, made it back, and scrambled into the tumbleweed. Bowlegs did his drag-ass routine, griped every step of the way, and complained constantly about how poorly he was being treated. I'd seen this same kind of behavior before. He was a dangerous man when loose, but a whining crybaby once you slapped the cuffs on him.

"You lawdogs mighta caught me, but that don't give you the right to treat me like some kinda goddamned Arkansas dog. Hell, I had better food the time I was locked up on a Louisiana prison farm out in the middle of a skeeter-infested swamp fer stealin' pigs from a state senator over in Shreveport. This biscuit, fatback, and molasses three times a day's done give me the south Texas trots. Feel like a man with one foot and an arm in a pine box, for God's sake. Few more days of this kinda barbaric treatment and I'll most likely go to my Maker on account of starvation."

Wanted to slap his face till his eyes rolled around like marbles in a barrel. "Why don't you shut the hell up, Wilson? Every time you get caught, we have to listen to your bellyaching bilge. All of us eat the same things you do. It ain't no easier for us, you know?"

"Let me tell you something, Mr. Tall-Hog-At-The-Trough Marshal Cecil from Fort Smith. None of yore problems mean a pile of weevils' dung to me. Be worried 'bout my personal eatin' habits, and I'm gonna complain to Judge Parker when we get back to town. This here kind of treatment is gonna stop, by God."

"Yeah, Wilson, you're probably right. When Maledon stretches your neck this time, it's a pretty safe bet you won't have to worry overmuch about that bottomless piece of gut you call a stomach ever again." That kinda shut him down for a second or so. But he never was one to keep his mouth closed for long if you gave him the least opportunity to yammer at you.

I held the steel-barred door open for him. He stepped up with his left foot, but stopped and shot a leering grin at Judith, who stood near the back wheel on the far side from me. "Wish I'd a-knowed you was around back there when we did our dance with yore stupid family, pretty girl. You are one fine-looking black-haired twitch. I'd a done for you just like I done for yore mama. Personally, cain't think of nothing matches a hot-blooded woman. Hell, she loved every second of the humpin' Wilson Bowlegs put on her. If'n I hadn't of kilt her, yore mama woulda follered me all over the world wantin' some more." Then he laughed. One of those kind of laughs that don't leave any doubt he was making fun of her and as far as he was concerned, there warn't a thing she could do about it, 'cept stand there and listen to the trash spilling from that filthy mouth of his.

Ain't no two ways about it. Anyone who'd ever studied at university would've declared Bowlegs an idiot after about five minutes of the hastiest kind of inspection. Man owned a piece of stupid as big as a number-three grain scoop. But Judith didn't have five more minutes to give the sorry wretch. She'd listened to the evil son of a bitch spout that kind of filth from the second we caught him. Guess his smutty mouth just finally pushed her over the edge. Looking back on it, suppose that wasn't much of a trip for her at the time. Couldn't have been more'n a baby step or two at the very most.

Her upper lip quivered a bit, at first. I barely noticed it. But Bowlegs must have spotted what he determined a weakness, and was the kind of no-thinking savage to take advantage, if he thought he could.

"You gonna cry, pretty girl? Gonna do that female boo-hoo thang right here in front of all us big bad men? Like my bandanna to wipe yore snotty nose?" He jerked a blue and white piece of rag from his pocket, held it out, and jiggled the thing like some kind of bait.

Don't guess she was as bad off as he thought. Her eyes narrowed up on him like the sights on one of those old rolling-block rifles. Her lips curled back like a mother wolf protecting newborn cubs when she said, "Damn you to an eternal burning hell, you sorry piece of human trash. You murdered my entire family." Her eyes blinked real fast a couple of times, and tears coursed down her cheeks right before she screamed,

"You even killed my mother, you low-life scum-sucking dog!"

Then, as God is my witness, a short-barreled Remington .44 appeared in that angry gal's hand like a sideshow magician's rabbit. Still don't know to this day where she had it hid. Hell, I'd seen her nekkid as a day-old baby and didn't notice that pistol. Course, just to stay on the side of truth here today, have to admit I wasn't looking for guns or knives at the time.

Big, bad Wilson Bowlegs turned toward me with this twisted, surprised look on his face just as her first slug caught him dead center. She was so close to that sorry weasel, the concussion damn near knocked both of us down. Massive chunk of slow-moving lead came out his back, and scorched a smoking rut four inches long in the right sleeve of my shirt. Second round dispelled any doubt anyone might have had that Judith Karr was a damned fine shot.

The ever-lovely Mr. Bowlegs, former killer, rapist, and thief, clutched at his chest with both hands, started making watery coughing, wheezing sounds, and was on his way to the ground. She took a half step toward him, and put one in his head—just above the right eye—that splattered a considerable wad of his brains all over the ground near my feet.

Well, as anyone with the most rudimentary smarts at all should gather, I went to thinking real fast there for a second or so. Guess I burned up brain cells aplenty tryin' to figure out some way to keep her from doin' me in too. Sure as hell didn't want to move too fast, or do the wrong thing, and wondered if she might blast ole Albert "Bully" May for good measure. He'd scrunched himself up in the farthest corner of the tumbleweed he could find, covered up with Judith's very own feather mattress, and went to screeching like a barn owl being tortured with a sharp stick.

"Oh, God, Marshal," he squealed. "Please don't let her kill me. I didn't hurt any of her family. Just watched." Went on like that for some time while I kept an eye on Judith to see what she'd do next.

But she only stood there, and shook all over 'bout like someone in the worst throes of malaria. Pistol out at arm's length like she just wanted to make sure Bowlegs was good and dead, but ready in case he jumped up, started cussing again, or grinned at her or something.

She hovered over her handiwork like he didn't amount to much more'n a snippet of crochet she'd just finished, stared hard at the body for a bit, then pitched the pistol on the ground beside it. Said, "Good," and walked off into the trees like nothing wayward had occurred. Soon's she turned her back, I snatched that .44 up and shoved it under my shirt.

Well, as you can surely imagine, ole Carlton J. Cecil felt like a man trying to put up a Chinese tent in a Texas thunderstorm. For about fifteen seconds, I didn't know whether I was getting' up or going to bed. Then all that yelping from Bully May brought me back to bloody reality.

Climbed into the tumbleweed, snatched him up by the collar, and pushed the barrel of my pistol into his left ear. Trick I learned from Hayden. Said, "Bully, Marshal Bird will be coming back shortly. He probably heard those shots. No matter what happens, you are gonna agree with everything I say to him. Do you understand me, you low-life cur? If you so much as hint at anything other than what I describe as having taken place, I'll tie you to Irene's open muzzle and send parts of your sorry hide to rain down from heaven on folks in Kansas."

Thought for a second or so I was gonna have to pick his eyeballs up off the floor. He gulped real hard a couple of times like I'd strangled him, and finally managed to blurt out, "Tell him whatever the hell you want, Marshal Cecil. I'll swear it happened just the way you say. You can claim that gal's pa came to life, dug his way out of the grave, followed us here, and took ghostly revenge on ole Wilson for all I care. Far as I'm concerned, don't make a damn how God came and got him. Just don't let her shoot me."

"That's real good, Bully. You keep your mouth shut, and I'll see what I can do for you when we get back to Fort Smith. Maybe I can keep Judge Parker from hanging your miserable, worthless self. But whatever happens, from this minute till everything manages to sort itself out, just remember, I'll be watching and listening. If I hear anything, even one wayward word, I'll see to it you die in a way that'll make you wish your mother had never brought you into this world. People in hell won't suffer like you will before you go meet 'em. Do we understand each other?"

"Oh, you betcha, Marshal Cecil. It all happened just the way you said. Whatever that turns out to be."

"Good." After I'd said all that, it came to me I must've sounded a lot like Judith when she rubbed Bowlegs out. Hell, I didn't care. Meant every word of it. Not real hard to get rid of someone like him back then, if you really wanted to.

Locked him inside, and then pulled the wagon about twenty feet up the trail from the body. Took a raggedy piece of tree limb, and messed the ground up all around where we'd been walking back and forth. Judith strolled up from her meditations in the woods. Girl looked like she'd retreated back to the same place she went the first few days after we found her.

Grabbed her by the right hand, pulled her to the seat on the wagon, and whispered in her ear, "Whatever you do, don't say anything. Leave it all to me. Just pay attention, and repeat whatever I tell Billy if he has any questions. Do you understand?"

"Yes, I understand, Carlton. I'll do exactly what you say." Her answer sounded like it came to me from the bottom of a half-empty rain barrel. Her hand was a block of ice with fingers. She never blinked when we spoke. Couldn't tell if she really heard me or if she just reacted the way I wanted her to.

Anyway, I barely had time to hop down and run back to what was left of Wilson Bowlegs when Billy charged up and jumped off his horse. Stood beside the useless scalawag's oozing corpse, and made like I was reloading my pistol when he dashed up and stopped beside me.

"What the hell happened, Carlton?" He strolled over to Bowlegs, and pushed at the body with the toe of his boot.

"Well, I stopped to let these boys take care of their twa-lett. Got Bully back inside, but Wilson didn't want to go. He whacked me on the side of the head, and started running. Chased him to about here, and we kinda wrestled around some 'fore I felt like he was about to get the best of me. Had to shoot the big son of a bitch."

Bully May hugged the bars and yelped, "Yessir, that was the way it happened, all right. Bowlegs and Marshal Cecil flopped around for almost five minutes afore the marshal had to pop ole Wilson. He'd of kilt yore friend fer sure if'n he'd a got a chance." Then, he shot a quick look my direction and smiled.

Billy stared at the outlaw's body, kicked a cloud of dust that direction, and said, "You got him good. He ain't coming back from them shots. Don't blame you, though. Hell, I'd have dropped him soon's he started running. Ain't about to get in no fistfight with a man like Bowlegs if they's any other way out of it." He gandered around some after that, but if he had any suspicions the tussle hadn't gone down the way I described, he didn't say anything. In fact, he never even mentioned the thing again till we got back to Fort Smith, and then he told the story exactly the way he'd heard it from me. Good man, Billy Bird.

'Fore we put the evil wretch in the ground, I did what Hayden'd tole me to do with anyone we couldn't bring back. Slapped a gob of ink on his palm and pressed it to the back of a John Doe warrant. I'd already done as much for Loftis Green Grass. Normally, we wouldn't have been able to collect anything on a dead outlaw, but Hayden had something going with the Judge I didn't understand at the time. He could even get us paid for those we had to kill.

Late that night, after we'd made camp and had a

little bite to eat, I crawled into my bed and drifted off
to sleep. Woke up, and found Judith all snuggled next
to me. She smelled like fresh rainwater, and kissed me
when I turned toward her. Thought for a second or so
all the ammo in my pistol belt was gonna fire off at
the same time.

She whispered in my ear, "I want to thank you for
not telling Marshal Bird what really happened this afternoon." She hugged me closer and said, "Tonight I'll
do anything you want."

Well, as just about any man with a beating heart
would probably understand, that night I wanted it all,
but couldn't get myself to take advantage of her. She'd
seen horrible things happen to her family, and had
killed the man most responsible for those atrocities.
Girl had an awful lot of heavy-duty emotion bubbling
around in her soul. Takin' what she offered would have
been so easy, but afterwards I'd of felt like the sorriest
kind of low-down cad.

So, I kissed her on the forehead and whispered back,
"Sweet, beautiful Judith, perhaps another time. Think
you should give your mind a rest. You've had way
more'n most folks to think about for the past few days.
We can talk about your offer later, if you still want to.
But Judith, I'm thinking that now just ain't the right
time."

"Don't you want me?" Hell, boys, the invitation in
her voice was unmistakable. Things that had filled my
fantasies ever since my spell hiding in the woods and
watching her bathe were right there for the taking. But
I just couldn't do it.

"Oh, hell, girl. Don't think I've ever wanted a

woman anywhere near as bad as I do you. But maybe we should wait for a bit. Believe you need some time to think this one through. Tomorrow morning you might look back on what happened here, and decide you made a terrible mistake offering yourself to me like this."

That's what I said, but I remember thinkin', if my luck held, maybe in a few days she'd make a second pass at it. By then, I should have been able to figure out some way for us to have some privacy. Wondered how that would sound to her. For the most part, women who feel the majority of the earth's nasty men can only think about one thing are pretty much right.

She made this noise almost like a tired cat purring, nuzzled up against my shoulder, and fell to sleep so fast I couldn't believe it. Guess she just needed some assurance everything was all right.

Next morning, we headed for Big Cougar Bluff as fast as good horses could pull that clumsy tumbleweed wagon and all its attachments. It'd been a hell of a trip up till then. But Jesus Christ Almighty, nothing and nobody could have got me ready for what was waitin' up ahead. And with God as my witness, any ideas that had entered my poor sorry brain that might have led me to think I had some understanding of women in general, and Judith Karr in particular, were just a few days away from being shaken right down to their roots. 'Fore our Red Rock raid ended, that gal made an impression that has lasted right up till this beautiful late fall morning.

•   •   •

Carlton had been whackin' at his tale for quite a spell when he started to sag. 'Bout the time his antique old self got to the part where Judith pulled her magic trick on Wilson Bowlegs, he'd almost done himself in all together. I waved Junior off. Motioned for him not to ask Carl any more questions. We'd been runnin' buddies long enough for me to recognize when his main spring had about run down. Caught Ruth's eye as she passed, and waved her over to my chair.

"Ruthie, I think Mr. Cecil might be gettin' a mite tired from the day's storytelling session. Reckon you could wheel him back to his room?"

She ran her fingers over the few remaining hairs left on his ancient head, leaned over, and almost whispered, "You ready to call it a morning, Mr. Cecil? Bet you'd love to take a little nap about now, wouldn't you? Got cool, crisp new sheets waiting for you."

He eyeballed the front of her heavily starched white uniform, cupped a hand over his right ear, and yelped, "Cat? Haven't seen Black Jack lately."

She bent forward about another foot. Her ruby-colored lips stopped a few inches from a hair-filled left ear. His nose, which was almost buried in her cleavage by then, twitched when it detected the delicate perfume she'd applied there. She didn't yell, just raised her voice a bit and said, "No, Mr. Cecil, I said you would probably like a little nap about now."

His head swiveled toward Junior and me like a rusted weather vane on top of a Kentucky horse barn. Just enough so we could see the snaggle-toothed grin on his face. Then, he leaned back ever so slightly to get a better view of her exposed bosom and growled,

"You're right there, little darlin'." He waved a bony arm back in our direction. "Have wilted a bit. These jugheads damn near wore me out. Kept forcing whiskey on me and made me spend the whole morning talking about good women, bad men, and evil behavior. Kinda work has a tendency to make me feel like an empty shuck. Guess I'll have to finish up some other time, boys." Last few sentences trailed off to a point where I barely heard him.

Junior stood, and took my old friend's withered hand as Ruth moved behind Carlton's chair. "Thanks for your time, Mr. Cecil," he said, "It's been quite a ride. Can't think of a better way to spend a morning. You've told us quite a story. Quite a story."

Carlton kind of wiggled all over like an old dog when you scratch the right spot on his belly. "Hope you'll forgive my early leave-taking, Junior. But my constitution just ain't as well constituted as it used to was. Hell, once you push past ninety, plus a few on top of it, ain't nothing what it used to be. Life gets to the point where it's more a problem than you're actually willing to deal with on some days." He tried to turn his head again so he could see the sparkling girl behind him. "Ruthie's usually right. Might be best if I take a break. Maybe after a nap, we can make another run at it."

The chair spun around in a tight circle. Couldn't keep my own eyes off that blond gal's beautifully rounded hips as she leaned into the load. I've often wondered if the day would ever come when a man gets too old to care about such things. Carlton was still a fine judge of females even at his advanced age.

He dangled a flapping arm over the chair's side, waved, and called over his shoulder, "Hayden can finish up for me. He's the only other person alive what still knows it all. You boys take it easy. I'll see ya'll in the mornin'. Good Lord willin' and the creeks don't rise." A raspy chuckle filtered back our direction as they disappeared down the hall.

Junior called it a day too. Said he had another appointment that afternoon anyway, and needed to get moving to make sure he arrived on time. Seems our governor, the former turkey farmer, wanted to talk with him about some of his previous and less-than-flattering columns. He left Black Jack and me sitting on the sun porch—just the two of us again—with the potted plants, and all my thoughts about what we'd talk about when the boy came back.

Didn't take dinner with the other prisoners that afternoon. Spent the whole time chewing around at the edges of the past. Hadn't used up too much space in my brain box over the years with that story Carlton dropped on Junior. He'd told me the whole thing soon's we got together up on Big Cougar Bluff. We kept it a secret all the years that'd past since that time. Now, pretty soon, everybody who could read an Arkansas newspaper would know about it. God, but life is funny. One day something as important as how a no-account, blood-letting outlaw like Wilson Bowlegs checked out of this world is all you can think about or worry over. Fifty or sixty years later, it just don't matter. Hell, it didn't really matter then, but we thought it did.

Truth of it is that the only thing about life that ever

does actually mean a hell of a lot is the people closest to you. You know, we get these teary-eyed do-gooders coming through Rolling Hills about twice a month blubbering about what they can do to help all us "poor neglected old people." Ain't much can be done by them—or anyone else. Everyone we ever cared about is gone. The one true thing virtually all the ancient souls in this Greyhound station for the last big trip need more'n anything else is just, very simply, some company. Other people. Folks like Junior. Someone to talk to us. Another living, breathing person who would take a few minutes to listen. People to share our final days amongst the living with.

That's why Carlton played such an important part in my life. We were old friends, getting older by the minute—together. We mutually watched and waited for the appearance of the one Carl called the ole bony-fingered dude. Time was running out on us. Carl knew it better'n I did. Bony Fingers had tried to carry him away about once a week for the past four or five years.

And that's why I'll have to admit—it didn't come as any real great surprise, or shock, when Chief Nurse Leona Wildbank tracked me down while I slept in my favorite chair, and woke me up at about two o'clock that morning.

"Mr. Tilden," she whispered, "Mr. Cecil is in a bad way and has asked for you. Could you come with me, please?"

Woman sounded about as serious as a heart attack. Her face was a mask of pain, and she looked to have been crying. That part surprised the hell out me. Never figured Leona for one who cared much for any of us.

I mean, she took good care of everyone, but she just never seemed to care for us. Don't know whether that's clear or not, but maybe you get my drift.

Followed her down the hall, toddled up to Carl's room, and waited by the door till she came back, led me inside, and left me standing at the foot of his bed. They had him hooked up to about a dozen different kinds of liquid at the time. A doctor who looked about twelve years old hovered over that old man's shrunken chest, and delicately shoved a stethoscope from one heaving spot to the next. Carl's breathing came in short, hoarse gasps.

Didn't notice them at first, but several of his favorite nurses stood in the shadows. He'd cheated death so many times before, but I knew this was serious because some of those beautiful young women wept and dabbed at their noses with white tissues. He'd been a constant source of considerable entertainment for them over the past few years. Think a few actually loved the randy old letch.

After about a minute or so, his teenaged doctor shook his head, hung his stethoscope around his neck, and moved away. Leona motioned for me to come forward. Shuffled up beside the bed and took his wasted hand in mine. Must have stood there for about five minutes, called his name several times, before he finally, and with considerable effort, forced his eyes open. Barely made out what he said. His voice was clear but weak and the words came in spurts.

"Well, *mi amigo viejo*, about time . . . to give up . . . my gee-tar. . . . Don't reckon . . . can hold . . . him off . . . much longer, Hayden. Awful tired . . . you know? Let you . . . talk me . . . out of this . . . last time. But you know . . . kinda tired . . . of fighting him off. Son of a bitch . . . is relentless . . . won't . . . leave me be. If'n I . . . had my pistols . . . put some holes in . . . his bony ass." He tried to laugh at his own joke, but went into a racking fit of coughing.

"Yeah, Carlton, I hear you. Understand completely. We've had a helluva ride together. Haven't we, old man?"

"Helluva ride. Gonna come back . . . to life . . . because of you . . . Hayden. Everyone's . . . gonna be famous. . . . People . . . all over . . . gonna know our names. . . ." His eyelids drooped and, for a second, I thought he'd finally bought the ranch for sure, but then they snapped open like the lid on a kid's jack-in-the-box, and he came back all fierce and new again for a few seconds.

"Remember what I said from the beginning? Tell it all. Don't . . . leave . . . nothin' . . . out. Things we done. Don't matter . . . who knows . . . now. Long's you've got . . . that pink-faced boy . . . on the hook . . . tell it all. See you on the other side, old man." He drifted away again for a second or two. Then shocked the hell out of everyone in the room when he tried to sit up. Clear as a dinner bell he yelped, "Elizabeth said to tell you not to worry. Everyone's waiting for you, and it's beautiful there."

A crooked grin creaked across his face as he eased back onto his pillow. Made motions like he was feeling around on the bed and said, "Where's my guns? The son of a bitch is coming!" His eyes fixed on mine for another second or so. Then he made that sound. If you've ever heard it you know what I mean. From somewhere deep inside his used-up, antiquated carcass, a righteous spirit turned loose and escaped, darted past his lips, flew over my shoulder, and went back to God.

Couple of the beautiful little girls in that barren room wept like babies. Ain't ashamed to say I cried too. Thought, it sure would have been nice if he could have had his pistols and saddle there with him when he went out. Course, they wouldn't have fit in very well with our dying-old-fart décor here at the Rolling Hills Home for the Aged.

He'd been my oldest and closest friend. And he'd done exactly what I told him to do. He'd stayed alive just long enough to tell Franklin J. Lightfoot Junior his part of our story. Suppose you could say, I kept him alive for a day or two longer than he'd actually planned on being with me to begin with. That didn't make his departure from this life any easier for me. Hell, I'd known it was coming. But like the man said, "We're never ready for death when he shows up." Whether it's you he's after, or someone close, we've got to be the most ill-prepared inhabitants on the planet when it comes to a showdown with the Maker.

But Carlton, now there's a very different tale. He had postponed the eventual at least a dozen times over the past year. His departure didn't come as any surprise at all to that old man. Personally, I'm pretty sure he might have planned it all that way. Be just like him.

Next morning Leona helped me make all the arrangements. Carlton didn't have any living family to take care of such things. Hell, I'd been looking out for him for almost thirty years as it was, and his funeral amounted to nothing more than the logical extension of those responsibilities. Felt like his father, for Christ's sake, in spite of the fact that he was damn near five years older'n me.

We had a memorial service at a crematorium out on the west side of town somewhere north of 65th Street. Hadn't ever been out there before, so I can't remember the exact location. Me and Lightfoot, Leona, Jerimiah Obediah Samuel Henry Jones, a few others who worked around Rolling Hills, and a whole bunch of pretty little nurses accompanied by very confused-looking husbands were the only folks who attended. Heddy McDonald wept like ole Carlton had been her best friend. Guess you could say he had a right nice send-off for a man who just had one *real* friend left in the world.

Lenoa got Rolling Hills' resident chaplain to do a kind of one-fits-all ceremony that actually worked out considerably better'n I would have ever thought it could. He did this whole song and dance where he compared our lives to taking a trip on a steamship and how all those who'd gone before waited for us on the other side. Seemed totally appropriate to me.

Don't know where he got it but, while we stood by Carlton's rented box and took our last look, Franklin J. Lightfoot Junior pinned a genuine silver-plated deputy U.S. marshal's badge on our friend's chest. Damned fine gesture on the boy's part. My respect for Junior went up about fifty points. Carl would have loved it.

Couple of days later, back out on the sun porch, Leona strolled up and handed me a highly polished wooden box. Inside I found a cobalt-blue jug that had a silver tag on the side with Carlton's name, date of birth, and date of death stamped into it.

In what had to go down as the most respectful voice that big ole gal could muster up, she said, "Mr. Cecil's mortal remains."

Thought seriously 'bout keepin' them mortal remains with me in my room, then got to figurin' he wouldn't have liked that at all. He'd never cared a whole lot for being warehoused in this holding pen for folks who'd been shucked right down to the cob. Decided what he most likely would have absolutely loved would have been for me to chase some of those nurses down the hall, and throw what was left of him on them. But I couldn't see myself doing anything like that. So I talked Franklin J. Junior into a little road trip. He had a well-kept gray 1937 Chevrolet Coupe. We drove out west of Little Rock to a spot on the Arkansas River named Pinnacle Mountain.

Folks over there had one of the last remaining ferryboats still operating in the state at the time. Called her the *Queen Willowmena*. Rode her across the river. I'd found one of Carl's old hats in his closet. When we got about halfway across, I held the sweat-stained thing by the brim, and Junior dumped the contents of that blue bottle into it. Always thought you ended up with fine ashes when someone got cremated. But that ain't the case. What came out of his jug was about a double handful of what looked like pieces of chipped-up bone and a rough-edged lump of silver that had once been a deputy U.S. marshal's badge.

Lightfoot leaned over and under his breath said,

"This is just a mite illegal, Mr. Tilden. Let's don't make a big deal out of the thing. Just get him in as quick as you can."

Pretty cold that morning, but I moved as far away as I could from the few other passengers on board. Took his old Stetson by the brim, and sent it sailing out over the water. Sun rode the tops of the trees, and threw a red-tinged golden glow over the river's fast-moving surface. Ole Carl dropped into that frosty stream on a beam of light that shot through the trees and followed him till he disappeared from view.

Lightfoot stood with his right arm around my narrow, sagging shoulders. I said, "Don't know about you, Junior, but I kind of like to think Judith came back just now and got him."

He smiled and waved in the direction of our old friend's watery grave. "Sure enough looked that way to me, Hayden. Sure enough looked that way to me."

9

"Lucius by God Dodge"

GUESS CARLTON'S PASSING had a more profound effect on Junior than I first thought. At least that's the way it seemed to me at the time. After our ferry ride over at Pinnacle Mountain, he brought me back to the home, and didn't come around again for more than two weeks. But his seriously shaved face finally meandered in on an ice-cold Monday just after Thanksgiving. Those days General Black Jack Pershing and me had the porch to ourselves, but we were happier'n horned frogs in an anthill because we'd inherited all of Carlton's former girlfriends. They checked on us constantly, and saw to our every need. Kept us covered up with a nice thick blanket one of the ladies on the second floor left when she cashed out a couple of winters before. Brought us coffee, or Hershey's hot cocoa, and cat treats anytime we wanted 'em. Hell, we got to thinking life couldn't get much better'n that.

"Appreciated the phone call Thanksgiving Day, Junior. Mighty nice of you to keep me in mind."

He examined each of the chairs along the wall like an old spinster buying flower seeds at her favorite feed store and mercantile before he found the one he favored. Then, he dragged it over next to me and Black Jack, screwed himself down into it, grinned like he was just tickled plumb to death, draped his heavy coat over still-cold legs, and pulled out the ever-present pad and pencil.

"Sorry I couldn't get by in person, Hayden. My wife's family expects us to show up at their house for holidays. We have to drive down to Shreveport again Christmas Day. They never come up here. Carmen and I've been married five years, and my in-laws have never set foot in my house. But by God, if we don't show up on their doorstep anytime I have a minute off, there's hell to pay. Besides, I had something special I've been working on for you, and had to see to it."

Before I realized what he'd said, I blurted out, "You don't have to explain, son. I understand." That just kind of sat there between us, for a second or so, till my brain caught up with the conversation. "Did you say you'd been working on something *special* there, Junior?"

His entire face lit up, and one of those expressions that almost screamed how pleased he was with himself plastered itself over his smile. "I've been looking for an old friend of yours. There for a spell, feared he might have already passed on. But turns out he's like you. A tough old bird who'll probably still be around long after I'm gone."

Well, that made about as much sense to me as watching a woodpecker trying to shoe a horse. "What the hell are you rambling on about, boy? Ain't nobody alive now 'cept me. Of all Parker's marshals, deputies, posse men, and other lawdogs from back during my time, Carl and me were the only two still around. Now, it's just me." Thought about that for a second or so and added, "At least, till a minute or so ago, I always thought I was the only one."

Must have sounded a bit testy, 'cause his face got red, and he looked embarrassed for about a second. "I know, Hayden. But you've forgotten somebody." He held his pencil by the eraser end and pointed over my shoulder, back toward the nurse's station. I twisted so far around in the chair, Black Jack got irritated and jumped down just to get away from the discomfort. Took a second for my eyes to tell the rest of me what I saw. Couldn't believe it at first, but there he stood. Poor son of a bitch was so old, he looked like the Dead Sea wearing cowboy boots and a raggedy-assed felt hat.

Hoisted my ancient carcass out of my chair, and the two of us stumbled toward each other like hundred-year-old babies trying to figure out how to walk for the first time. Have to admit, though, he still moved mighty damned good for a man in his late eighties.

We fell on one another's necks and blubbered around for a bit. Don't know where he came from, but a feller carrying an ugly box camera—topped with a shiny flashgun—started running around us. He must have popped off about a dozen of them damned eye-burning sizzlers. Neither of us weepers could say much of anything that made any sense for a bit, except how glad we were to see each other, and how great it was to still be alive. Then, of course, there was a lot of joshing around about how both of us thought the other one had already bought the ranch.

Finally, had to get us moving toward something like a rational conversation myself, after we staggered back to the porch and Junior helped us get settled into our individual nests. The boy's photographer buddy had dwindled into a carefully selected shot every once in a while. Seemed to be trying for a postcard, portrait, or some such thing. Irritating little ferret was still burning up those eye-poppers when my old friend asked for a cup of black coffee. One of the nurses brought it to him, and smiled when he told her how pretty she was. Soon as she turned her back, a bottle of Kentucky's finest popped out of his dress-coat pocket. He doctored that mug of belly-wash up to the point where I figured it'd probably grow hair on any saddle that survived the Seventh Cavalry's debacle.

"Lucius By God Dodge. Would have sworn on big stacks of King James Bibles your mother dropped you next to a mesquite tree ten years before Moses got born, old man. You should have gone home to glory aeons ago. Hell, back in 1925, friends of mine from Austin told me a Mexican bandit shot the hell out of you in some out-of-the-way pimple down in south Texas called Poteet. Way I heard it, that hot tamale sent you straight to the devil so quick you never knew what hit you."

With the kind of effort eight and a half decades can bring, he crossed his denim-covered right leg over his left, dropped his mangy hat onto the toe of his boot, and took a deep swallow from that beaker of wickedly doctored Folger's. A smile of profound contentment spread over his leathery, crag-creased face as he savored the potent treat.

"Yes, sir, Tilden. That he did. Name was Jose Alphonso Guiterrez. Taco-bending son of a bitch went on a thievery-and-mayhem rip that lasted almost three months 'fore I caught up with him. Figured the Mexican bastard for a thief, not a murderer. Cornered his sorry ass in a stick-and-mud hacienda 'bout sixty miles south of Poteet out on the Frio. Thought he was gonna give it up and come in peaceable. Hell, he had his wife and kids there with him."

He took a long pull from his cup, glanced at the boy and me—to make sure his audience was displaying the right degree of attentiveness—then went on. "Anyway, we kinda wrasseled around for a bit before I got him by the scruff of the neck and headed him toward a horse. Snaky son of a bitch pulled one of those double-action, hammerless Smith and Wesson pistols from somewhere under his serape, and put four .38 slugs in my crusty hide. Who'd have guessed it? I mean, a knife, you bet. Maybe even an ax or long-handled hoe. But a pistol warn't part of that recipe. Guess he musta stole it from somewheres. Anyway, that south Texas *pendejo* managed to shoot the hell out of me afore I tore his ticket for a trip to a spot way south of Mexico. Egg-suckin' *hijo de puta* almost kilt me. Hell, I was sixty-five years old, and still tougher'n most of them

candy-asses carrying a badge down there. Been sher-
iffin' for all them ungratefuls in Atascosca County for
about five years at the time. Took me almost a year
and a half to recover from them holes Alphonso put in
me."

He shook his head like he still didn't believe it, took
another sip from that cup of heavily doctored coffee,
then went on like he'd never even slowed down. "Had
to retire after that 'un. Living on a middlin' horse ranch
I inherited from my uncle over on the Sulphur River,
not far from Texarkana. Been raising them spotted
horses. All them little cowgirls love my Appaloosas.
Your young friend managed to run me down over a
month ago. I've got family here in Little Rock, and
come up on the Flyer every so often. One of my daugh-
ters, and her brood, live over in The Heights right off
Cantrell. Tried to make it up this way when Lightfoot
and I first talked. Sorry I couldn't get here 'fore Carlton
passed." He'd started with so much enthusiasm, but
ended like it tired him out, or maybe memories of Carlton and the past just caught up with him all at once.

For several seconds, Cecil's hoary ghost oozed up
through the cracks in the floor and settled around our
shoulders like an old shawl. But Lucius, who'd never
been one to take a lot of time ragging around over the
dearly departed, or any other departed for that matter,
put Cecil behind us in a hurry.

"Heard you've been piling it on pretty scary for this
whippersnapper of a reporter, Tilden. I still recall how
good you got at telling this stuff as you put more experience under your belt. Judge Parker always said you
made the best witness he ever had testify. But I thought

maybe I should come over and make sure you don't mislead the boy overmuch. Gotta watch him, son." He flashed a sparkling smile and clicked what looked like a brand-new set of store-bought teeth at us. "Even when he's telling the truth—it can be so fantastic most folks won't believe him. But when he's lying—it's a sight and sound to behold. Think he learned it from being around Carlton for so long."

"Looka here, Lucius, if you showed up to keep me honest, that's just dandy. Ain't nobody else alive that can remember, or for that matter ever knew, exactly what happened up on Big Cougar Bluff or over in Red Rock Canyon at Big Eagle's nest. You can jump in any time you feel like I'm off the mark or your rusted-up old bones can stand the heat."

He smiled, fired up a cigarillo, and said, "Wore my best boots, and they's spurs in my duffel. So get it on, big boy."

Guess Junior's photographer finally finished his dance. He leaned over and whispered in the boy's ear for a second, nodded, and bowed himself off the porch while Franklin scribbled like a madman. Suppose he wanted to get every syllable his two very own private antique man-killers said just in case they both did a Carlton on him and jackknifed off into the great beyond that night.

His pencil had almost set his paper to smokin' when he said, "Where is Big Cougar Bluff? I've looked, boys, and it's not on any map of Oklahoma I've seen so far."

Lucius nodded, stuffed his hat back on his head, and pulled at the brim like he'd tipped it and said, "Go ahead, Tilden, I'm just here to listen and keep you honest. Way I've got it figured, you'll slip up pretty quick, and I'll have to rein you in." He sipped at the steaming liquid in his cup, made a smiling grimace of a face at us, clicked his shiny new teeth again, and looked happier'n a kid sittin' in Santa's lap down at Dillard's Department Store.

Hell, I ignored him, and jumped right back into my story. "You won't find Big Cougar Bluff on the maps, Junior. It's nothing more than a steep spot over a bend on the Canadian really. Kind of thing some law-enforcement types today would probably call 'locally known as Big Cougar Bluff.' 'Bout twenty miles east and a little north of Red Rock Canyon."

When Cecil and Billy finally showed up, they had this black-haired, hot-eyed gal named Judith Karr with 'em. Told us most of that wild-assed tale you heard from Carlton about their run-in with Wilson Bowlegs and his bunch of Sunday afternoon churchgoing picnickers. A slouched dunce named Bully May sat in the tumbleweed looking pitiful, and spent most of his time whining and complaining about what he called his "sit-chi-ation." But that didn't stop him from offering up a heartfelt "amen" or "praise God" to every word that came out of Carlton's mouth. The girl didn't say much of anything, just sat and mooned around over Carlton like he was the only man living.

Didn't know for some time whether he understood it or not, but little Miss Karr's infatuation with Carlton beat anything I'd witnessed between a man and woman in all my years up till then. Remember thinking, at the time, that she'd have walked through fire and swallowed hot coals for him if he'd asked her. Truth of it all was that by the time that raid came to its bloody conclusion, she played a part in the festivities that none of us could have foreseen with a crystal ball, Gypsy tea leaves, or Tarot cards.

Billy's feet hadn't hit the ground good when he said, "Where the hell's Handsome Harry? I've missed that prissy-assed Boston son of a bitch. Can't wait to tell him about how much fun me, Carlton, and Judith had shooting the cannon at Wilson Bowlegs." He jerked his gloves off, stuffed them into his pistol belt, and anxiously glanced over my shoulder for our missing friend.

Well, Lucius, Old Bear, and me just hung our heads and couldn't say anything there for a bit. Charlie Three Bones couldn't speak English anyway, so he didn't count. I ended up having to be the one who told him and Carlton how Harry bit the dust, and all about our shootout with Brutus Sneed and those with him at Broken Hand's place.

Billy chewed his bottom lip till it bled. Stingy tears carved pained trenches down his dust-covered cheeks. He'd known Harry longer than any of the rest of us, and I think the news of our friend's death hardened the boy in a way like nothing that had happened to him before—or for a long spell after.

He even went to blaming himself for it. "Damnation, Hayden, I shoulda been the one what went with you."

Lucius put a soothing hand on Billy's skinny shoulder in an effort to comfort him. I said, "It wouldn't have mattered, Billy. What happened out there just happened. There's nothing anyone could have been done to stop or change it."

But he wouldn't let it go. "I'm better with a gun than Harry. If'n it had been me, none of them ole boys woulda cleared leather 'fore I blasted the hell out of 'em."

All I could do was offer up as much comfort as possible with: "Maybe, Billy. But we can't live the rest of our lives on maybes. Harry was a man, full grown, and he knew all the dangers in doing this job. He damn near bought it when we chased Saginaw Bob to Dallas and Tollman Pike shot him out of his saddle. Besides, it could have been any one of us. Like a good many before him, his carefully guarded ball of luck just came unraveled someplace close to where Brutus Sneed was standing. Same thing could happen to you, or me, tomorrow. Near as I can figure, living has always been the primary cause of dying, and the sooner we all accept that simple truth, the better off we'll be."

Well, our entire company was a pretty miserable bunch for the rest of the day. Billy stayed gloomy and morose for weeks after that. But by the time we got him, Carlton, and Judith set up for camp, and fixed a special spot for Miss Karr to take her ease, the initial shock of the thing had begun to wear off some. Honestly, though, I can't recall Billy Bird ever mentioning Harry's death after that. From then on he talked about ole Handsome like the man was still with us.

We waited till the next morning to go over our plans for Martin Luther Big Eagle and his crew of Red Rock Canyon bad boys. Old Bear said it would be best to let everyone get a good night's sleep before we jumped

into any heavy-duty discussions in that area. I trusted
his instincts and, as always, it proved a good decision,
although I'm not sure any of us slept very well that
night, especially Billy Bird.

When a smoldering yellow sun got us up that morning, Judith Karr fixed the best breakfast we'd had since
we left Fort Smith. That dark-eyed gal could make mir-
acles with coffee, a slab of bacon, biscuits, and flour
gravy. She even came up with a dozen eggs from
somewhere. Carlton claimed she slipped away one
night on the trail, and raided a poor unsuspecting
farmer's henhouse. Could tell he admired such independent methods in the girl. None of us cared much
where those cackle-berries came from. We were just
glad to get them.

Being as how Billy knew more than any of the rest
of us about the canyon and the area around it, it naturally fell on him to get the ball rolling on how to go
about our planned raid. He sat on a rock the size and
shape of an inverted water bucket, picked up a tree
branch about three feet long, and went to scratching in
the blood-red dirt while the rest of us listened.

"This here is the Canadian." A long line that ran
from left to right in front of him followed the stick as
he dragged it through the thick layer of dust at his feet.
"About twenty miles west of where we're sitting right
now, and maybe five miles south of the river, you'll
find Red Rock Canyon." He glanced around, and
locked eyes with each of his attentive deacons for a
second. "If you ain't never been there, this is gonna be
quite an education, boys. So pay strict attention."

The stick snapped up and pointed at the wagon.

"You can climb up on top of the tumbleweed and look west, and the only thing you'll see is rolling hills, knee-high grass, and a few trees in the sheltered areas along ravines and creeks—mainly cedar, pecan, hickory, and some maple in those places. Actually, there's more trees down in the canyon than anywhere between here and there. Fact is, we'll be right on top of that bloody trench before we even know we've found it."

He stood to emphasize what he said next, and even used his stick to point at each of us as he swung it around the circle. "I mean it, boys. If it was dark, and you didn't know where this little sucker was, you could walk right off into it, and break your neck before you even realized you'd found it. This thing is just a crimson sandstone scar in the ground about a mile and a half long. It's two hundred and fifty or maybe three hundred feet across at its widest, and anywhere from fifty to a hundred and fifty feet deep. Years back, some of the Plains tribes, like the Sioux and Cheyenne, used it as a spot to winter. Helped get them out of those icy northern winds blasting in from Canada. Then, for several years, forty-niners made it one of their favorite stopping places on their way to California. Cattle thieves, killers, and lawbreakers of every stripe know about it today, and head this direction every time they can't think of any place else to run. Other parties of Judge Parker's marshals have chased individual pieces of scum in there before, and it was considerably less than a picnic just getting them shook loose. Once a man gets inside, he can be harder to bust free than an Alabama tick. This is my third trip out here. But to be absolutely truthful, I don't have any real clear idea what we'll find tomorrow. All the rumors we've heard claim that Big Eagle has come up with something special in the way of fortifications down there. That's why Hayden and Carlton brought the cannon."

Held my hand up. "Any water in there, Billy?" I hoped we could use a lack of supply against that band of thieving killers just in case things worked out to a waiting game.

"The canyon's fed by crystal-clear springwater that supplies a sparkling creek. Runs right through the middle of the whole shebang. 'Less these ole boys have managed to get more stupid than usual, they don't have to worry much about water, as long as they stay down there."

We watched, wrapped in our individual thoughts on the problem, as he squatted again and continued to enhance his artwork in the dirt. He mapped that still-raw scratch on the earth's ancient hide and its relation to the Canadian—along with the creek that ran through it, and what looked like hidden coves gouged into various places along its easternmost wall.

Lucius asked what had to have been the most obvious question. "How do we get down into this place?"

Billy pushed his hat back, leaned over with his elbows on his knees, and shook his head. "Well, that's the problem, Lucius. Only entrance I know of is on the west side, and it's a real snaky son of a bitch. I was down in there a couple of years ago, but neither me nor any of our feller marshals has ever really seen this so-called 'fortress' we've heard so much about. What we're going on here is strictly based on recent rumor, fuzzy-mouthed legends, and probably a goodly number of downright lies. But I can tell you this. If Big Eagle has the entrance over here very heavily guarded—and there's no reason to think otherwise—we'll have to fight our way down that winding path to the gorge's floor, before we can set the cannon up and do any damage to whatever they've got waiting for us."

Old Bear sat beside Charlie Three Bones and translated the discussion as the two of them watched Billy's diagram develop. They ragged it around a good bit before he nodded toward his friend, pulled his big bowie, touched the tip to a spot on the east side of Billy's drawing of the chasm, and grunted, "My friend Charlie Three Bones and I agree. Your map is accurate—this spot in center is place for fort. Hard to get at, if it's there, from any direction. But Charlie Three Bones says we might find open spot on canyon wall opposite this site. Maybe we shoot down on them from other side." He jabbed at a spot along the west wall of our friend's dirt map just south of the entrance.

Billy thought that over for a second. "Old Bear's dead on. This spot inside is located almost in the exact center of the place. There's a deep depression in the sandstone walls that would be a great place to put up a fight, whether you've built yourself a stronghold down there or not."

Lucius turned reasonable again, blew out another cloud of heavy smoke, and asked what must have been on his mind for some time. "What the hell were you boys thinking when you decided on this trip? Didn't anyone sit down and plan this out before we left Fort Smith?"

Billy, Carlton, and I busted out laughing at the same

time. I said, "Hell, Lucius, if we'd of given it too much in the way of thought before we left, we'd all probably still be in Fort Smith right now. Carlton could be having a lemon pie with his buddy Barnes Reed down at the Napoli Café; Billy could be trying to carve a sailboat out of a stick of stove wood; and I could be eating dinner with my beautiful wife and looking forward to a much-desired night in her arms."

Once we'd all got a good snicker in at his expense, I went on. "We had a crude idea of what we'd face here, but nothing definite. Couldn't really make much in the way of serious plans because of that. And besides, you've already seen that nothing ever happens out here the way we expect or want. For all intents and purposes, fate won't let go till we get back to civilization. It's just the Nations, Lucius. Just the Nations."

Carlton picked it up from there. "Truth has always been, from the very beginning, that we don't know what Big Eagle's got cooked up for us down there— if anythin'. All we've heard is stories. Have to wait till we get inside tomorrow and take a look-see for ourselves. By then, we should have a pretty fair idea of what we'll have to do, and how to go about it."

I know he probably didn't plan to do it, but Carlton even got serious on him for a bit. "You can bet all them pistols strapped on Hateful's back that whatever's in Red Rock Canyon, it won't be an easy fight, and some of us might not come back from it."

Everyone in the circle, except Charlie Three Bones, glanced around at his friends, then snapped his eyes back to the drawing on the ground. After a second or two of silence, I got us going again with: "Here's what we know for certain, boys. Big Eagle has some kind of hidey-hole either in the canyon, carved into one of the sandstone walls, or on a hill nearby. Whichever it turns out to be, that's why we brought the heavy artillery. If the past is any indication, Big Eagle can most likely count on an unknown number of accomplices and cohorts who accompany him. We're fairly certain one of those men is Smilin' Jack Paine, and there's the distinct chance that W. J. McCabe, the louse Lucius came out here looking for, is there too. God only knows what kind of other scoundrels, miscreants, and malefactors we'll find once we get inside."

Each of my fellow lawdogs nodded. I went on. "There might be one small complication we haven't had a chance to discuss." Fleeting looks darted back my way. "Before we left Fort Smith, I developed a piece of information that led me to believe Big Eagle might be holding a woman against her will. Her name is Birdie Mae Blackwell."

That one dropped right into the middle of everything like one of Carlton's Ketchum grenades. Billy didn't waste any time getting his feelings out in the open. "Good God, Hayden. If that's true, what'll we do if they threaten to kill her? Or what if they start torturing her? What the hell are we gonna do then?"

"We'll just have to play it by ear, Billy—'bout the same way as everything else that's happened up till now. We'll take care of those problems any way we have to when the necessity arises. You've done the same thing a hundred times before. This won't be any different."

He snatched the hat off his head and spun it around

on the end of his trigger finger. "It's always a problem any time a woman gets involved in this kind of thing. You know I'm right on this one, Hayden. Hell, it's bad enough we had to bring Judith along with us, but we couldn't leave her back there on the trail with her dead family. Don't get me wrong here. I'm not complaining. It's just that women always make matters worse than they already are when the shooting gets cranked up real good. Once the air fills with gunpowder and quick death, men tend to careful up enough to get themselves killed when a woman plops down in the middle of everything."

Carlton, who'd been pretty quiet up till that point, hooked his thumbs in his pistol belt, kicked at a spot on the ground, and said, "Take my word on this 'un boys. We don't have to worry over much about Miss Karr. She don't need a whole lot of lookin' after. Pert sure she can take care of herself. Hand that feisty little gal a pistol, and you'd better hold on to your sombrero, amigo. She's a shooter, if I ever seen one."

Course none of the rest of us had any idea where his testimony came from, and all of us could tell it didn't come anywhere close to satisfying Billy. But he let it go anyway. Man wasn't blind or stupid. He could see the attachment that had grown up between Carlton and the girl. Their growing affection for one another was absolutely obvious to our entire party. It tended to be a daily source of speculation and discussion among the rest of us who either held out hopes for such female fondness for ourselves, or whose hearts secretly pined for the women who awaited our arrival back in Fort Smith. The kind of love those two were seriously working at was always envied by other men in the wild places. Leastways, by any man in his right mind.

We spent the rest of the afternoon, and that night, in preparation for what we could only guess awaited our arrival in Red Rock Canyon. Everyone made sure all his weapons got cleaned and loaded. Took Lucius longer than the rest of the party put together, what with all the weapons he dragged around. A man has to expend a lot of time and effort to clean and load ten pistols and a rifle. He oiled and wiped for hours, and was still at it when I turned in for the night.

Civilized roosters slept like week-old chicks when we struck out at first light. A cloudless night had left heavy dew on the grass that rose up and caressed the bellies of our animals. My boots and pant legs were soaked in less than ten minutes.

For all the dime-store cowboys out there who never got any closer to a horse than a mounted cop, you should know that dragging an iron-barred wagon—like a tumbleweed—around the Nations never could be described as anything that resembled a simple proposition. Add a cannon and caisson to the mix, and things got considerably harder. But once you got west of the spot on the Canadian that ran almost due north for a ways, the countryside out there changed so dramatically as to be almost unbelievable.

Good thing about it, our progress from that point was considerably easier. The dark, dense woodlands, and real mountains of Arkansas and the eastern Nations, vanished as a swaying curtain rose from the rolling prairie to reveal an ocean of grass that stretched before you in endless waves that seemed to heave and ripple to the other side of the world.

Handsome Harry had studied that kind of stuff at one of those well-known universities back east. Harvard or Yale, I think he said. Called himself an amateur botanist. Whatever in hell that was. He never missed a chance, before his untimely passing, to instruct me on what we saw as our animals tromped it into the ground. And he claimed that what all us ignorant jaybirds simply referred to as grass was comprised of several different varieties, and had actual names. Little bluestem, big bluestem, foxtail, cord grass, and others I can't even remember. Course, I recognized Indian grass and buffalo grass when I saw it anyway. So it didn't come as any real surprise that some poor goober, with not much of anything to do, used up his life hanging tags on every stem, berry, twig, rock, tree, and bush we passed in our deadly travels.

An observant and mildly educated man who crossed that barren place could spend a good part of his storytelling endeavors doing the most fleeting description of the flora and fauna of a mile long stretch of what now makes up western Oklahoma. But back then, we didn't give a hoot in hell what kind of grass lapped at us like waves on a peaceful sea, or what kind of trees grew in the depressions, cuts, gullies, and canyons.

Bad men demanded our presence in those places. Those men of blood would murder any one of us, just like Sneed and his bunch killed Harry, and they wouldn't lose one wink of sleep over it. Lawlessness, gunfire, and death followed everywhere we went and, to be totally forthright about it, my concern, or thought, for the passing scenery at the time, amounted to little or not a goddamned bit at all.

Billy took us north of our objective by several miles. Once we got past our final destination a bit, we turned back south, and approached the canyon's entrance from the west. Pulled everything to a halt behind a nice rise about half a mile from our target, and spent most of several hours before the sun started down squinting through our long glasses at anything that moved. Just before full dark, Old Bear and Charlie Three Bones snaked their way up to the entrance, disappeared inside for about an hour, and came back later with a surprise.

We all sat close and talked in whispers that night as he told us what they found. "No guards at entrance. Made our way to gorge floor. Saw no one."

"Well, at least that's something," Billy muttered.

Then came the downside. "But plenty of movement and noise up near the spot we picked out on Billy's map. Did not get all the way there. Sounded like at least a dozen men. Charlie Three Bones thinks maybe more. We backed out. Quick as we could."

Lucius groaned. He hadn't been able to roll 'em and smoke 'em since the sun went down, and was well on the way to being edgier than a pistol-toting pig in a meatpacking house. "Well, I say we take it to 'em Indian-fighter-style. Let's blow in—all guns blazing— and let God sort 'em out when the last one stops twitching."

Think everyone else knew we couldn't do it his way. I'd been mulling around about it all night, and had my mind made up on how we'd tackle the problem, if we could. "Look, Lucius, we can thank a merciful God

they must not know we're here—at least not yet. Pretty
safe bet these ole boys expected us a week or so ago.
All our delays, and side trips, might well have worked
to our advantage. Appears our luck has come back, and
this bunch has got a bit sloppy. You can bet your un-
spent reward money for W. J. McCabe, everyone down
there knows we're out here somewhere. So, here's
what we'll do.

"Tomorrow morning, when it's just coming light,
you, me, Billy, Old Bear, and Charlie Three Bones go
in first. We'll make our way in one at a time, and form
a solid wall at the base of the entrance. Once we get
established, Carlton can bring the cannon down. We'll
do what we can to muffle it down some, but it'll still
be noisy and sure to wake someone, who'll put the rest
on alert. By then, if our luck holds, it'll be too late.
Once we get inside, they're done for."

Carlton glanced at Judith and said, "What about the
tumbleweed and Miss Karr, Hayden?"

"We'll leave the tumbleweed here. No point trying
to take it with us. It'd be too much trouble and way
too hard to maneuver around. Miss Karr can guard
Bully. Wouldn't want him to raise a ruckus after we
leave, now would we?"

The girl's boldness showed itself an instant before
Carlton was about to object. "Leave me a pistol and
rifle, Marshal Tilden," she said. "No one will get to
me, long as I'm armed, and if Bully gets restless or
starts yelping, I'll see to it he quiets down."

Carlton's prisoner had been trying to hear everything
we'd said since we pulled up behind the rise. Didn't
matter to me if he knew what we had planned or not.

Long as he stayed chained to the floor of the tumbleweed and kept quiet, I made sure no one bothered him.
But I also let him know he'd better keep on his best
behavior.

"You make a sound, Bully, or manage to give us
away somehow, and I'll turn Old Bear and Three
Bones loose on you. Trust me, you wouldn't like the
result. Couple of days staked out on an anthill with
some carefully applied wounds calculated to help you
slowly bleed out, and you'll wish you'd never seen any
of us." I stood less than ten feet from him—and he
heard every word. He made it a point to let me know
I didn't have anything to worry about from his filthy
corner of our rolling prison.

"Oh, don't you worry none 'bout me, Marshal Tilden. Ole Bully'll be the quietest man alive till you tell
him to talk again." He made a clamping motion over
his lips with his fingers, and made out like he'd
snapped a padlock closed on his mouth.

'Bout that time, Charley Three Bones got to making
frantic signs and jabbering away at Old Bear. The two
of them made shussing motions at everyone, and darted
over to the north side of our camp. A dozen weapons
came out cocked and ready for action. Bully May
flopped down in his corner and crawled under the pile
of clothing, bedding, and other stuff piled up there.
Pretty soon, it got so quiet, the only thing I could hear
was crickets making love in the grass.

I stayed all wound up and ready for action so long
that my hands and arms started cramping up on me.
Then Old Bear and his friend led a huge figure into

camp. Old Bear whispered, "Guess you look hard, you find almost anything out here."

Barnes Reed reached around him, grabbed me by the arm, squeezed, flashed a toothy grin, and chuckled. "Been missin' you boys. 'Fraid there for a while that I wasn't ever gonna find you."

Carlton popped out of the dark and they hugged each other like family at Christmas dinner. "Damn you, Barnes. What the hell are you doing out here?" He slapped his friend on the back, and led him to the center of our gathering.

"Cain't be away from my favorite pie-eating compadre for long, and besides, I got me to figurin' that if this here roost of robbers was as infested with scumsucking vermin as everyone claimed, you children might need another gun or three. Besides, I missed my chance at Martin Luther Big Eagle 'bout a year ago. He owes the United States of America some of his sorry hide for murdering an Arkansas whiskey drummer named Balthus Smoot over at Winding Stair. Cut the man's heart out with a hatchet."

The only way he could have been a more appreciated sight and sound, to me, was if he'd brought Elizabeth along for the ride and had her hid somewhere in his war bag. His surprising arrival seemed to have the most profound effect on Billy. The boy was so happy, he looked like a two-tailed puppy about to wag himself to death.

Unfortunately, by the time we explained our situation, and told the story about Harry Tate's death again, Barnes Reed's cheery deportment had abandoned him. Course he hadn't known Harry as well as the rest of us, but that didn't matter. Anytime another member of the brotherhood of the badge went down, we all felt it. But I've got to hand it to him. Barnes was a professional, and immediately set out to take our minds off the bad news.

"Came out here thinking I'd meet you boys on the way back to civilization. Figured what with your cannon and all, you most likely had Big Eagle and his boys whipped down by now. Talked with some folks at McAlester's Store, and found out you'd split up and gone in different directions. Kept after Billy and Carlton. They was just naturally the easiest to follow, what with dragging that piece of artillery around behind 'em and all. Discovered the spot where you camped over on Big Cougar Bluff yesterday. Realized then you'd finally hooked up again. When I didn't hear any gunfire, or shelling from the cannon, figured I could still catch you in time to make it to the dance." He almost laughed into the sleeve of his shirt, but caught himself and squeezed it off to a short bearlike snort of pleasure.

Didn't take him long to get a handle on the situation, and from all indications, he was itching for a fight. "Hey, I been wantin' to put another hole in Smilin' Jack ever since that little fandango over at Drinkwater's near the Arbuckle Mountains. Hayden owes him for Thunder, and I owe him for not falling when I put at least one slug in his sorry hide as he made his getaway."

Might have got about ten winks of sleep between us that night. We were all so tired, I don't think any of us would have woke up at the time we wanted if it hadn't been for Barnes. When we set out that morning,

I remember thinking how I felt like one of those Plains Indians, who'd lived and hunted there a hundred years before, as we silently snaked our way through the waist-high grasses and crept up on the men below. Light from another blazing sun carved a gleaming red slit across a wine-colored sky above Red Rock Canyon. It crept across the surging, grassy plains on silent padded feet and, just about the time we all arrived at the gloomy entrance, some of it spilled over on to the chasm's bloody pockmarked western wall.

Beneath the light, though, it was like looking into a well. A misty gray fog hovered over the creek below, and we had to walk our horses down the twisting trail that led us into darkness. Somewhere at the bottom, hidden from view in the murk and fog, unseen and perhaps only a few feet away, fate awaited our arrival. Open-armed, wings spread, he looked a lot like death in my dreams.

10

"THE BATTLE OF RED ROCK CANYON"

LUCIUS BY GOD Dodge rode beside me as we eased our animals over the lip of that fog-shrouded crater and started down the short twisting trail to the bottom. He leaned in his stirrups and whispered, "Darker'n midnight under an iron skillet in there, Hayden. Be getting up toward seven or eight o'clock 'fore this mist burns off and we're able to see everything we really need to see." His assessment hit that horseshoe nail right on its boxed head. Martin Luther Big Eagle could have had an armed killer behind every bush, tree, or rock, and I wouldn't have been able to see any one of 'em.

Sank into the gloom and shadows in pairs. We'd kind of reshuffled our order of movement what with Barnes showing up and all. Old Bear and Three Bones led. Lucius and I followed them. Billy and Barnes came behind us, and Carlton brought the cannon up as quietly as he could.

He and Judith had spent several hours of extra effort greasing every part that turned. They'd tied down all the bits and pieces that might rattle, clink, or bump against one another. Covered the trace chains in strips of cloth ripped from Judith's mattress, and muffled the wheels with a layer of prairie grass twisted over the iron bands on the rims, then wrapped the grass with rope.

Just before he climbed up onto the ammunition chest, that feisty little gal grabbed Carlton and laid a lip-lock on the man that almost set his longjohns to blazing. He had it tough leaving her that morning. I knew exactly how he felt.

Last time I glanced over my shoulder, she had her rifle up at waist level, and motioned for Bully May to move back to his corner. Man might have had about as much in the way of brains as a wagon load of rocks, but he jumped over to his assigned spot real quick, scrunched up in the corner, and acted like he knew she would do exactly what I'd told her to do if he didn't. Just to be on the safe side, I left Caesar with her. Told him to bite Bully's ass off if he moved.

We pulled our animals up at the bottom of the craggy, rutted trail, dismounted, and waited for Carlton. Everything had gone so well, at first, it caused us to let our guard down a bit. Got a mite cocky, I suppose. But there were still no guards or lookouts in evidence. Couldn't hear any movement ahead. Place seemed deserted in spite of Old Bear's claim he'd heard noise about half a mile down the trail, and speculated at least a dozen men were somewhere ahead of us in the haze.

Since Three Bones wasn't actually an official member of the group, we left him to guard the horses, and the rest of us set out on foot. Pistols, rifles, and shotguns came out all around. Every weapon we carried was already primed and ready for action. I took my Winchester. Course Lucius favored his pistols, and must have been loaded down with at least six of 'em. Barnes lugged a long-barreled Greener with him. Carlton slid in behind us with Beulah/Irene, and kept the animals pulling the rig to something around a slower-than-molasses-in-January speed. Altogether, we were loaded for bear and itching for a fight.

Once the trail bled out into the gorge, a heavy crop of scraggly trees that desperately clawed upward for the sparse light closed in on both sides. Most of those leafy poles pushed their way out of the hard soil beneath our feet, but some clung precariously to the canyon walls by way of roots that grew from million-year-old cracks in the rusty-colored sandstone rock. Dense undergrowth about waist high clogged the limited space beneath the plants we silently passed, and a goodly bit of the scruffy stuff grew up the tree trunks and competed with the larger shrubbery for any available sunshine.

After about thirty minutes of creeping along like snails on walking sticks, visibility got considerably better. The foggy mist lifted to the point where I could make out individual bushes and rocks. We'd just brought everything to a halt at the edge of a stagnant, scum-covered pond on our right when unexpected things started popping.

From ahead of us, a clear strong voice with a slight halting quality to it charged up the trail and slapped us right in our surprised faces. "You—lawdogs think to come here—unknown. We hear 'bout you—weeks back."

Everyone scattered, and found himself a crusty rock or ivy-draped tree to hide behind as our unseen greeter went on like he was inviting us to an English tea party. Lucius had one side of a fractured depression in the easternmost wall, right next to me.

The voice got bolder. "Been—gettin' things ready— for you, Til—den. Yes. I know you. Me and Smilin' Jack—good friends—of Saginaw Bob Magruder's. Watched you and that Yankee disgrace Parker—kill our friend."

Guess Billy Bird had heard all he wanted. His patience with thieves and killers hadn't grown the slightest during the whole time I'd known the man. From behind a broken rock that looked like a totem pole about forty feet forward of my position, he yelled, "If you're so damned smart, then you know we're a posse of deputy U.S. marshals from Fort Smith. We have enforceable warrants for anyone we find in this rat's nest. You might as well throw your hands up now, and save us killing some of you."

Our invisible rival didn't miss a beat. From somewhere around an outcropping in the canyon wall on our left, he chuckled and fired back, "You funny man. Maybe you get job—with dancing bear act—I seen it once—in Fort Smith. You tell jokes. Do card tricks.

Dance a little jig. Sing some songs. Make people laugh. Pass the hat."

That really got Billy's goat. "You come out from behind that corner and we'll see who does any kind of a dance, you son of a bitch." A second or so passed and a deep-throated chuckle, followed by hearty laughter from several other concealed adversaries, floated down the canyon. Their amusement was loud enough even Three Bones should have heard it.

Out of the corner of my left eye, saw Barnes pressed against the canyon wall doing his version of the Comanche tiptoe in the direction of our otherworldly opponents. He made it to the shattered corner and peeked around about the time we all got an invitation. "You boys—come on in. Martin Luther Big Eagle, Smilin' Jack, W. J., and almost twenty more—we been waitin' for you. Soon as the sun gets some higher, Til—den, my boys up top gonna give you hell."

Lucius snapped a glance above us to a spot where the canyon's knifelike edge sliced across the sky. "Don't see anything, Hayden. But if he's got guns up there, we're gonna be in horse fritters eyeball-deep in about twenty minutes."

'Bout then, Barnes snaked his way back to our hollow from his scout. He weaseled up to me, squatted, and said, "You ain't gonna believe what I just saw, Hayden." He pointed to the bend in the sandstone wall he'd recently abandoned. "Once you get around that corner up ahead, there's a sharp break and a shallow depression that goes back about sixty yards. They must have moved a hundred ton of rock, dirt, and logs from somewhere. Made themselves a good-sized hill, and built a double-deep log-and-boulder castle on top of it. Here, it looks like this."

He took a stick and drew a straight line for a bit, then made a kind of half circle and continued on. Inside the depression he dropped a flat rock and said, "The fort's on top of the rock. It's backed right up against the canyon wall, and must have at least fifty gun ports sprinkled hit-or-miss fashion all over the front. Our talkative friend is standing in a kind of bell tower, right in the middle of the structure." He threw the stick down. "This is gonna be a real humdinger, Hayden."

Billy had scrambled his way back to us in time to hear Barnes's description of what waited. "Look," Billy said, and pointed to a spot across from Barnes's corner, "let's move Carlton's toy over to that point in front of the pond. We'll have a clear shot at *whatever*'s back there." He turned, scratched around in the dirt some, then smiled before he went on. "And just to give them something to think about, let's limber Beulah up right now and put two or three balls into the canyon wall over there where Barnes stole his peek at 'em. It'll rattle their eyeteeth right down to the sockets, and maybe make a few chinks in some of their smart-assed bluster."

Everyone nodded his individual agreement for the idea, and to setting it all up real quick. Carlton wheeled the gun around. We detached her from the ammo box, moved her to the flattest place we could find, and in pretty short order, Billy and Carl had beautiful Beulah loaded and ready to roar.

When I gave the signal, that big popper bellowed to

life and sent a shattering blast that ricocheted from one end of that gulch to the other, like the crack of God's own doom during a Kansas cyclone. It was the first shot fired in what would forever after be referred to as the Battle of Red Rock Canyon.

Got to give proper credit to our amateur artillery-men. They couldn't have launched that first ball into a better spot if they'd climbed up the wall on a rope and placed it by hand. That big lump of black iron hit the brittle rock about twenty feet from the canyon rim. The unnerving sound of cracking stone fell on everything below, and a giant column of it snapped from the force, split away, and moved almost five feet from the spot where it had been attached.

Carlton and Billy whooped and laughed like things insane. They lowered the barrel a bit, loaded her up in what had to have been a record minute or so, eyeballed everything one final time, and sent the second shot into the new crevice they'd just created. Must have hit the exact perfect spot right down to the smallest possible grain of dirt. That crimson, tree-shaped pillar looked like it had grown feet and could walk. When it finally stopped moving, the newly shaped post made it appear as though the canyon wall had grown itself a chimney. We all froze in place like bird dogs on the point.

Billy whispered, "I'll be dipped in snuff. If that won't blow air up your dress, I don't know what would."

"By Godfrey, I think I'm getting that Cletis Broad-bent disease." Carlton cackled and stroked Beulah's barrel as though she lived, breathed, and could purr.

Billy looked puzzled. "What disease is that?"

Carlton grinned like a possum eating peaches. "Think he infected me with his love of blowing thangs up. Hell, this is about as much fun as I've had in years without being drunk, completely nekkid, and covered with molasses."

From a spot only Barnes had seen so far, we heard panicked shouting. Then, a ferocious volley of rifle and pistol fire kicked up dust and chinked rocks forward of our position, but hell, they were just shooting at nothing.

The stupid gomers didn't have any better view of us than we did of them. But, hey, we had a much bigger fire-stick.

Then, Barnes came up with another great idea. "Let's move her up as far as we can and still be on this side of the corner. Carlton and Billy can put a couple of big'uns into the wall, back over on the south side of those boys, just to rattle their resolve a mite more. Bounce a few around over there, and I'd be willing to bet they get a lot more nervous than they already are—and pretty damned quick."

Lucius had himself all geared up for the fight, but observed, "I think maybe our talkative friend was lying about people up above. We might have caught them with their pants down, and he's just out to throw a bluff on us if he can. Bet they never got around to sending anyone up top. If he had guns up there, they'd already be dropping lead all over us. So I think we can do whatever the hell we want, and not have to worry overmuch about it."

Old Bear, who had come up and squatted beside Barnes, said, "Me and Three Bones saw no sign of men along canyon rim. Lucius is right. They might have known we were coming." He picked at his teeth with a splinter of wood and added, "But they didn't expect us today." He grinned like a man so happy he could barely stand it and added, "It's a good day to shoot a cannon, Tilden. Let's blast the hell out of 'em."

Everyone grabbed a piece of Beulah and leaned into the move. We got her set up, while our friends inside the stronghold kept pouring pointless torrents of lead into the ground and all around a spot about forty feet in front of the howitzer's newly established position. Some of them even decorated our recently transformed feature to the landscape with shots that accomplished absolutely nothing. Guess it must have made them feel better about their situation in the process. Carlton and Billy primed the gun again, while the rest of us found anything available to hide behind and covered our ears. Billy set her off that time.

Think someone might have added a thimble or so too much powder to the cartridge used on that shot. Or maybe it had held up better than its ancestors over the years since Cletis found it. Anyway, thunderation ruled. Boxed in like we were, that thing made a hell of a noise. Can't begin to imagine what those poor stupid devils inside their stick-and-stone refuge must have thought. Concussion sent red waves that looked like the ocean for sixty feet in front of the muzzle. That six-pound slug shot across the opening in front of their hidey-hole, hit a shelf of sandstone about fifty feet square on their south side that shattered, dislodged, and came down like a deafening echo of Beulah's report.

When the dust finally started to settle, things were

considerably quiet back there. Didn't hear any more of the smart-mouthed taunting we'd got at first. We formed up next to Beulah, and talked it over again. Lucius scrunched in beside me, and pointed to a stand of scruffy trees nicely grouped around a pile of waist-high boulders and rocky rubble that would give us a nice barricade of about twenty feet across. Located some thirty paces in front of the pond, the rocky refuge directly faced our objective and seemed to be awaiting our arrival. From all appearances you would have thought someone had known we'd need a place to set Beulah up and made sure we got it.

The lanky Texas Ranger stood with his thumbs hooked in his pistol belt. "We're gonna have to get over there, Tilden. Only place I can see where we'll have a completely clear shot at 'em from down here. If that don't work, we'll have to move Beulah back up top." His terse Texas drawl gave the impression we might have been discussing the various gradations of how to roll a handmade, rather than where best to locate an instrument designed to bring death and destruction to everything in front of its open mouth.

Barnes agreed. "What we can do is, two of us can wiggle over and lay down a little cover—maybe take they minds off what the rest of us be up to. Those back here will get everything set, and make a quick push to move the whole kit and caboodle into place."

Carlton scratched his chin. "It'll take two trips. Have to make one run for the gun, and another for the ammunition chest. Could get truly hairy out there, boys. Especially on our second jaunt. Them ole boys up the hill will have the range by then. Might get dusted pretty good. But what we could do is load Beulah up before the initial move, and then some of us can tote a few cartridges and balls for at least two, maybe three, additional shots."

Billy stood, glanced in the direction of our objective, and said, "Well, we ain't gonna get over there by sittin' here talking about it. Let's do it."

He and Old Bear volunteered to make the initial dash. Both of them carried an extra cartridge and ball. Lucius, Barnes, Carlton, and I were left to bring the cannon over. We had a relatively level, unobstructed track to run till we got to the trees. Getting everything under cover would be a minor problem. We were going to have to do it with a curtain of blue whistlers drilling deadly holes in the air all around us.

Our friends ducked from rock, to tree, to boulder, to stump, to anything they could hide behind till all the decent cover ran out. Then, they made the short sprint for the trees. My God, but the first seriously threatening shower of fire from that nest of vipers stunned us with its power and concentration. Billy and Old Bear had scarcely made cover when a lead scythe cut a deadly swath through everything around them. Tree limbs fell in piles and a steady shower of perforated leaves that looked like they'd been swarmed by a horde of angry cutworms dropped all around them.

Lucius shook his head. "Sweet jumping Jesus, Tilden, this little Pecos promenade might get a whole lot tougher'n we figgered."

Barnes jerked his hat off, and swabbed the sweat from his huge head with a blue and white bandanna. "When we starts in that direction, Hayden, we're gonna have to go fast. Not stop for nothin'. We get slowed down for a second—they'll chop us up like the kinda stuff you'd feed that big yeller dog of yours."

Carlton pointed to the space between our position and the trees. "If we're fast enough, they won't be able to see us but three, maybe four, seconds at the most. Let's give everything twenty minutes or so to die down a bit, then surprise 'em. We'll get Beulah primed and ready to fire, run like hell, set her up, and throw one their direction as quick as we can. It'll scare the blue-eyed hell out of 'em."

Lucius went to checking all his loads again. He'd not yet had chance to fire a shot. "You Arkansas boys got a thicker layer of bark covering your crusty asses than I ever imagined. Scares the hell out of me just thinking 'bout getting across that stretch of ground alive, after the last round of fire them boys delivered." He twirled a pistol on his finger, dropped it back into its holster, and grinned. "But hell, I'm the gamest rooster in the barnyard, so let's get to it."

We signaled Billy and Old Bear as how we were gonna wait a bit to come over. Once the general gunfire died out, the four of us—two on either side—lined up, grabbed a spot on Beulah's carriage tail, and on a silent signal from Barnes Reed, ran like Satan and all the imps from hell itself chased us. For two or three seconds, we must have caught Big Eagle's bunch flat-footed and unprepared. But they woke up and, good God Almighty, a hailstorm of bullets chinked or blasted damn near everything around us.

Lead bounced off Beulah's barrel, took chunks out of her wooden wheel and spokes on the side closest to the shooters, put holes in Barnes's hat, shirt, and pants leg, burned a nasty trench in Lucius's upper left leg, and left hot creases in a variety of places on all four of us.

Fortunately, as it turned out, they could lay down a blistering wall of fire, but couldn't shoot worth a damn. I landed beside Old Bear like a felled moose with a burning groove across my left shoulder and the back of my neck. Carlton lay beside me, twisted at the waist in an effort to get a partial view of his backside.

"Look at that." He was madder than a bucket of red ants, and pointed to a spot just below his pistol belt. A fuzzy, ragged rip across his behind had almost cut the canvas pants off the man. "One of them sons of a bitches come nigh on to shooting me in the ass! I been shot by the best of 'em in some pretty tender places, but damnation, ain't nobody ever shot me there afore! Something like that could make a man look real bad to other folks, Hayden."

In spite of all the rips, cuts, holes, and such, we had managed to make it to safety relatively undamaged. But that cavity in the seat of Carlton's pants really pissed the man off. He scuttled over to Beulah like an angry horned toad, and started jerking on the carriage tail in an effort to get her pointed the right direction. Man swore a purple streak from the ground all the way to heaven's gate during the process. We all stopped checking our individual gashes, tears, and bloody places, and helped him get her swung around. Took a few more minutes, hunkered over behind the pile of rocks that protected us, for Billy and Carlton to get the old girl lined up and sighted in to their recently acquired expert-cannon-shooter satisfaction.

Our friend lit his match and was about an inch from
setting her off when Barnes stopped him. "Carlton,
hand that'n to Old Bear. Let's give him a chance to
shoot her this time. Soon as she goes off, it's gonna
put up a curtain of smoke, and hopefully scare the living hell out of those boys over yonder. While they're
ducked for cover, the rest of us will go like hell for
the ammo box. When we get set to come back, you
send another one their way, and we can sneak over
behind more panic, confusion, and dust."

Well, everyone liked that suggestion a bunch. We
dropped most of our personal artillery, except for a
pistol apiece, and got down like runners about to start
a footrace at Fort Smith's Forth of July celebration.
Billy counted off from three, and Old Bear jammed the
match into the fuse hole. Behind a billowing cloud of
burnt black powder, rattling rocks, and flying dust, we
ran like hell. Big Eagle's bunch, up on their little man-
made hill, must have thought God himself had come
to visit when that ball hit the front of their place. They
didn't fire a shot. Not one!

Glanced their direction as I lumbered toward the
caisson. There couldn't have been more than 250 feet
or so from the cannon's muzzle to the front of the
rustic log castle. Beulah's present didn't lose any of its
velocity, and hit a spot dead center of the sixty-foot-
long front wall about three feet above the ground. The
resounding crack against the wood-and-rock-reinforced
barrier echoed out and up in an ear-rattling umbrella
of noise. The muzzle blast sent waves that vibrated
along the canyon floor like the ocean sweeping in on

a gale-racked beach. But the most surprising thing about the entire outlandish scene was, for all the accompanying noise, clouds of black smoke, and red dust, the damned ball bounced off that bark-covered barricade like a kid's marble ricocheting off a board fence.

Needless to say, I was disappointed with what appeared to be the final effect, but there was one positive result. Guess it scared the bunch of cutthroats inside bad enough. We managed to reach the ammo box with nothing more than a handful of poorly aimed rifle shots being thrown our direction. Lot of yelling, swearing, and hollering from behind their pile of logs and rocks while we got a grip on the caisson's tongue, and moved it into a good spot to launch our sprint back.

Once Billy had Beulah loaded and ready, he counted down on his fingers so we could see him. Got to one and set her off again. We jumped like a team of spooked horses, and managed to move the heavy wheeled chest to our natural fortress before Big Eagle and his boys even knew what happened.

Billy and Carlton had a field day for about the next hour or so. They must have loaded and fired that thing ten or fifteen times. The barrel got so hot, Lucius lit smokes off it, and Carlton decided he'd better stop for a while and let her cool off. When the noise, dust, and general hubbub finally died down a bit, we were stunned with what we saw. All that blasting had barely made a dent in the place. You could actually count the spots where the balls hit. Splintered eruptions in those stacked tree trunks stood out like puffy white clouds against a storm-darkened sky.

Carlton summed it up for all of us when he made clicking sounds between his teeth and mumbled, "Damn. I would never've believed we hadn't done any more damage than that. Guess Barnes was probably right from the beginning. That front wall has got to be at least two, maybe three, logs deep."

Barnes chuckled. "Yeah, but can you imagine what it must be like inside that place right now? Bet them ole boys is messin' they britches like a bunch of scared kids. Hell, I know I would be, if'n someone was blasting away at me with this leftover Civil War thunder boomer. Every shot you and Billy sent their way hit home. Rocked the entire canyon and house right down to its foundation. Might not look like we did much damage, but you can bet the farm they're shaking in their drawers right now."

Billy snorted and said, "Hell, these ole boys never figured on anything like Beulah. When the last rock went up against them walls, I'd bet everything I own they felt like nothing could ever get at 'em. That's why they let us in here without a fight. Way they had it figured, wasn't nothing to worry about, as far as they could see. But Martin Luther Big Eagle, Smilin' Jack, and all their sorry friends made a single, but serious, mistake in judgment. They didn't come anywhere close to planning on the hardcase likes of Hayden Tilden and Carlton J. Cecil showing up with a cannon."

Carlton sat with his back to Beulah's left wheel. "Well, fellers, we do have one surprise for 'em that even Tilden doesn't know I brought along." He grinned all around, crawled over to his mobile arsenal, fumbled about inside for a bit, and came back carrying two odd-looking cannon balls. "Cletis Broadbent slipped these to me on the side, Hayden. Said I might try 'em out just for the fun of it. Called 'em case shot. They're filled with gunpowder and slugs. Thing screwed in on top is a timer. You punch a hole in it, light the fuse, ram her down, and shoot. Six seconds should be about right. That'll give us time to get her loaded and ready to fire. We'll elevate the barrel so the ball explodes above the roofline. So much lead's gonna fall on those fellers, they're about think they're in an Arkansas hailstorm."

Don't know about anyone else there, but it sounded a shade on the risky side to me. "You sure about this, Carlton? We never tried one of these things when Cletis taught us how to shoot Beulah. From the sound of it, if you don't know what you're doing, you could blow us all to smithereens while you're trying to get her loaded." I could picture the cannon scattered around on the ground in jagged pieces on top of all our mangled, broken, bloody bodies if he made a mistake.

He cradled both balls in his left arm, pushed his hat to the back of his head, and winked. "Don't worry, Hayden. You sissy boys can hide behind this stingy pile of rocks while I try the first one. If it don't work, won't damage nobody but me. If it goes off like Cletis said it would, I've got five more of these killer weevils, and we'll send one their direction every so often to give 'em something else to worry about."

Well, naturally, Billy jumped in and offered to help him with what the rest of us felt bordered on a suicidal endeavor. Since Barnes had the most distinctive voice,

Carlton selected him to count off the seconds so he could get the fuse lit and the gun fired at the exact right moment. Things got damned tense around our hastily made cannon bastion and fortress for a bit. Fire from Big Eagle's bunch had died off to nothing more than some random sniping, if they thought they had a good target. Had to hand it to ole Carlton. It was a great time to come up with a plan like that. When I squatted down behind those rocks, hoped it would all shake out to our advantage, and I'd come up happy that he and Cletis had slipped something past me.

With my fingers in my ears, I peeked from my shelter, and watched as they swabbed the barrel out and loaded the cartridge. Billy's hand shook as he ran the pick in, poured some powder down the fuse hole, and got ready to fire. Carlton's face was drenched with sweat and rivers ran from under his hatband. But he flashed a big grin, struck a lucifer, and pointed to Barnes, who ducked and yelled "One!" On his easily heard shout of "Two!" Carlton lit the fuse, rolled the ball into the barrel, and pushed it home on "Three!" Billy fired it on "Four!" We all jumped up and snatched a peek over our wall of boulders, whispered "Five" and yelled "Six!" at the same time.

Damnation, it was something awesome to behold! That thing exploded about thirty feet above those bad boys' nest and sprayed lead in every direction. Slugs splattered into the sandstone wall overhead and behind their hideout. Billowing clouds of dust kicked up in front, on top, and all around their well-made fortifications in a solid sheet of instantaneous devastation and potential death. Looked like five hundred deputy

U.S. marshals with Winchester rifles fired on the place at the exact same moment.

Needless to say, got damned quiet over in the Big Eagle camp. In fact, they didn't throw another shot our direction for almost two hours. Guess they were talking the whole deal over at the time. That's one powwow I'd really liked to have been able to sit in on. Those ole boys thought no one could take them 'cause of the way they had their den of thieves and killers built. They'd evidently been controlling the canyon, and the area for fifty miles around, for more than a year. Guess Billy was right. Martin Luther and his lieutenants never figured on anything like our bunch and Miss Beulah, showing up outside their door with a death-dealing invitation to come out and play with the big boys.

Carlton and Billy acted like ten-year-old kids at a picnic. They giggled and slapped around on each other with their hats, then launched off into a deep and thought-provoking discussion about what they could do next with their toy. The jaw-wagging session finally ended when Billy said, "You know, Carlton, it's a shame Cletis didn't have any of that stuff they called canister shot. God Almighty, but I'd bet some of that stuff would get their undivided attention." They sat next to each other with their backs against the carriage tail, laughed, and started slapping on one other with their hats again.

Carlton finally stuffed his bonnet back on his head and muttered, "Canister shot. Son of a bitch! Why didn't I think of that? I'll bet Cletis had a pile of the stuff hid somewhere in that armory he called a barn. Hell, if we'd kept digging around, and asking questions, he'd probably have come up with a good-sized, flatcar-mounted field mortar or maybe one of them boats that can go underwater. Ain't no telling what that man's got hid out there on his place."

Billy looked confused and scratched his chin. "What the hell would we do with an underwater boat? Better yet, what the hell *is* an underwater boat?"

Carl looked up at me and winked. "Forget the underwater boat, Billy. Let me tell you one thing for sure-fire certain and true, though. I wouldn't want to be anywhere close to that battlefield pilferer of an Arkansas bootlegger's hardscrabble farm if his barn ever exploded. Probably kill every livin' soul for three or maybe even ten miles around, and leave a crater the size of downtown Fort Smith. Hayden and me came away from there with Beulah and some other goodies, but God only knows what else the man had hid. Bet he's probably got a Gatling gun in his chicken house."

A wistful look swept over Billy's face. "Damn. A Gatling gun. Now there's one toy I'd love to get my hands on."

Didn't take long after that for things to settle into one of those "You shoot at us some, you sons of bitches, and we'll shoot back at you for a bit" kind of dances. "And, oh, by the way, if you make us mad enough, we might hit you really hard with another of these six-pound slugs or a cascade of lead from one of Carlton J. Cecil's surprise case shots."

Once we managed to get at least some predictability built into everything, I sent Barnes back for Judith, Three Bones, and Bully May. They brought everything down, and set us up a fine camp and headquarters far enough back toward the entrance to be out of the line of fire. Stayed in a Mexican standoff for about four days.

Then, the morning of the fifth day, Big Eagle and his bunch woke up and realized they'd made an incredibly stupid mistake. The closest spot to them in that sparkling, spring-fed creek was at least fifty feet from any cover. That's when Smilin' Jack came out front carrying a white flag, and waited till I got to about twenty feet from him before he started laying it all out the way he saw it.

The evil son of a bitch had a ragged scar that ran across his neck from ear to ear. Looked like someone had tried to cut his head off with a hatchet. Man could barely speak above a raspy whisper. "Well, Tilden, you're still alive. I had hoped someone would've kilt you by now. Tried my best back when we first met at Drinkwater's Store."

The fingers of his right hand danced around the grips of the Colt pistol strapped high on his waist as he glanced over my shoulder. "See you brought that big nigger Barnes Reed with you. Actually, I thought I'd done for him and you at the same time. Coulda swore when I got away from Drinkwater's, you was both deader'n Methuselah. Have to admit I'm somewhat surprised you badge-totin' bastards are still amongst the living." His ear-to-ear grin made that hideous scar look like a second mouth. Man obviously felt like he held the pot winner, and didn't see any need to curb his tongue. That was the first time I'd been close enough to him to see the neck wound or that several teeth had gone missing from the front of his mouth.

"Well, Jack, I'm gonna be sure and tell Barnes what you said. I'm certain he'll find your reference to his heritage interestin' and informative."

He might have been dumber than a snubbin' post, and meaner'n a box of teased rattlesnakes, but the man knew an insult when he heard it. "Listen to me, you smart-mouthed son of a bitch, we've got a woman in here and not much water. So what we're gonna do is send her over to the stream any time we need a drink. If you or any of your men try anything funny—we'll shoot her right on the spot, and the deed'll be on your head."

Had to do some damned fast-on-my-feet thinking right then and there. Only thing I could come up with was: "Well, we've got a woman with us too, Jack. I'd like to send her over when Birdie comes out, so the two of them can talk a bit. Want to make sure you haven't mistreated your reluctant water-carrier."

"How'd you know my woman's name?"

"What difference does it make? Can Miss Karr come over or not? She'll stand on our side of the creek so as not to pose a threat to any of the big, bad men you have escorting Miss Blackwell."

He thought that one over for almost a minute before he finally relented. "Send your woman, Tilden. But make damned certain of one thing. You law-bringers take a stab at something like trying to rush my men and steal Birdie, and I'll have her guards cut 'em off at the knees. You git my more-than-obvious drift there, Marshal?"

"Sure, Jack, I understand. Couldn't get any plainer."

"Tell them others over there with you what I said. I

mean it, Tilden. My men'll be instructed to blast 'em
to kingdom come if any of your marshals step out
when the women are by the stream. Won't be no mercy
given."

When I got back and talked it over with Judith, she
couldn't wait. "Sure, Marshal Tilden, I'll do anything
you want. I'd do it anyway. God only knows what that
poor woman's had to deal with locked in with that
bunch of murderin' scum."

While the plan worked for me, and she couldn't have
been more willing to help, it didn't sit well with Carlton at all. I understood. Hell, if it had been Elizabeth,
I don't think I would have allowed it to be considered
for the first second.

He elbowed his way up between us and said, "Wait
just a damned minute there, Hayden. This whole idea's
nutty as hell. You can't be serious about sending Judith
out there. Ain't no way to predict what might happen
with this bunch of cornered barn weasels. Some of
those men are nuttier than a bag of circus peanuts."

She took him by the elbow, and kind of guided him
off to the side. Don't have any idea what she said, but
after that he gave up on the thing. I mean, you could
actually see it on him. He had this kind of sunken,
defeated look. Know it was just because he fretted for
her safety, but she wasn't to be denied, and tried to
soften her stony resolve about the whole thing with a
tender kiss on the cheek. Don't think it helped him
much, but personally I admired her for the gesture. No
way around it, Judith Karr proved herself a woman
with an impressive well of strength.

After the first few days watching poor Birdie Mae

scamper back and forth under the guns of her hairy, rough-as-a-shucked-cob escorts, I got to worrying that she could easily end up with less in the way of a pulse than a pitchfork. Then, the hard-as-nails Judith strutted back from one of their meetings with a rescue plan that shocked all of us right down to the soles of our boots. When Carlton heard what she had in mind, his cheeks turned a color you could have only duplicated on the face of a corpse and, honest to God, I thought he would pass out. Poor man swayed on his feet, and stumbled away like he'd had a stroke or something. Made garbled mumbling noises, flopped down on a rock, and cradled his head in his hands.

Billy shook his head. "It could work, but do you really want to do this, Hayden?"

"No! Have to admit I'd rather not. But the truth is we don't have any choice, Billy. Way things have gone so far, we could be here when the leaves fall if we don't do something—and damned soon. It's riskier than dancin' with Beelzebub's girlfriend, but I can't see any other way."

Billy's eyes narrowed down to slits. "Who the hell's Beelzebub? Or maybe I should have said what the hell is a Beelzebub?"

"Man from England wrote a poem 'bout two hundred years ago named *Paradise Lost*. Satan's right-hand man was a devil named Beelzebub. My mother used to read to me from that poem when she wanted me to behave myself. Scared the hell out of me."

"That's the reason I never miss a chance to go out on one of these tea parties with you, Hayden. I always learn something I never knew before. You're a walking, talking education all wrapped up in one man."

Judith's gaze swung from Billy to Carlton, and back to me. So I said, "If we could figure any other way, your offer probably wouldn't get the first consideration, Miss Judith. But I think we need to get Birdie away from that den of snakes as soon as we can. So, we'll try it."

Looked like someone put steel in that girl's already stiff spine. She stood ramrod straight with her shoulders back and said, "Good, now hand me two pistols and get everything ready. When the shooting starts, I don't want anyone back here making the kind of mistakes they'll end up regretting somewhere down the road. Does everyone understand?"

Gotta tell you, a pretty solemn bunch of tired, wrung-out marshals muttered, "Yes, Miss Judith."

11

"That's Smilin' Jack out Front"

JUNIOR SNAPPED A quick glance up from his scribbling and zeroed in on Lucius. The old Ranger had just finished doctoring his coffee again. He snaked the bottle back to its hiding place, and stirred the contents of his cup with the index finger of a trembling right hand.

"Is that the way you remember it, Mr. Dodge?" The boy winked at me as if to indicate he wanted my permission to include Lucius in the tale. I nodded and winked my total agreement right back at him.

"Well, son, you are one lucky man," said Lucius. "Anybody else, we're talking Carlton J. Cecil here mostly, would probably have a hell of a lot of fun out of this story, by padding it up with all kinds of self-enlarging heroics and blazing bullshit. From what I understand, there's still a good market for that kind of stuff. But I gotta hand it to old Tilden. He's keeping you pretty much on the straight and narrow path. Can't say as I've heard anything yet I'd strongly disagree with. But you know that's to be expected. Heard more than one of them other Arkansas lawdogs say Judge Parker loved it when Hayden had to testify in his court."

The still-steaming cup rose to meet his smiling lips, and hovered there like a drunken hummingbird for a second, while he puckered up and blew whiskey-scented steam my direction. Before he partook of the treat, he said, "Yes, sir, I remember Carlton telling me, one time, the Judge always said if only one man worked the Nations whose word he could absolutely trust—that man was Hayden Tilden." The cup lightly touched his lips. He sucked and slurped at the hot liquid a time or two before he sighed his approval, took a healthy gulp, then wiped his lips on his sleeve.

Lightfoot glanced back at me, and ran his fingers through rapidly thinning hair. Found something he didn't like and scratched at it for a moment and said, "There is one thing that really bothers me about this fracas so far, boys."

"And what might that be, Junior?" I knew from the way he squinted and stared at the ceiling fan that a seriously thought-out, but likely idiotic, question was about to follow.

"Since hindsight is perfect, don't you think that Big Eagle and his men were just a shade stupid to let themselves get hemmed up at the bottom of a box canyon the way they did? I mean, you know, it sounds like when it comes to stupid, that decision was the equivalent of going fishing with a shotgun."

Lucius kind of chuckled from somewhere deep in his belly, then back up through his chest till he laughed so hard he almost dropped his heavily spiked mug of go-juice. Good thing he didn't. That stuff could have stood up on its own and walked around the sun porch.

He coughed, wiped his chin with a bandanna he hauled from his hip pocket, and said, "Hell, yes, Mr. Lightfoot. No doubt about it. When it came to smarts, if that whole damned crew's brains had been made out of printer's ink, they wouldn't have collectively had enough thinker power to put the dot over the first *i* in one of their own wanted posters."

Then, he made a flashy production out of lighting one of those long thin cigars he'd always liked so much before he continued with his rant. "See, you made the same mistake decent folk always do when it comes to bloodletters and bad men. Most people just naturally think thieves and killers are downright intelligent. Hell, boy, I'd be willing to bet that Hayden and me ain't seen more'n two or three smart outlaw types between us. Guess maybe the most inspired thing Big Eagle and Smilin' Jack pulled in Red Rock was sending that poor girl out for their water. We couldn't shoot her, and even though we didn't really believe they would carry through on their threats to rub her out, we couldn't take a chance and grab her ourselves. After about the fourth or fifth day, she had to make that trip a half a dozen times, every morning and every afternoon. All we could do was sit behind our rocks and watch while Judith Karr ran out to meet her and talk a little."

Knew outlaw stupidity couldn't be all my young reporter friend had on his mind, because he still looked like a dog lying in the yard with something between his feet he'd never seen before. "Where were their horses during all that initial shouting, shooting, and general mayhem?" he asked.

Lucius motioned at me with his cigar like he'd talked all he wanted for a while and was inviting me to jump back in. "Now that's a good question, Junior," I said. "But you're gonna have to wait a bit for a definitive answer. See, we wondered the same thing after we'd been at the bottom of Red Rock Canyon for little more than an hour or so. None of us could figure it out at first. But Birdie had to make so many trips every day, I got to figuring Big Eagle must have his animals inside the fort or behind it somewhere."

We put the final showdown off until the fifth day after Smilin' Jack laid down the law about Birdie's water-gathering. Almost started the fandango on the fourth day, but it took Carlton and Billy most of that one to get into a good position. They carried our box of Ketchum grenades, and made their way out of Red Rock and around to a spot on the east side of the canyon wall. Way we had it planned, when they finally settled in, they'd be directly above Smilin' Jack and Big Eagle's den of thieves like a pair of bomb-throwing guardian angels watching over us. The delay kind of lulled that bunch of low-life slugs into a false belief that they had us over a female barrel, and we'd eventually have to give it up, turn tail, and drag our failed asses back to Fort Smith.

Carlton didn't like leaving Judith a damned bit, but I finally persuaded him it would be better for the safety of both of them if he went with Billy. Personally, given the plan she'd outlined, I feared he might do something impetuous and dangerous enough to get them both killed if he stayed. We'd laid it on for Billy and him to hold off taking any action until they heard the first cannon shot, once our Pecos promenade got started. When Beulah spoke, they were to toss all those paper-tailed rockets over the edge as fast as they could, get back down to the canyon floor quick as their horses could carry them, and shoot the hell out of anybody they didn't recognize along the way.

Damn near broke my heart as I watched him and Judith say their good-byes. She took Carlton by the hand and led him to a shaded spot under a huge maple tree near the creek. Know they thought no one watched, and I probably shouldn't have done it, but couldn't help myself. Their parting reminded me of how much I missed Elizabeth, and her fears for my safety.

An amazing thing occurred as they whispered their newly found love in each other's ears. I saw one of those hat-sized orange and black butterflies land in Judith's hair. Strange, because I'd not noticed any of them before that moment, and didn't see another afterward. Somehow Carlton coaxed the thing onto his finger, then presented it to her like a living gift more precious than all the gold in California. Sunlight, filtered through a wispy curtain of mist and dust, formed a halo around them as they kissed good-bye. Others may think what they want, but I took it as a sign of blessing from a power far beyond anything most of us ever understand, and knew from the moment their lips parted everything would work itself out.

They talked for so long, I began to think he might not go. But I guess she persuaded him it was the best thing for everyone concerned. Over the course of her numerous visits with Birdie Mae, she'd developed a close connection to Elizabeth's unfortunate friend. And though it might have been wrong, I got the impression Judith felt a deep need to help the poor woman, even if such actions might result in the forfeiture of her own life.

Took Billy and Carlton the rest of that day and most of the night to get to the spot we'd all agreed would be to our best advantage when the shooting started up again. Next morning, I spotted them through my long glass. They both waved a Ketchum to let us know they were ready for the dance to start.

Judith strolled over and visited with Birdie Mae, the first three times she made the water runs that morning, like nothing was amiss. After her third trip, she slipped past me and said, "Get everything ready, Marshal. We'll start this Arkansas shootaree the next time she comes out."

Lucius, Barnes, and Old Bear manned Beulah. They'd all seen enough to know as much about firing her as any of the rest of us, and I felt comfortable with the decision. So, at about one o'clock in the afternoon, Birdie and her escorts made their way around the south end of the stronghold. She had a wooden bucket in each hand and, even from a distance, had a bone-weary look on her that started with sagging shoulders and drooped downward in a wave of obvious exhaustion.

Judith didn't hesitate a second. She stepped from our wall of rocky cover and hurried toward the stream. Behind her back, tiny hands filled with pistols rested on her swaying hips. She made it to the creek at a point that might have been a little over a hundred feet from our position. It was as close as she could lure them in our direction and not arouse suspicion. Birdie and her guards ambled over to the spot Judith picked—and never gave it a second thought.

While the obviously drained and agitated hostage filled her first bucket, Judith laughed, talked, and passed the time the same way she had on numerous prior occasions. Then, as I watched though my glass, both her hands came up at the same time. The guns were already cocked. For about half a heartbeat both those boys got a look on their faces like they had put their bucket down a well and pulled up a skunk. Before they were even able to twitch, that ironbound girl blasted those bandits quicker'n you could blow out a candle. Most men I knew weren't that great firing from each hand at the same time. Judith made it look easy. Those boys were still on their way to the ground when she stuffed the pistols into her belt, jumped into the middle of that three-foot-deep stream, grabbed Birdie by the hand, and started pulling her toward safety.

I turned to Barnes and yelled, "Let 'er rip." He jammed a flaming wick into Beulah's fuse hole. Before anyone in Big Eagle's camp had a chance to blink twice, our Civil War holdover roared to life, and delivered the six-pound message Carlton and Billy were waiting for. Ball smacked into Big Eagle's front wall just as Judith and Birdie Mae fell safely behind our pile of stacked shale and busted rocks.

Never saw any of them Ketchums fall, but my glorious God, explosions ripped from one end of that log fort to the other so fast it even shocked me. Judith grinned as both women covered their ears.

Think we had eight of them Ketchum-type bad boys. Guess they were so old, several didn't go off. But at least five blew holes in the roof. A couple started instantaneous, quickly spreading fires, and even knocked a pair of gaping fissures in the massive front wall.

Well, that's when we found out where they'd hid their horses. 'Bout thirty seconds after Judith jerked Birdie to safety, at least ten mounted men poured from behind their wrecked, burning fortress and headed for the entrance in a dead run. All of a sudden, Big Eagle's nest looked like an anthill some mean-assed kid had stomped on for fun. Those murderous bastards rode with the reins in their teeth and pumped a stream of buzzing death our direction from pistols in each hand. Since there was only about a hundred feet between our position and the rock walls, they went by us to our left in single file. Offered up a series of mighty inviting targets.

Over a deafening den of racket from the combined screaming, shouting, and shooting, I heard Barnes yell, "Dammit, Hayden, that's Smilin' Jack out front!" All of us jumped up and fired their direction as fast as we could thumb 'em off. Three of their horses went down at the same time, and the four immediately behind stumbled over those. Pretty quick we had seven men on foot, some of them wounded. Two from the tail end of the parade managed to make it past the tangled pile of men and thrashing animals that heaved and flopped in every direction. Smilin' Jack and that amazingly lucky pair of bandits who didn't stumble got to the trees before we could drop any of 'em.

Lucius started running and screaming at the same time. "One of them three sorry sons of bitches was W. J. McCabe." The two of us made it to Hateful and Gunpowder at about the same time.

Barnes tried to keep up, but realized someone had to stay behind. Heard him shouting directions at Old Bear and Three Bones to get all those wounded or dazed under the gun as quick as they could. Lucius and me kicked hell out of our animals, and headed for the canyon entrance.

We boiled out of that hole in the ground like Mexican scorpions on the prowl. Lucius let Hateful have her head. Gunpowder and me had a tough time keeping up. Smilin' Jack, W. J., and a fancy-dressed outlaw who wore a derby hat were about half a mile ahead of us going straight for sunset. They blasted through the grass on those rolling hills like a Kansas City fire engine.

We chased 'em as hard as horses could run. Then, when things finally started to slow down some, that Indian-fightin' Texican put them silver rowels to Hateful for one final spurt of muscle-burning energy. He tied his reins to the saddlehorn, snatched a couple of those Colt's Dragoon pistols from their pommel holsters, and shot two of their horses from under them quicker'n small-town gossip at a Baptist church social.

We pulled up to a clod-scatterin' stop on W. J.

McCabe and the derby-wearing feller. Lucius had 'em covered before they could get their wind back from the fall. He grinned and said, "Well, I got mine, Tilden. Yours is still running." He waved in the direction of Smilin' Jack, just as the man disappeared into the cover of a gully. Few seconds later he reappeared, but had slowed considerably as he fought for a path up the next hill about five hundred yards away.

"You're right about that one, Lucius. But he ain't gonna be running too much longer." Pulled the .45–70, stepped down, and flipped the peep sight up in the same motion. Stroked Gunpowder's neck to get him settled, rested the rifle on my saddle, put some spit on the front sight, and while Smilin' Jack struggled up the steep rise, I waited for about ten seconds to get a clear shot.

By that point Lucius had his captives completely corralled and properly humbled. Pretty soon everything around me got about as still as a sack of flour. Just before I pulled the trigger, I whispered, "Owe you this one, Jack. Consider it a serious equine retribution from a horse named Thunder." Winchester delivered a massive hunk of metal that hit that poor bangtail nag just behind the withers and knocked it sideways about a foot. Unfortunate beast landed on the hard ground like a village blacksmith's anvil dropped from the roof of a barn. Got to hand it to Gunpowder. Big sucker didn't even twitch when the rifle went off. He'd definitely done more than his share of hunting somewhere before we met.

Lucius pushed his hat back with the barrel of one of his Dragoons and said, "Sweet Jesus, Tilden."

Sheathed the rifle, and jumped back on board. "Yeah, Lucius. Those are my sentiments exactly. But he had that one coming—in spades. Be back shortly."

Eased up on Smilin' Jack real slow. Somehow he'd managed to get himself under the horse when it landed. He kept shooting off his pistol at any sound he heard, but given the man's limited range of motion, he didn't do much but damage the air in general.

Stopped thirty yards from the belly side of his dead animal and shouted, "Better give it up, Jack. You know I'll kill you—for damn sure—if you don't stop all your indiscriminate blasting."

"You can go to hell, Tilden. I've got enough kat-ridges to hold you off for a week."

"You'll be dead in exactly ten seconds if you don't toss your pistol over to me, Jack." For all his huffing and puffing, he got pretty quiet after my gritty threat. Counted off the time from ten. Told him I'd blow his brains out on one. When I got to three he cursed my mother, my father, all my living—and dead—relatives, Judge Parker, several former Presidents of the United States, and everyone else he could lay his tongue to. That streak of blue language by its lonesome should have assured his place in Satan's banquet hall. Pistol came flying over his dead horse like a wounded bat when I shouted "two!"

Slipped up on him afoot. Made certain he didn't have any more weapons at hand. Afterward, it took me, Lucius, and both those other boys to get that poor dead hay-burner off the busted-up outlaw. Fall broke both Jack's legs and mashed him up pretty bad. We scrounged around, and found enough limbs down in

the gully to build a pole drag to get him back to Red
Rock. Man screamed and moaned every step of that
short trip.

Lucius and I felt certain he would never make it
back to Fort Smith. Hell, I didn't give a tinker's damn
whether he got back to civilization or not. More the
sorry bastard suffered, the better I liked it.

Barnes, Old Bear, and Three Bones had all Jack's
living friends shackled and chained by the time we
made it to the canyon floor again. Amazingly enough,
we'd only killed two of them. Martin Luther Big Eagle
got himself blown into several fairly equal chunks
when one of Carlton's grenades hit the roof right above
his head and scattered him all over about half his
stunned cohorts. According to an introducing scamp
named Parrot Head Johnson, he'd been standing not
ten feet from Big Eagle when the explosion shot down
through the timber and mud-covered roof like God
himself had stepped on his unfortunate friend's head.

Johnson's hands still shook when he said to me,
"Damnedest thang I ever done seen, Mr. Tilden. Didn't
get to do no fightin' back yonder in the Civil War. So,
I ain't got nuthin' to compare it against. But I gotta
tell ya, Marshal, it can sure as hell get a man's attention
when the feller he's a talking with's head disappears.
I'm still thankin' Jesus it didn't fall on me."

Final count came to twelve captured—four of them
wounded—two extremely dead, and most everyone
with his share of cuts, bruises, scratches, and bloody
wounds. Didn't get anywhere close to the twenty or
more Big Eagle had claimed the day we arrived. Far
as I was concerned, it was just further evidence he

rarely opened his mouth without lying. When Billy and
Carlton made it back, we put the eight who could still
get up and around to scratching in the wreckage, just
in case they might have forgot about some of their
companions. But they didn't find anyone else.

Most remarkable thing about that whole episode was
the corral cut into the stone behind their stronghold.
The room proved large enough to hold at least twenty
animals, and couldn't be seen from our position down
by the pond. But I gotta tell you, it smelled mighty
bad by the time we blasted them boys out of that place.
Don't take long for that many horses to produce
enough meadow muffins to pile up pretty deep and
odiferous.

Started back for Fort Smith the next day, after Billy
and Carlton planted dynamite everywhere they could
find a hole in the ground. Set an extremely long fuse,
and we had gone almost a mile east of the entrance
before we heard the explosion. My God, but it shook
the ground like one of them earthquakes I'd heard they
have so often out in California. Blast couldn't have left
more than three or four twigs stacked on top of each
other. Those fun-loving boys put so many of them
flame-red sticks under what was left of Big Eagle's
logs, their final efforts at blasting turned the whole
thing into a hazy cloud of blood-tinted powder that
shot up over the invisible canyon rim like a Pacific
Island volcano belching gas and fire.

Barnes went back out to Red Rock about a year after
our adventure. He told me you could barely find a
stone fragment left down there that was much bigger
than a saddle blanket for a brown dog tick. Said those

last few detonations caused the cave those murderin'
thieves used as a stable to collapse and create a massive
cavity in the east side of the canyon. Left a scar that
had been considerably smaller before our arrival.
Guess some folks might call our activities destructive,
but we didn't want to have another bunch come in right
behind Big Eagle and get resettled anytime soon. Besides, Barnes said travelers used the spot as a shelter
when they camped there on the way west, and had
named it Tilden's Hole.

Hard to believe, but folks on those western treks
even named the sandstone totem Carlton and Beulah
created with the first two shots. Called it Walking
Rock. Still standing today, from what I hear. Got trees
growing in the fissure, but you can find it if you look
hard enough.

Old Bear and Three Bones stayed around until Carlton and Billy's final display of fireworks. The little
Kiowa really enjoyed all the noise, dust, and movement. Three Bones pointed and talked in his own language for long stretches. Old Bear smiled and patted
his friend on the shoulder. Think he got almost as big
a kick out of Beulah as Carlton.

Maybe an hour or so after the last big explosion,
they pulled up and dismounted. Old Bear led his friend
over to me and said, "Three Bones has something he
wants to say before we head south."

Mahogany-skinned fighter held his arms out like he
wanted to hug me. When I extended mine, he clasped
me by the elbows and spoke for almost a minute before
he stopped. Then, he smiled, nodded, and stepped back
beside Old Bear and waited for the translation.

"He says—this best time he's had—since his people forced to come to the Nations. Reminded him—of the life he's missed—for many years—life of a warrior— life of a man respected by those who fear him. If you ever need his help—if you have need of a *warrior*— you send word." Old Bear placed his left hand on his friend's shoulder. "Says he would be honored to die with you, Tilden."

Well, a lot of men have said a lot of things to me over the years since the day we stood on that grass-covered hill. Good and bad. Don't think anyone else ever told me it'd be an honor to stand by my side and die with me. Powerful stuff. For a while, I couldn't think of anything to say in reply. How do you respond to a man who honors you in such a fashion?

Finally, I managed to mumble, "You tell Three Bones I won't forget him, and that it has been a great privilege fighting by his side. We will meet again. And tell him I'd be honored to have him with me anytime." Hugged Old Bear 'cause I didn't know when he'd show himself in my life again. They mounted up, waved their rifles in one final salute, and kicked it south for the Kiowa, Comanche, and Apache Nations.

Every one of the evil sons of bitches we brought to book was wanted. Five of them bad enough to have posters out that offered nice rewards. Most valuable of the group, after Smilin' Jack and Big Eagle, was a killer named Orpheus Black. Orpheus had been cap-tured before. Even got jerked up short with a convic-tion of murder for killing a farmer named Abraham Neely and a Negro woman in his employ. Poor folks lived on a vegetable and grain farm over in the Chickasaw Nation near the town of Stonewall.

Orpheus stopped at Neely's home on a lightning-spiked night back in '78. Killed the poor man with an ax he found in the yard, then beat Jezabelle Boston to death with a stick of stove wood. Stole a pair of boots, Neely's coat, and the woman's pantaloons. Neighbors who testified at the trial said the poor woman had so many splinters in her scalp, they thought she might grow leaves. Judge sentenced him to hang, and Maledon braided up a rope for him. But he got loose, killed a jailer in the process, and stayed out on the scout until we brought him down at Red Rock.

Court found him guilty of another killing done after his bold escape. Judge Parker sentenced him to hang again. But late in 1883, that got commuted to life over at the federal penitentiary in Detroit, Michigan. Sorry son of a bitch should have hung at least twice, but got off because men with a lot less intestinal fortitude than Judge Parker got their bleeding hearts involved, and saved his worthless hide one more time. But thanks to Providence, it just didn't matter. Another convict caught ole Orpheus sittin' in the outhouse one day, and stuck a piece of sharpened water pipe in his left eye that punched a hole in his brain and ended his days on this earth.

Story of our adventures got to Fort Smith ahead of us. The *Elevator, New Era,* and the *Western Independent* were full of it. Even heard some of the Indian papers like the Atoka *Indian Champion* and the Vinita *Indian Chieftain* ran extravagant versions of the tale. Must have been a hundred people on the ferry dock when we arrived. Spotted Elizabeth while I was still on the other side of the Arkansas. She almost waved her arm off before I could get to her. Don't think anything in the world feels like holding a woman who loves you. I kissed every square inch of her glowing face. Then turned and said, "Brought someone you know back with me."

Birdie Mae Blackwell rushed past me, fell on Elizabeth's neck, and burst into grateful tears. Never seen two people cry like that. Elizabeth stroked the poor girl's hair and mouthed "Thank you" at me. Altogether, it was the best reward I ever got. Money just can't match a blond-haired, blue-eyed woman with tears streaming down her cheeks whose gratitude would be flowing my way for some time to come.

We put W. J. McCabe down in the holding cells with all them other black-hearted villains. Lucius stuck around for about a week. Then one morning, he showed up on the porch for breakfast. Wolfed down six eggs, three biscuits, and most of a slab of bacon. Mixed some whiskey in his coffee, leaned his chair against the wall, gazed off toward the river, and said, "You are one lucky man, Tilden. Beautiful wife who loves you, house on the hill with a view right out of a dream, and a town full of people who think you walk on water. Don't get much better'n that. Hope you're properly grateful."

Poured myself a cup, motioned for his bottle, and said, "Lucius, if you had told me things would come out like this on the day Saginaw Bob shot me over at Winchester, I would have laughed right in your face. Probably sound like a court-certified loony from the state hospital for the criminally crazy over in Little Rock." Leaned over and tapped my cup against his.

He finished off his coffee and shook my hand and said, "If you ever make it to Fort Worth, look for Company B of the Texas Rangers. They'll help you find me no matter where I am. By the time you get down there, everyone who knows me will know who you are. You'll be treated to the best Texas has to offer in hospitality and respect. It's been a privilege, Marshal Tilden."

He did his Texas mosey across the plank floor and down the steps. Big Mexican rowels on his silver spurs sang a right nice song when no one was shooting at us. Pulled the reins loose from my hitch rail, turned like he was lost in deep thought, and said, "You know, think I just might swing by Willard Rump's place and visit for a bit with Eleanor Little Spot. That is, if her daddy and mama will allow it." He grinned, tipped his palm-leaf sombrero, jumped on Hateful, and hoofed it to Fort Smith. Billy said our Texican friend picked up ole W. J. about an hour later, and headed back to the Lone Star State. Several years passed 'fore we saw each other again.

Cecil and I took Beulah back to Cletis Broadbent a few days after that. He damn near had a stroke when he saw all them bullet holes in her wheels and carriage. But when Carlton started peelin' ten-dollar bills off a stack I'd given him before our arrival, ole Cletis's eyes got about the size of pewter dinner plates. He quickly settled for a lump-sum payment, and a nice bonus, for the piddling damage his plaything had sustained. Hell, the scruffy bootlegger was happier'n a hog in slop when we left him standing in his nasty yard, knee-deep in screaming kids, barking dogs, and chickens.

Of course, us deputy marshals had to testify at the trials of all those worthless gobs of spit we'd caught out there at Red Rock. Spent a lot of time sitting around on cane-bottomed instruments of torture waiting to tell the same story over and over again. Don't remember a whole lot about most of those trials, because they involved petty criminals of the thieving and bootlegging variety. But I do remember what Judge Parker said the day he sentenced Smilin' Jack.

He leaned over the edge of his desk and almost shoved his index finger up Paine's nose. Thought there for a second the Judge would hook it into one of Jack's nostrils and jerk him off the floor. "Your numerous crimes have been proven in this court beyond any question. Evidence has shown you to be a man of repulsive and abhorrent character. The jury heard grisly tales of murder and rape by your hand. These lurid accounts have inflamed local citizenry to the point where open discussions of lynching have been reported to my own ears. Such actions on the part of the public will not be necessary, or tolerated, so long as I sit on this bench. It is only through respect for the law, and the certain belief that justice will be carried out by it, that you are not today hanging from a tree somewhere outside the city limits, and already in the hands of your close friend Satan.

"The enormity and stunning wickedness of your criminal activity leaves no ground for sympathy, sir. You can expect no more compassion than experienced by those victimized by your dastardly behavior. Perhaps God can bestow mercy upon your head. His infinite understanding, care, and grace can wipe out even your horrible crimes. The sinful activities for which you are guilty rest upon your hateful soul. I beseech you to seek atonement for your revolting actions and sincerely hope you find it.

"But it falls upon this court to carry out the sentence required by the laws that you have broken. Listen now to the sentence of the law, which is that you, Alonzo Jackson Paine, for the crimes of murder and rape committed by you in the Indian country and within jurisdiction of this court, and of which you stand convicted by the verdict of a jury in your case, be deemed, taken, and adjudged guilty of said crimes and hanged by the neck until you are dead.

"The Marshal of the Western District of Arkansas, by himself, or deputy, or deputies, shall cause execution to be done in these premises upon you on the thirty-first day of October 1882, between the hours of nine o'clock in the forenoon and five o'clock in the afternoon of that day. May God, whose laws you have broken, and before whose tribunal you shall then appear, have mercy upon your immortal soul." He punctuated all that with a gavel rap that sounded like a pistol shot.

Paine, who still suffered mightily from the injuries he'd incurred when his horse fell on him, gathered up enough fire to snap back, "I want to appeal my verdict to the Supreme Court, Your Honor."

A wicked smile snapped across the Judge's face. "Thought you would, Alonzo. But believe me when I tell you, sir, my prosecutors will fight it tooth and nail.

In the end you will hang, and everyone who is even remotely interested will get to watch your departure from this life."

Unfortunately, that happy dream didn't come to pass. Alonzo Jackson Paine, called Smilin' Jack by those who feared the son of a bitch, died in his jail cell from a bout of pneumonia barely a month later. Needless to say, Mr. Maledon, the court's official hangman, and his admirers expressed considerable dismay and disappointment at being cheated of their entertainment.

Jack's passing made Carlton so mad he went on a spitting fit you could only match by watching tomcats fight. Think that's part of the reason he never forgot about Paine. And then again, it might have been because about six months after our return, he and Judith Karr stood before Judge Parker in the living room of my home and got married. The way those two looked at each other that day was enough to give even the most downhearted hope for the future.

Elizabeth held my hand, wept, and repeated her vows in my ear as we stood and watched. That beautiful couple stayed together for over fifty years. Think when Judith died it damn near killed Carlton too. But something kept him alive long enough to finally rise above the black funk that fell on him. Maybe it was the fact he spent most of that time with me. Don't know. No point in trying to understand God's plan. We just have to live it.

Birdie Mae lived with Elizabeth and me for almost a year. Thought she'd recovered fairly well. Then, suddenly, she jumped up and moved to Kansas City. Said she wanted to be somewhere a bit more civilized than a dusty frontier outpost like Fort Smith for a while. Personally, I've always held that the married man she ran off with, Marvin Upshaw, was the sole and only reason for her departure. Unfortunate decision, actually. In 1893, if memory still serves, she stepped into Westport Road right in front of the Wyoming Street Saloon and got hit by a runaway team of horses pulling a beer wagon. Killed her deader'n a cut-glass doorknob.

Elizabeth cried for a week. Never had the heart to tell her how local authorities wrote me that Birdie took the road of the soiled dove and was well-known to all the men of local law enforcement. Seems Marvin heeled it for parts unknown about six months after they arrived, and she took to heavy drink and certain easily obtainable painkilling drugs. Tragic, just damned tragic.

Don't think Junior's pencil made a mark during the entire time I tied everything up for him. Stared at me like a man who'd been hit in the face with a ten-pound bag of meadow muffins.

He finally made this kind of strangled frog sound and said, "God, every time I think you can't shock or surprise me anymore, you manage to do it again, Hayden. Carlton's assessment of the Nations was dead accurate. Hell on earth. Seems like everyone touched by the place suffered the tortures of the damned while still among the living."

After dragging himself out of his chair, he started for the door, but stopped and turned back toward the two empty shucks whose stories had helped fill his notebook. "How is it, do you think, that what Carlton described as 'hell in the Nations' didn't have the same effect on you boys as it did on all these other poor people?"

I turned to Lucius and shrugged. His watery, red-rimmed eyes squeezed a single tear loose that trailed down a cheek the boy couldn't see. "Oh, make no mistake about it, Mr. Lightfoot," he said. "It affected us as profoundly as it did any of these others—perhaps even more so. The most telling difference between Hayden, or men like me, and them, was we had the responsibility of trying to save everyone we could, and didn't have time to dwell overmuch on our individual tragedies." He stopped long enough to consult the contents of his cup again, then added, "Course we outlived all of them too."

Lightfoot took a step back into the room. "What individual tragedies did you suffer from all this, Lucius? From what I've heard so far, you came out of the whole affair in pretty good shape."

My old friend stared into his cup for a second and took another heavy swallow. "Well, one thing Hayden, gentleman that he still is, didn't say anything about was how my visit with Eleanor Little Spot went."

Lightfoot's eyes narrowed down on the old Texas Ranger like drawn pistols. "What the hell does that mean?"

Lucius ran his finger around the rim of his cup. It made a soft humming sound. "When I got there, her parents took me straight out to visit her grave, son. Seems she'd stepped on something sharp hiding in their chicken-shit-covered yard. Got the lockjaw.

Sweet, beautiful girl died a horrible death. Still remember how she looked when she smiled at Handsome Harry and me. Even after all these years, her face still pops up in my better dreams."

For several seconds, it got so quiet you could hear the schoolhouse clock out at the nurse's station. Twisted toward Junior and said, "That'd be a great title for this chapter, don't you think?"

He looked surprised. Like I'd snapped him back to reality from someplace he'd visited before, but hadn't thought of much. "What would be a great title?"

"*Hell in the Nations,* Junior. *Hell in the Nations.*"

His face lit up like a ball from a Roman candle. "Damn, you're right." He turned and ran for the door. Over his shoulder he shouted, "Look for it about a month from now. *Hell in the Nations—Chapter Two in the Life and Times of Hayden Tilden!* Good God, boys, people are gonna love this stuff."

EPILOGUE

LUCIUS SPENT A whole week with me. Stayed in a guest room right there in the Rolling Hills Home for the Aged. Hell, he was as bad as Carlton when it came to nurses and young women in general. Actually, sometimes he was worse, because he'd managed to stay in a lot better shape than Carl, and those poor girls had a harder time hoofing it away from him. He could still dance pretty fast for an old dude.

Silver-tongued elf talked me into going back to Texas for a visit on his Sulphur River ranch. Since I enjoyed the freedom commanded only by inmates voluntarily committed to that cell block for those awaiting eternity, it didn't take much in the way of expended effort to persuade Leona to turn me loose. Oh, I did have to threaten to shoot her in the foot a time or two, but she finally relented. Mainly 'cause she had good-sized feet. Think we sealed the deal in her office one afternoon when Lucius whipped out one of them big ole .45's, and told her he was still a pretty fair shot even at his advanced and decrepit age.

Took the Flyer from Little Rock to Texarkana. Had a great time on the way down. Met a couple of real nice-looking middle-aged ladies in the club car who came out to the ranch and visited with us twice while I was there. One of them was a blue-eyed blonde. And hell, you already know my feelings 'bout girls like that. Her name was Kathleen.

Lucius had an ancient rattletrap of a truck parked in the depot lot. Surprised the hell out of me that he could still drive. Took us about an hour and a half of paved back roads that bled out to gravel, then turned into dirt trails, 'fore we finally arrived. But, hell, bubbas, it was damned sure worth it. Barn, corral, and all were in fine shape. Well-kept and recently painted, from all I could tell.

Ranch house had a screened back porch that looked right out onto the river, and we spent every evening snugged down into a couple of broken-down wicker chairs, sipping our coffee and remembering all the things we missed about the past. Mostly, though, it was the people. Ain't much about living back then that was real good—'cept the people we loved. And some we very definitely hated.

When it got too cold outside, we'd move to his tiny living room where he kept a tin stove. He'd fire it up red-hot, and keep it going all night. You city boys should know that nothing smells as good as burning oak on a cold night.

After a couple of days building up to it, he even managed to get me back on a horse a time or three. But as Carlton always liked to say, it warn't good judgment. My poor aching ass hurt all the way up to my shoulder blades, and I'd be willing to bet I didn't spend twenty minutes in the saddle—all totaled—at the end of my stay.

Got to admit, though, that after about a month of roughing it, I missed green Jell-O and Leona Wildbank so bad I couldn't wait to get back. He hugged my neck just 'fore the train pulled out. Said he'd see me again on the other side. Man had tears on his cheeks when the train pulled away. Guess maybe I might have had some on my face too.

'Bout three weeks after I got back to the Home, a twine-tied bundle of big, thick *Arkansas Gazettes* showed up one Sunday morning. Had a pull-out feature section inside named *Hell in the Nations—Chapter Two in the Adventures of Hayden Tilden*. Thing sported lots of pictures of Lucius and me hugging each other and wiping our faces with big bandannas. Some of me and Junior. Junior and Lucius. Lucius and the nurses. One of 'em showed Leona with a look on her face like she might pinch the photographer's nose off.

Lightfoot's article hadn't been out more than a week or two when a feller named A. Maxwell Vought started calling me long distance from California. Said he wanted to discuss the possibility of making a movie about my life based on Franklin's newspaper piece, and my first-hand recollections. Hinted that maybe me and the boy could come out to Hollywood and visit with him. Said he'd pay for the whole shebang. Something he mentioned got my brain to chewing over the Brotherhood of Blood for the first time in years.

I sat there and thought, what in the hell is Franklin J. Lightfoot, Jr., gonna do when he finds out about Hayden Tilden, Carlton J. Cecil, Charlie Two Knives, and the Brotherhood of Blood? Sweet Jesus, now there was a hell of a story. Horse manure and gun smoke galore.

Too bad Carlton won't be around to help me tell it. Damn his sorry hide for dying. Heddy McDonald, General Black Jack Pershing, and I miss that randy old bastard.